ADMISSION OF INNOCENCE
The 11th Bernie Fazakerley Mystery

by

JUDY FORD

Bernie Fazakerley Publications

ADMISSION OF INNOCENCE

Published by Bernie Fazakerley Publications

Copyright © 2018 Judy Ford.

Madonna and Child image © 2018 Catherine Young

Scripture quotations are from New Revised Standard Version Bible: Anglicized Edition, copyright © 1989, 1995 National Council of the Churches of Christ in the United States of America. Used by permission. All rights reserved worldwide.

ISBN13: 978-1-911083-53-5
ISBN10: 1-91-108353-8

DEDICATION

Dedicated to

Save the Family

(a charity providing support to homeless and vulnerable families in the Chester area)

Father of orphans and protector of widows
is God in his holy habitation.

Psalm 68:5, NRSVA

CONTENTS

GLOSSARY OF UK POLICE RANKS

Uniformed police

Chief Constable (CC) – Has overall charge of a regional police force, such as Thames Valley Police, which covers Oxford and a large surrounding area.

Deputy Chief Constable (DCC) – The senior discipline authority for each force. 2nd in command to the CC.

Assistant Chief Constable (ACC) – 4 in the Thames Valley Police Service, each responsible for a policy area.

Chief Superintendent ('Chief Super') – Head of a policing area or department.

Police Superintendent – Responsible for a local area within a police force.

Chief Inspector (CI) – Responsible for overseeing a team in a local area.

Police Inspector – Senior operational officer overseeing officers on duty 24/7.

Police Sergeant – Supervises a team of officers.

Police Constable (PC) – 'Bobby on the beat'. Likely to be the first to arrive in response to an emergency call.

Crime Investigation Department (CID) – Plain clothes officers

Detective Superintendent (DS) – Responsible for crime investigation in a local area.

Detective Chief Inspector (DCI) – Responsible for overseeing a crime investigation team in a local area. May be the Senior Investigating Officer heading up a criminal investigation.

Detective Inspector (DI) – Oversees crime investigation 24/7. May be the Senior Investigating Officer heading up a criminal investigation.

Detective Sergeant (DS) – Supervises a team of CID officers.

Detective Constable (DC) – One of a team of officers investigating crimes.

These descriptions are based on information from the following sources:
[1] Mental Health Cop blog, by Inspector Michael Brown, Mental Health co-ordinator, College of Policing.
https://mentalhealthcop.wordpress.com, accessed 31st March 2017.
[2] Thames Valley Police website,
www.thamesvalley.police.uk, accessed 31st March 2017.

PLAN OF 26 WILBRAHAM AVENUE

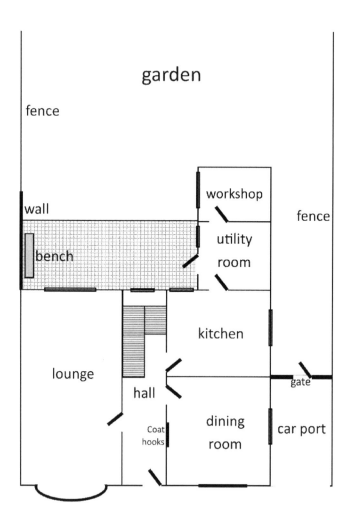

garden

fence

workshop

wall

fence

bench

utility
room

kitchen

lounge

hall

gate

Coat
hooks

dining
room

car port

1. PRAY FOR US SINNERS

Hail Mary, full of grace.
The Lord is with you.
Blessed are you among women,
and blessed is the fruit of your womb, Jesus.
Holy Mary, Mother of God,
pray for us sinners,
now and at the hour of our death.
Amen.

Traditional Catholic prayer.

'Come in, Peter,' Father Damien Rowland greeted his friend, standing back to allow him to enter the presbytery. 'Thank you for coming over.'

'It's no bother,' Peter assured him. 'The kids are with their mum this morning. She's on a late shift, so I haven't got them until after lunch. And you were so mysterious on the phone that I'm agog to hear what this is all about.'

'Come through to the study and I'll explain.' Father Damien opened a door on their right and ushered Peter into a bright room with windows on two sides, bookcases lining the remaining walls, and a round table in the centre.

Peter had spent many hours sitting at that table during the months of his instruction before being admitted into membership of the church the previous Easter. Now, he saw an unfamiliar figure occupying his usual seat opposite the door. The clerical collar and black shirt suggested that this interloper too was a priest, but these garments were offset by a jaunty striped blazer, which seemed incongruous – irreverent almost. He got to his feet as the door opened and leaned across the table holding out his hand towards Peter.

'Let me introduce my good friend from our seminary days,' Father Damien said, gesturing towards the stranger. 'This is Gerry Casey. He's parish priest of St Monica's in Evesham. Gerry – meet Peter Johns. As I was telling you, he used to be a detective inspector with Thames Valley Police and he's got lots of experience investigating murders. Why don't you both sit down and get to know one another, while I fix us all some coffee?'

He went out, leaving the door open. The other priest resumed his seat and Peter sat down opposite him.

'I gather you're quite a new Catholic?' Father Gerrard said, after a short pause. 'Damien was telling me that you were confirmed at the Easter Vigil this year.'

'That's right.' Peter tried, and failed, to think of anything more to say. Smalltalk was not one of his strengths.

'And you used to be a police officer?'

'Yes. That's right,' Peter said again.

'Do you miss the work, now you're retired?'

'No. I've got plenty of other things to fill my time. My grandchildren, for a start,' Peter became more expansive now that he had discovered a topic upon which he felt confident to make conversation. 'My son and daughter-in-law moved back here from Jamaica a couple of years ago and they're none too flush with cash; so I look after their two kids, which means they can both go out to work full-time. And then there's the house, and I've got a teenage step-daughter too; so I don't have time to miss the old job – not like some police officers, I could mention!' he added with a wry smile, thinking of Jonah, the ex-colleague who lived with them and who had yet to come to terms with a new life of leisure. 'If you're hoping to get a bit of private detective work done, you'd do better talking to a friend of mine who's just retired this year and is still suffering withdrawal symptoms!'

'Well, as it happens …,' Father Gerard began, smiling across the table at Peter.

'You're serious?' Peter asked, suddenly comprehending the purpose of Father Damien's summons. 'You've got a case that you want me to investigate?'

'That's right,' the priest admitted quietly. 'One of my parishioners has been accused of-'

'You really ought to take it to the police,' Peter interrupted. 'Whatever accusations have been made, if it's something criminal it ought to be investigated officially.'

'That's already been done.' Father Gerard sighed, leaning his elbows on the table and clasping his hands together in front of him. He leaned his chin on his hands, thinking for a moment or two, before continuing, 'but they came up with the wrong answer.'

'How can you be so sure?' Peter was torn between curiosity as to what this was all about and a feeling that such scepticism about the conclusions of a police investigation should not be encouraged.

'I know the people involved.'

'Sometimes people act out of character,' Peter suggested cautiously. 'If I had a pound for every time someone has said to me, "I can't believe he did it – it's so unlike him!" …'

'No, but it's more than just that,' Father Gerard insisted. 'It's … well it's difficult to explain, except to another priest. But you surely can agree that the police do sometimes get it wrong? And miscarriages of justices do sometimes occur?'

'Oh yes!' Peter smiled. 'We get it wrong often enough and it can sometimes even mean people get wrongly convicted – although I'd say that it's more common for our mistakes to allow criminals to get away with it.'

'So it can't do any harm to have another look at the evidence, can it?' the priest argued gently. 'Just in case…?'

Peter was spared the need to answer immediately by

the return of Father Damien with a tray. He set it down in the centre of the table and started handing round coffee.

'Here's your disgusting muck,' he said cheerily as he passed Father Gerard a large mug with a photograph of St Cyprian's Church on the side – one of a large consignment produced to help raise funds for the restoration of the organ. 'I hope it's strong enough for you. Help yourself to sugar from the bowl.'

His friend took the mug and reached out for the sugar. 'I just like to be able to taste my coffee, that's all,' he protested with a smile. 'I can't understand why you always used to insist on watering it down with milk and spoiling the flavour.'

Peter watched the priests' banter, realising that this was a long-running difference of opinion dating back to their student days, which had been revived as part of the process of re-establishing their friendship after a length of time apart.

'And here's yours, Peter,' Father Damien continued, setting down a matching mug in front of him. 'Like mine – white, and no sugar because we're both sweet enough without! And help yourself to biscuits, both of you. These are home-made shortbread from a parishioner who thinks I don't feed myself properly and need building up. Have as many as you like – she'll probably have some more for me on Sunday.'

Peter and Gerry obediently each took one of the biscuits and nibbled them. Damien sat back in his chair with his coffee mug cradled between his hands and looked round at them.

'Have you told Peter what it is we're hoping he might do for us?' he asked at last.

'Well, I started, but …'

'Father Gerry said that he's worried that someone may end up getting convicted for something they didn't do,' Peter continued, as the priest tailed off. 'But I don't know who or what or why you think I might be able to help.'

'Typical Gerry!' Damien snorted in mock derision. 'You never could get to the point, could you? I remember Father O'Keefe describing one of your homilies as, "a winding road that always promises sight of its destination round the next corner but eventually peters out leaving the listener stranded in an impenetrable forest of metaphors." Get out that paper you were showing me earlier and let's start with that.'

Gerry reached into a battered briefcase that lay on the floor beside his chair and took out a newspaper. He laid it down on the table, moving the tray to one side to make room for it. Peter saw that it was a local paper covering a region of Worcestershire around Evesham. He read aloud the headline on the front page: 'Local woman kills her husband.'

Then he looked up at Gerry. 'Is that the case you're worried about?'

The priest nodded. 'Carry on,' he urged. 'Read the rest of the report.'

'Mother of one, Mrs Vanessa Wellesley, attended South Worcestershire Magistrates Court on Monday to be charged with murdering her husband, Christopher Wellesley, by stabbing him in the chest with his own screwdriver. She was remanded in custody pending consideration of her application for bail by a crown court judge.' Peter paused to scrutinise the photograph below the headline. It was of a woman in a black dress, flanked by two uniformed police officers. Her straight black hair hung down to her shoulders on either side of her face. The picture was too small for him to distinguish any facial features or to make a guess at her age. He looked up at Gerry. 'Vanessa Wellesley is your parishioner, I take it?'

'That's right. I've known her since she was a teenager. Her family have been there since way before I came to the parish. Her mother is head teacher of our school and her father is our treasurer. The whole family are real stalwarts of the church.'

Peter decided against suggesting that none of this precluded Mrs Wellesley from being capable of killing her husband. He turned back to the newspaper.

'When the emergency services attended the Wellesley family home in the Greenhill area of Evesham last Saturday,' he read aloud, 'they found Christopher Wellesley (40) lying unconscious in a pool of his own blood. The murder weapon, a large screwdriver, which had been driven into his chest, lay beside him. Paramedics attempted to treat him at the scene, before rushing him to the emergency department at Worcestershire Royal Hospital. He was pronounced dead on arrival without having regained consciousness.'

'What it doesn't mention,' Gerry interjected, 'is that it was Vanessa herself who called the emergency services. According to her, she found him like that when she got home from the shops.'

'See page 5 for an exclusive interview with her sister, Louise O'Shea,' Peter continued to read. 'Should I look at that too?'

'Yes, go on,' Gerry urged. 'That'll put you in the picture.'

Peter turned the pages and found the interview. It was illustrated with a head-and-shoulders photograph of a woman in her twenties or early thirties with long black hair and dark eyes. He scanned down the page, reading silently and picking out sentences here and there.

'Ms Louise O'Shea doesn't mince her words when it comes to her brother-in-law,' he commented. 'Look at this: "While I'm totally convinced she didn't do it, I wouldn't blame Vanessa if she had killed him." … and this: "He was a vicious bully and made her life hell. He deserved what he got." … and here: "It was all his fault that she lost her baby." This is hardly designed to convince a jury that her sister is innocent!'

'That's what I said,' Damien chipped in. 'That definitely reads like she knows she did it, but only because he drove her to it.'

'That's what everyone thinks,' Gerry agreed. 'Nobody is disputing that Christopher was an abusive husband. Vanessa's parents have been worried about his controlling behaviour for years. The obstetrician who treated her when she went into labour prematurely and delivered a stillborn baby last April was suspicious at the time and is now prepared to give evidence that she had bruises on her abdomen that suggested that she had been kicked or punched. Her GP confirms that she was suffering from post-natal depression and that she had several times in the past presented with injuries typical of domestic abuse. Vanessa herself always used to insist that there was nothing wrong, but since Christopher's death, she's admitted that he was systematically abusing her both physically and mentally. Everybody agrees that it would have been completely understandable if she had suddenly snapped and …'

'If everything's as clear cut as that – and if the prosecution is willing to accept that her husband was the vile abuser that her sister portrays him as – surely the best thing for her to do would be to plead guilty to manslaughter and appeal for leniency because of all the mitigating circumstances?' Peter suggested.

'That's exactly what her legal team keep telling her!' Gerry answered. 'They're confident that she'd get away with a non-custodial sentence, because of Christopher's treatment of her and because sending her to prison would be unfair on her little girl.'

'And because there's no possible reason to suspect her of being a danger to anyone else,' Damien added.

'So where's the problem?' Peter asked. 'Why doesn't she take their advice?'

'Because she didn't do it,' Gerry repeated. 'She told me that she didn't kill him, and I believe her.'

'Oh! I get it,' Peter said, after a brief pause. 'That's what you meant by it being difficult to explain except to another priest. You've heard her confession and she didn't confess to killing her husband?'

'As I'm sure you are aware,' Gerry answered, poker-faced, 'I am not permitted to reveal anything about what is said at the sacrament of reconciliation – or even to confirm that an individual has come to me for that purpose. However, I'm not breaking any rules by telling you that, if a penitent confesses to a criminal offence, I would require assurance from them that they will hand themselves in to the authorities and accept whatever punishment is meted out to them under the law, before agreeing to pronounce absolution. And any of my regulars would be able to confirm that Vanessa Wellesley rarely misses my Saturday afternoon confessional time.'

'I understand,' Peter grinned. 'It's one of those, "you might well think that; I couldn't possibly comment" occasions. OK. So your Vanessa is innocent of killing her husband. But presumably the prosecution must think they've got a good case against her. Under the circumstances, she might still do better to plead guilty to manslaughter – on the grounds of loss of control or else because she was just using reasonable force to defend herself.'

'But that would mean telling a lie in court,' Gerry argued. 'And that's something she can't in all conscience do.'

'And surely you're not suggesting that she ought to?' Damien added.

'No, I'm not,' Peter assured him, 'but I am saying that that might be the pragmatic way of minimising her sentence – assuming that the real killer can't be found.'

'And that's exactly why Damien suggested talking to you!' Gerry broke in. 'We need someone to find the real killer. That's the only way of convincing people that Vanessa didn't do it.'

The two priests looked hopefully towards Peter, who dropped his eyes and seemed to be busily studying the newspaper again. They waited in silence. Eventually Peter felt that he had to say something.

'I'm not at all sure I'm the right person for the job. I've never investigated a crime without a team of police officers behind me. Can't this Vanessa's solicitor find a proper private detective to do it?'

'I told you – they think she ought to plead guilty,' Gerry replied quickly. 'You're our only hope. Damien thought you'd understand Vanessa's predicament.'

'I suppose I do,' Peter sighed, 'but that doesn't mean that I'm going to be able to do anything to help. If the police haven't found any evidence that anyone else was involved, then it's very unlikely that I will, working on my own.'

'But it's got to be worth a try …,' Damien suggested.

Peter sat uncomfortably in his chair, conscious of the silent scrutiny of the two priests.

'I'll have to think about this,' he said at last. 'I've never been asked to do anything like this before.'

'Sure. Take your time,' Gerry said, detecting a softening in Peter's resolve, 'but if you could come up with a decision before I go back this afternoon, I'd really appreciate it.'

'I'm sorry. I really don't know.' Peter wrestled in his mind with conflicting emotions. He had a deep respect for Father Damien and did not want to refuse any request from him. He also felt sympathy for this woman whom everyone seemed to agree had suffered at the hands of her husband and did not deserve to be sent to jail for his murder. Yet, it did not seem right to be questioning the meticulous police work, which he knew his colleagues must have carried out in order to reach the point at which she was being prosecuted. Not that the police always got it right – and with such an obvious suspect, perhaps they would have been tempted not to look too hard for an alternative. And then again, if he were to take on this commission, would that just be raising false hopes? What chance was there that he would find the real culprit when the official enquiry had failed?

'I'm sorry,' he repeated. 'I – I – I'm going to have to ask Mary about this.' He got up and made for the door. 'I'll try not to be long.'

Gerry stared after Peter as he left the room. Then he turned to look at Damien, raising his eyebrows in a questioning manner.

'Don't worry. He'll be back.'

'But … who's Mary? I thought you said his wife's name was Bernadette.'

'Ah!' Damien smiled enigmatically. 'Peter has a special relationship with Our Lady. He's off into the church to have a word with her.'

'How d'you mean?' His friend stared in disbelief and astonishment. 'You're joking, right?'

'Wrong. What's up? Prayers to Our Lady are hardly revolutionary, are they?'

'I – I suppose … Look, I know that the church has always accepted the idea of … but, in this day and age! I mean …'

'Come on, Gerry,' Damien chided gently. 'You're not telling me you don't say the Hail Mary or –'

'But that's different! It's all part of a long-established liturgy. It's … and to be honest, I do have trouble justifying it to our ecumenical colleagues. But, actually praying to a saint – and expecting an answer – that's just too … And I thought you said Peter was a new convert. This is more the sort of thing I'd expect from my Irish granny!'

'Well, of course, converts are always the most extreme and the most enthusiastic, aren't they?' his friend smiled back, amused at his brother priest's apparent discomfiture with this aspect of traditional Catholicism. 'But in Peter's case it's not that. He chose the Catholic Church precisely *because* it's the only one that takes the veneration of Mary seriously, and he has a special reason for that.'

'Oh? Enlighten me, do.'

'Last summer – not the summer just gone, I mean 2017 – his baby granddaughter was snatched from her pram.[1] During the period when she was missing, Peter wandered into St Cyprian's. His step-daughter, Lucy, wanted to light a candle for them and he came with her. We've got a rather unusual Madonna-and-Child statue – I'll show you it later. The infant Jesus has dark skin and curly black hair. According to Peter, he's the spitting image of Peter's son Eddie – the one whose baby went missing. Anyway, Peter was standing there looking at it when Our Lady spoke to him, and he promised her that he'd become a Catholic if little Abigail came home safe.'

'Whew!' Gerry whistled through his teeth. 'And I gather the baby was recovered OK?'

'Yup! The police tracked her down and got her back safe and sound a couple of days later. So you can see why Peter feels a special bond with the BVM[2], can't you? He'll be there now, checking what she thinks about this story you've just told us.'

'But …,' Gerry began, unsure what to make of this. 'But … surely he can't really …? I mean … Look Damien,' he began again, speaking more seriously now, 'are you sure he's the right man for this job? You don't think maybe he could be past it? I mean, a man who talks to statues is hardly going to carry much weight with the lawyers, is he? Or the jury, for that matter.'

'O ye of little faith!' Damien sighed, but with a smile on his face. 'Trust me – Peter has got his feet very firmly planted on the ground. He's exactly the person you need: bags of experience in the police force and total commitment once he makes up his mind to something. And he is absolutely not going ga-ga, however much he

---

[1] You can read about this in "Sorrowful Mystery" © 2017, 2018 Judy Ford, ISBN 978-1-911083-46-7.

[2] Abbreviation for "Blessed Virgin Mary"

may remind you of your Irish granny!'

The sound of footsteps on the quarry tiles in the passage heralded Peter's return. He stood in the doorway, glancing round a little sheepishly at the two men seated at the table. Damien looked back at him enquiringly.

'Did you say this Vanessa has a child?' Peter asked, looking towards Gerry.

'Yes. A little girl called Leah. She's two.'

'And they'll be separated if Vanessa's convicted?'

'That's what the lawyers say,' Gerry confirmed. 'If it's murder, there's a statutory life sentence.'

Peter took a deep breath. 'OK,' he said as he let it out again. 'I'll have a go – but I'm not sure what good it'll do.'

'That's great!' Gerry got to his feet and squeezed past the back of Damien's chair to reach Peter. 'I can't tell you what a relief it is to have you say that,' he continued, grasping him by the hand. 'I just know Vanessa didn't do it, and it would be a travesty for her to be sent to jail.'

'Like I said, I don't know that I'll be able to do much good,' Peter repeated. Then, after a brief pause, he went on, 'and you ought to know – it won't just be me you're taking on. If I'm going to be chasing murderers across Worcestershire, there are a couple of other people who are going to expect to be doing it with me.'

'Oh?' Gerry looked at Peter and then round at Damien, who was smiling broadly.

'There's my wife, Bernie, for a start,' Peter went on, 'and then there's Jonah.' He paused. It was difficult to explain how Jonah fitted into their family. 'He's a friend of ours, and another ex-copper. He lives with us. He only retired a few weeks ago and he's still getting withdrawal symptoms. There's no way he's going to let me keep a case like this to myself!'

'He's talking about DCI Jonah Porter,' Damien explained. 'You may have heard of him. The press call him *the wheelchair cop*. He was shot in the spine about a decade ago, but he refused to be pensioned off[3]. Peter and Bernie took him in when his wife died.'

'Oh yes!' Gerry said excitedly. 'I remember! Didn't he solve a murder in one of the Oxford colleges a few years back?[4]'

'That's right. And he was in charge of finding out who that corpse was that turned up under our organ a few months ago[5]. I told you about that, didn't I?'

'Yes, but you didn't mention that you'd had a celebrity investigating it!' Gerry answered with undisguised delight at the prospect of meeting the famous police officer who had defied his superiors and insisted on returning to his job after life-changing injuries. He turned back to Peter, trying not to sound as relieved as he felt that they would not be relying solely on him to find Christopher Wellesley's killer. 'That's great! The more manpower we can muster the better. We've got quite a tight schedule. The trial is set to start on the first.'

'The first of October?' Peter queried anxiously. 'That's less than three weeks away.'

'I know,' Gerry grimaced. 'It was when the date was announced that it really hit me that this is for real. I suddenly realised that if we didn't do something soon, it was going to be too late. So now – where do we start?' He looked round eagerly at Peter and Damien.

'I think the first thing is for me to meet this Vanessa and check that she wants us to try to help,' Peter said, more decisively than he had appeared up to now. 'And, if she does, then we ought to see her lawyers and be officially appointed to the defence team. That will give us the right to ask the police for disclosure of any evidence they've found that could be helpful to her case. Where's she being

---

[3] Jonah's life story is recounted in "Changing Scenes of Life" © 2015 Judy Ford, ISBN: 978-1-911083-09-2

[4] See "Awayday" © 2015 Judy Ford, ISBN: 978-1-911083-06-1

[5] You can read about this in "Organ Failure" © 2018 Judy Ford, ISBN: 978-1-911083-38-2.

held?'

'She isn't,' Gerry replied promptly. 'She's been remanded on bail – which just goes to show that nobody thinks she's a danger to anyone or has any intention of trying to abscond. She's required to live at her parents' house and to report to the local police station every few days. Like I said, her parents are stalwarts of the church. I know them well. I can give them a ring now and arrange for us to go over. Would tomorrow be OK for you?'

Peter hastily consulted the calendar app on his mobile phone. 'You're in luck,' he smiled back at the eager priest. 'It's an off-duty day for Crystal, so I don't have any childcare responsibilities.'

Crystal was his daughter-in-law and the mother of baby Abigail and her older brother, Ricky.

'Smashing!' Gerry reached into his briefcase and took out a mobile phone. Within a few minutes, he was turning back to Peter again. 'It's all arranged. We're going to meet them at half-ten. If you come to the presbytery first, I'll drive you over there and introduce you.'

'OK,' Peter agreed. 'We'll aim to be there by ten; but we'd better take our own car – Jonah's wheelchair won't fit in yours.'

'You're sure he's going to want to come then?'

'Oh yes!' Peter said confidently. 'He won't want to miss out!'

2. NEITHER DO I CONDEMN YOU

And Jesus said, 'Neither do I condemn you. Go your way, and from now on do not sin again.'
John 8:11 NRSV, Anglicised Edition

'That's it!' Gerry called out, pointing towards a modest semi-detached house on what had clearly once been a council estate. Like most of the other properties in the road, this one bore the tell-tale signs that it was now owner-occupied: the ubiquitous council house canopy over the front door had been replaced by a small porch, and the white plastic windows were of a slightly different design from those of its partner.

Bernie pulled up in front of the low privet hedge, which separated the small front garden from the road. She got out of the large, specially adapted car and went round to the back, where Peter was already engaged in unfastening the straps that held Jonah's wheelchair (with him in it) securely in its place. She opened the rear door and set up the ramp that allowed him to drive his chair out of the vehicle. Jonah's spinal injury had left him paralysed in all four limbs, apart from the first three fingers of his left hand; but technology, such as this state-of-the-art electric wheelchair gave him a large amount of independence, which he guarded keenly.

Gerry watched as the wheelchair descended to the road. Bernie immediately folded the ramp and stood there with it in her hand, while Peter jumped down to the ground and closed the door.

'You'd better go first,' he said to Gerry, 'and introduce us.'

Gerry led the way between beds of dahlias and Michaelmas daisies to the front door. It opened, before he could knock, to reveal a grey-haired woman in a full, below-the-knee skirt and a high-necked white blouse. She looked at them with deep brown eyes.

'Father Gerard!' she greeted Gerry warmly. 'I saw the car and I thought it must be you. It's so good of you to come! Come in all of you. The kettle's just boiled.'

'Deborah!' Gerry took the woman's hand between his and squeezed it warmly, before following her inside. Bernie immediately stepped forward with the ramp, unfolding it and setting it up to enable Jonah to drive his wheelchair over the step and into the porch. With a little more difficulty, and some help from Peter lifting at the front, he negotiated the smaller step from the porch into the house.

They clustered together in the small hall, rather dark because the only window looked into the porch. A child safety gate stood open at the foot of the steep staircase opposite the front door. Peter looked up and saw that the matching gate at the top was fastened closed. He deduced that Leah Wellesley, whom these precautions were presumably designed to protect, was most likely upstairs.

A tall, well-built man emerged from a room on their left. His hair was white and his eyes were blue – almost as clear blue as Jonah's were. He too greeted Gerry warmly and the two men shook hands.

'Pat, Deborah: may I introduce retired police detective Peter Johns? Peter: Patrick and Deborah O'Shea – Vanessa's parents.' The priest gestured towards Peter, who smiled back and held out his hand towards the couple, who shook it in turn.

'And this is Peter's wife, Bernie,' Gerry continued. Bernie also shook hands with the O'Sheas. 'And last, but not least, their friend, Detective Chief Inspector Jonah

Porter, recently retired from Thames Valley CID!' he finished, a note of triumph in his voice.

Mr and Mrs O'Shea looked shyly towards Jonah, who responded with a lop-sided smile and a tilt of his head. They all stood in silence for a second or two, before Deborah reiterated her intention to make tea and scurried away to the kitchen, leaving her husband to show them into the lounge.

'I'm afraid it's all a bit cluttered at the moment,' he apologised as he pushed one of the easy chairs into a corner to make room for Jonah's wheelchair. 'We'd forgotten how much mess having a toddler around the house makes.'

He moved aside a small pink rocking horse and then bent down to clear a pathway for Peter and Bernie between piles of brightly coloured plastic building blocks, so that they could reach the sofa.

'It's very good of you to offer to help us,' he added, settling down in a rather worn easy chair, which sagged visibly under his weight. Peter suspected that he had chosen this seat for himself in order not to subject any of his guests to the discomfort of sitting in it. 'We're at our wits end not knowing how to keep poor Vanny out of prison.'

'How is Vanessa?' Father Gerard asked, sitting down next to Patrick O'Shea.

'I don't know. I mean – health-wise she's fine, but ... I had hoped she'd go back more to how she was before ... I mean ... but I suppose it's going to take a while for her to ...,' he tailed off into incoherence.

'We can't promise to do anything until we've spoken to your daughter and she's agreed that she wants us to,' Peter told him seriously. 'Does she know we're here?'

'Oh yes!' Patrick assured them. 'At least, she knows you're coming and I expect she'll have heard you come in. She'll be down presently. She's just changing Leah.'

As if on cue, the door of the room opened and a young

woman came in, carrying a toddler in her arms. Peter detected a slight family resemblance to Deborah O'Shea in the angle of her nose and the shape of her chin; and the black hair that hung down both sides of her face might well be destined to turn to the steely grey of her mother's over the next few decades. Her eyes, however, were blue, like her father's. She stood in the doorway looking round at the crowded room.

'Come in, Van!' Patrick urged her. 'And sit down. These are the detectives that Father Gerry told us about. They're going to prove that you didn't murder Christopher.'

'Well, we're going to investigate what happened – if that's alright with you,' Peter interjected. 'We can't promise that we'll manage to prove anything. It all depends on what we find.

Vanessa picked her way across the room and sat down on a large beanbag, which lay on the floor next to her father's chair. She put her daughter down in front of her and began building a tower from the plastic bricks, which still lay strewn across the carpet. Leah watched for a few seconds and then joined in, crawling under her grandfather's legs to retrieve more bricks and attempting to attach them to the ones that her mother had already joined together.

Once she was satisfied that the toddler was engrossed in her game and would not interrupt the adult conversation, Vanessa raised her head and looked round the room, studying the face of each visitor in turn.

'Do you really believe that I didn't kill him?' she asked at last. 'No one else seems to.'

'We don't know,' Jonah answered for them all. 'The case against you looks fairly strong, but we haven't heard your side of the story yet, so we can't make a judgement.'

'Father Gerry is sure that you're innocent,' Peter intervened quickly, seeing a look of alarm pass across her face. 'But we need to hear it from you. And we need to know that you *want* us to try to find the truth.'

'Bearing in mind that *whatever* we find may have to come out in court,' Jonah added.

'Why don't you start by just telling them what happened?' Gerry suggested. 'We can talk about what they may be able to do to help afterwards.'

'OK.' Vanessa hesitated, looking round at each of them again. 'Where do you want me to start?'

'How about telling us exactly what you and your husband did the day he died?' Jonah suggested. 'Start from first thing that day. What time did you wake up?'

'About five-thirty,' Vanessa replied promptly. 'Leah woke and started singing in her cot, so I got up and went to quieten her, so's she wouldn't wake Christopher.'

Her narrative was interrupted by the arrival of Mrs O'Shea with a tea trolley. Patrick got up to make space for it next to the only remaining unoccupied chair. For several minutes, conversation ceased while tea and fairy cakes were distributed among the guests. Eventually, however, they were all settled back into their seats, and Vanessa resumed her story.

'She was wide awake, so we played together in her room for a bit and then I got her dressed and took her down for her breakfast.'

'And your husband?' Jonah asked. 'He stayed in bed?'

'Oh yes,' Vanessa confirmed. 'He never got up before eight-thirty on a Saturday. He always said he worked bloody hard during the week to keep us all, so he deserved an extra hour in bed at the weekend. I heard him moving about upstairs, so I made him his breakfast and then, while he was eating it, I went back up and had a shower and got dressed.'

'And this will have been what time?' Jonah asked.

'I don't know exactly. Before nine, but not much, I think.'

'OK. Go on.'

'I always do the supermarket shopping on a Saturday. It

keeps – kept – us out from under Christopher's feet. He loved Leah to bits, but she can get a bit irritating sometimes with her noise and all the mess she makes.' Vanessa looked round at the scattered toys. 'It must've been half nine or maybe a bit later. We went to Tesco on Worcester Road.'

'Did your husband say anything to you about his plans for the day?' Peter asked.

'Not that I remember. He was in the middle of making some shelves for Leah's room. I assume that's what he was doing in his workshop.'

'I'm sorry, I think I've missed a bit here,' Jonah cut in. 'What's this about a workshop?'

'He had a workshop at the back of the house,' Patrick O'Shea explained. 'It used to be an outside toilet and coalhouse, I think. That's where … where he was found.'

'I see. Thank you.' Jonah looked towards Vanessa again. 'And was he expecting any visitors that morning, do you know?'

'I shouldn't think so.' She shook her head. 'He doesn't – didn't – usually invite his friends round. He'd always meet them at the golf club or a wine bar or something. And he always saw clients at the office.'

'What about family?' Jonah pressed her. 'Did he have any relatives living close by who might have called?

'No.' Vanessa shook her head. 'There's only his sister, Paula, and she lives in Oxford. His parents are both dead.'

'It's their house that he was living in,' Patrick interjected. 'And didn't he love telling us about it!'

'When they got married, I thought he'd sell up and let Vanessa help him choose a house of their own,' Deborah added, 'but no: his house was perfect and he wasn't moving or letting her have a say in how it was done up. He wouldn't even let her choose new curtains for their bedroom.'

'Oxford isn't far,' Jonah persisted. 'It only took us just over an hour to drive. Could his sister have come to see him that morning, do you think? Did she ever visit unannounced?'

'Did she heck!' Patrick snorted. 'She'd got more sense than to have any truck with the bastard.' He broke off and looked apologetically at his daughter who had drawn in her breath sharply at this outburst. 'I'm sorry, Van, but that's what he was: a very cunning and devious bastard – very charming when it suited him – but a bastard nonetheless.'

He turned back to Jonah.

'They hadn't spoken for years,' he went on. 'She didn't even come to the wedding. I never realised he wasn't an only child until after Leah was born. He said something then about how he hoped she wasn't going to be as much trouble as his sister had been to his parents.'

'He was a misogynist. That's what he was,' Deborah put in vehemently. 'A misogynist and a bully.'

'OK,' Peter said quietly in the silence that followed this declaration. 'Getting back to that Saturday morning: you went shopping with Leah – in the car, I assume?'

'That's right,' Vanessa agreed. 'It's only just round the corner, but we always have such a quantity of stuff – what with Leah's nappies and everything.'

'And did you come straight back?'

'Yes.'

'About what time?' Jonah asked quickly.

'Like I told the police, I'm not really sure. I remember looking at my watch while we were still in Tesco's and thinking we'd better hurry because Christopher would be annoyed if the lunch was late. It was five past eleven then. I still had some more things to pick up and then there was a queue at the checkout … I'm sorry, I really can't remember. I don't think I checked the time again until after the ambulance came.'

'Never mind,' Peter reassured her. 'It probably doesn't matter exactly what time it was. Now, in your own time, tell us what you found when you got back home.'

'I called out to let Christopher know we were back. He

didn't answer, but he often doesn't when he's in his workshop. Some of his tools make a lot of noise and he doesn't always hear me.' She paused and looked round at them all.

'Carry on,' Peter said gently.

'I got the bags out of the car and put them all down in the hall. Then I got Leah out and locked the car. I sorted out the frozen food and took those bags through to the chest freezer in the utility room behind the kitchen. The door to the workshop was open, which was odd, because we had a rule that we always kept it closed to stop Leah getting in there. Now that she's walking, she's into everything and she could hurt herself on some of the things he has in there.'

'Mind you – he was probably more concerned about her doing damage to his precious tools!' Patrick put in scornfully.

'I put the stuff in the freezer and then I went through into the workshop to give Christopher his change and the receipt for the shopping.'

'He never let Vanessa have any money for herself,' Patrick O'Shea growled, seeing the looks of surprise on Peter's and Jonah's faces. 'He would get cash out on his way home each Friday for her to do the weekly shop and then he expected the change back and an account of what she'd spent it on.'

'She had to beg for money for clothes,' Deborah added, 'even for Leah.'

'It was his money,' Vanessa argued. 'He had a right to know what I was spending it on.'

'He had no right to keep you so short,' Patrick retorted, 'or to forbid you to accept any from us when you needed it.'

'Maybe we could get back to that Saturday morning,' Jonah suggested. 'You went into the workshop, and then …?'

'I called out to him first, in case he was busy and didn't

want to be disturbed. He didn't say anything so I peeped round the door – I said it was open, didn't I?'

'Yes, you did,' Peter confirmed.

'So, like I said, I looked round the door, and …' Vanessa tailed off into silence. She leaned forwards and put her arms around Leah and hugged her to her chest.

'Yes?' Jonah encouraged.

'He was there – lying on the floor. He wasn't moving. At first I thought he might be dead – a heart attack maybe; but then he moved a bit and groaned. I went in and looked closer, and there was this … there was this big screwdriver sticking out of his chest.' Vanessa lowered her eyes and seemed to be intent on studying the pattern on the carpet. 'I couldn't really believe what I was seeing and I was in a complete panic by then. People told me afterwards it was the wrong thing to do, but all I could think of was getting that horrible thing out of him. So I knelt down and got hold of the handle and pulled it out.'

She looked up and stared directly at Peter.

'I know it only made things worse, but that wasn't what I meant to do. I was trying to help him.'

'I believe you,' he assured her quietly. 'Now go on – what happened next.'

'Blood gushed out from where the screwdriver had been – all over my hands and on to my skirt. And then I heard Leah calling to me and I saw her standing there in the utility room. And then she started running towards me and she tripped over one of the bags that I'd left on the floor after unpacking and she fell over and banged her head on the freezer and started crying. And then I couldn't think of anything else except stopping her crying and getting her away from Christopher.'

'Of course,' Peter agreed. 'You didn't want her to see her father like that.'

'He always got so annoyed when Leah cried,' Vanessa went on, as if she had not heard him. 'The noise irritated him more than anything. I picked her up and took her upstairs to her bedroom, where he wouldn't be able to hear her. I gave her a drink and a biscuit and settled her to play in her cot. Then, when I was sure she wouldn't disturb him anymore, I went back down and had another look at him.'

'And?' Jonah prompted, as she paused and appeared to be studying her nails.

'He was still lying there like before. There was a lot more blood now – all over the floor. I went back in the kitchen and rang 999 from the phone on the wall there. They said they'd send an ambulance and I was to wait for it and try to stay calm.'

'Did you do anything to help your husband?' Jonah asked. 'Did you try to staunch the flow of blood by pressing on the wound, for example?'

'No.' Vanessa shook her head. 'I didn't think there was anything I could do, so I just got on with putting the shopping away.'

Peter and Jonah exchanged glances. That would not look good to a jury.

'Don't blame yourself,' Gerry intervened. 'People often do that sort of thing in a crisis. They go on to autopilot and just carry on with doing what they would normally.'

'Yes. That's right,' Peter agreed. 'Now, tell us what happened after the ambulance came.'

'The paramedics looked at Christopher and did some things to him and got him on to a trolley to take him to the ambulance. But before they got him out of the house, the police arrived and started asking questions. There were two of them. One of them went in the ambulance with Christopher and the other stayed with me and Leah. I gave Leah her lunch and tried to get her to settle for a nap, but she wouldn't, and then the policeman who'd stayed with us came up to her room and told me that Christopher was dead. Oh! I forgot to say – another police officer had turned up by then – a plain-clothes one – a woman. She asked a lot of questions and told me I mustn't touch anything.'

'And then Vanessa rang us and we went over and brought them both back here,' Deborah added.

'OK.' Jonah looked across the room at Vanessa, watching her carefully as she bent over her daughter, helping her to build the multi-coloured bricks into a tall tower. 'I think we've got an idea of the sequence of events. Now, please can you think back to when you first came in and found your husband on the floor. I realise it must be distressing to have to think about it, but if we're going to be able to help you to prove that you didn't kill him, you need to think hard and try to picture it in your mind and tell us exactly what you saw.'

'Take your time,' Peter added gently. 'I'm sorry we have to do this, but Jonah's right. If we're going to establish that someone else was there, before you got back from the shops, and attacked Christopher, we need to know if you saw anything that might give us a clue as to who that could've been.'

'I don't remember seeing anything,' Vanessa said, looking round blankly at them both. 'There was just Christopher lying there on the floor with this handle sticking out of his chest. I thought he must've somehow fallen on top of it. It never occurred to me that someone had done it deliberately – not until the police started talking about murder.'

'You said it was unusual for the door to the workshop to be open,' Peter pointed out. 'Was that the only thing that was different from normal?'

'I think so,' Vanessa answered uncertainly. 'I wasn't really noticing.'

'Was there anything at all out of place?' Jonah persisted. 'Or anything in the house that wasn't there when you went out?'

'No – nothing at all.'

'And nothing missing that you'd have expected to be there?' Jonah continued to press her.

'No, really – I can't remember anything.'

'Never mind,' Peter said kindly. 'Let's try another approach. Can you think of anyone who might have a grudge against your husband?'

'No,' Vanessa shook her head, but her father cut across her.

'There were plenty of people – us for a start! It's no good Vanny,' he added, seeing his daughter opening her mouth to protest. 'He was a wrong 'un and you're well-off shot of him. What's the point of pretending now? He had you under his thumb and it was doing you no good at all – or Leah either!'

'You told us he had a sister that he'd fallen out with,' Peter said, trying to steer the conversation away from Patrick's evident dislike of his son-in-law. 'Do you have any idea what that was about?'

'No.' Vanessa shook her head. 'It was all over before I met him. Christopher never talked about her – except when he said that thing about girls being a nuisance to their parents.'

'So, did she fall out with their parents as well, do you think?' Jonah asked with interest. 'And you say your husband inherited the family home. Could she have resented that?'

'I'm sorry,' Vanessa shook her head again. 'I really don't know. I just know that Christopher hadn't seen Paula for years. She never even sent a card at Christmas.'

They sat in silence, thinking about all that Vanessa had told them. Gradually, all eyes turned to look at Peter.

'Well, what do you think?' Gerry said at last. 'Will you give it a go?'

Peter got up without speaking and went over to Vanessa. He sat down on the floor and started helping to build the tower of bricks.

'I have to admit that I think your lawyers are probably right,' he told her. 'Your best chance of staying out of jail would be to plead guilty to manslaughter, based on loss of control due to his unreasonable treatment of you. But if you'd rather we had a go at finding who really stabbed him with that screwdriver …'

'I didn't do it,' Vanessa lifted her head and looked him in the eye. 'And I can't say I did when I didn't, even if …'

'Yes, I can see that; and we will try to help you – if that's what you want. But it has to be your decision. If we start digging around looking for evidence of who did it, there's no knowing what we may turn up. It could make things worse instead of better. Do you understand?'

For a long time no one spoke. Then Vanessa took a deep breath and looked directly at Peter again.

'I want to know the truth,' she said quietly but firmly. 'I know I didn't stab Christopher with that screwdriver and I would like to know who did.'

Peter put out his hand and squeezed hers briefly, before scrambling to his feet and turning to Jonah and Bernie.

'It looks as if I've got this commission – are you in it with me?'

'Of course!' Bernie declared with a smile. 'We're backing you all the way.'

'You don't think I'd let you handle a tricky case like this on your own, do you?' Jonah added. 'You're going to need someone with brains to solve this one!'

'We're tremendously grateful to you,' Deborah began, looking round, first at Peter and then at Bernie and Jonah, 'but we can't afford to pay much. I mean – aren't private detectives very expensive?'

'But we're not private detectives,' Peter said at once. 'Just think of us as friends.'

'That's right,' Bernie added, grinning round mischievously. 'And you're doing us a service, letting us investigate this case. Jonah's been a right pain ever since he retired from CID. A practically insoluble murder is just the thing to buck him up and stop him moaning.'

'Good! That's settled then,' Jonah declared. 'Now we'd

better go and start putting the wheels in motion.'

'Yes.' Peter turned to Vanessa again. 'We need you to get on to your solicitors and tell them we're on board. We need to be an official part of the defence team in order to get access to the police files. They're obliged to disclose evidence to the defence side, but not to any Tom, Dick or Harry that comes along.'

'OK.' Vanessa nodded. 'I'll give her a ring.'

'Are we done now?' Jonah asked, impatient to go.

Peter nodded agreement.

'I'll show you out.' Patrick got up and held open the door to allow Jonah to manoeuvre his wheelchair into the hall. Bernie and Peter followed. Then Patrick came through, pulling the door closed behind him. He approached Peter and spoke in a low tone.

'Do you really believe that she didn't do it?'

'Do you?' Jonah came back at him, before Peter could respond.

'Yes, of course!' Patrick replied quickly.

'Are you sure?' Jonah pressed him. 'Back there it sounded more as if you thought she did it, but he deserved it.'

'I – I …'

'Actually,' Peter said quietly as Patrick tailed off into silence, 'I do believe her. But I don't think that a jury will. And I think that, even if they come down on the side of manslaughter, the judge will feel obliged to impose a custodial sentence unless she admits fault and shows remorse. Her only chance of avoiding jail is if we can find out who the real murderer is.'

'And we don't have a lot of time,' Bernie added, sensing Jonah's impatience to be gone.

'Which is why we need to get off and get down to business right away,' he chimed in, following her cue. 'Let's cut the cackle and get stuck in!'

***

28

Too impatient to wait for confirmation from Vanessa's lawyers that they had been declared to be part of the defence team, so that he could go through the official channels, Jonah made his own arrangements for obtaining information about the police investigation. Sitting in the back of the car on the return journey, he used the mobile phone attachment on his wheelchair to contact a friend.

'Hi Jonah! How's retirement going?' DI Paul Godwin greeted him from his desk in the Shropshire Area Crime Investigation Department of West Mercia Police. He had worked with both Peter and Jonah in Thames Valley Police, before his transfer to West Mercia and he also knew Bernie well, having once been a lodger in her house.[6]

'I need you to do me a favour,' Jonah replied. 'We've been asked – well,' he admitted reluctantly, 'Peter's been asked, to help with the defence of a woman who's been accused of killing her husband. We've agreed to try to find out who really did it.'

'And where do I come in?' Paul asked suspiciously.

'The murder took place on your patch – well, sort of,' Jonah told him.

'How d'you mean?' Paul still sounded dubious. He knew Jonah well, and suspected that he was not going to like what was coming next.

'Evesham. A Mrs Vanessa Wellesley is accused of having stabbed her husband with a screwdriver.'

'Evesham! That's hardly *my patch* as you put it. It's miles away – South Worcestershire Area.'

'But it *is* in West Mercia,' Jonah persisted. 'I'm sure you could find the files for me – us,' he corrected himself. 'We haven't got much time – the trial starts in just over two weeks.'

'She's a young woman with a toddler,' Peter called out

---

[6] For more on Paul Godwin and his relationship with Bernie and her friends, see "Two Little Dickie Birds" © 2015 Judy Ford, ISBN: 978-1-911083-13-9

from the front passenger seat. 'And if we can't find out who really did it, she's going to go to jail for a crime she didn't commit.'

'What makes you so certain?' Paul asked sceptically. 'If the case is going to trial, presumably the police found evidence that she did it.'

'Her parish priest told Peter that she would have told him, if she had,' Jonah answered, with just a hint of derision in his voice. 'Something along the lines of not endangering her immortal soul by telling lies to her confessor.'

'She says that she didn't do it, and I believe her,' Peter said simply. 'So there must've been something that the police investigators missed. That's what we're hoping to find.'

'But we'll get there a lot quicker if we don't have to start from scratch,' Jonah added. 'So be a good boy and have a chat to your friends in South Worcestershire and get them to hand over the files, won't you?'

'Oh alright!' Paul sighed. Jonah was a difficult person to say *no* to and Peter … well, Peter hardly ever asked a favour from anyone. If he believed in this woman and wanted to help her, there must be something about the case worth giving a second look. 'I'll see what I can do and let you know. When do you need them?'

'Yesterday!' Jonah quipped. 'You know me – always in a tearing hurry.'

'If you can spare the time, why don't you both come over for tea on Sunday?' Bernie suggested. 'It'd be nice to catch up with you and Karen. We didn't get much chance to talk at Jonah's retirement do.'

'OK. I'll see what I can do,' Paul repeated. 'And I'll bring over whatever I can find on Sunday. Now, get off the line, will you? I've got real police work to do.'

3. ALL WENT TO THEIR OWN TOWNS

All went to their own towns to be registered.
Luke 2:4, NRSV, Anglicised Edition

What I don't get about that woman,' eighteen-year-old Lucy said, pointing towards the newspaper that lay on the table next to Peter's bowl of breakfast cereal, with the picture of Vanessa on the steps of the magistrates court showing clearly on the front, 'is why she didn't just take the kid and go back to live with her parents. Why did she stay with her husband if he was such a monster?'

'It's not as simple as that, love,' Bernie told her through a mouthful of toast. The family – Peter, Jonah, Bernie and her daughter, Lucy – were all sitting round the large kitchen table in their home in Headington, having breakfast together preparatory to Lucy's departure for her first term at Liverpool University.

'Your mam's right,' Peter agreed. 'I've seen this sort of thing before. The controlling partner in the relationship – usually the man – undermines the other one's self-esteem, so that they don't believe they deserve to be treated any better.'

'And they undermine their self-confidence so that they don't believe they're capable of getting out even if they tried,' Jonah agreed.

'And, in this instance,' Bernie added, 'there's the added factor that Vanessa seems to come from a very traditional

Irish Catholic family, who probably drummed it into her from an early age that marriage was for life.'

'Even when you're being beaten up by your spouse?' Lucy demanded scornfully. 'That's ridiculous!'

'I agree,' her mother replied, 'but I'm afraid that the Catholic church has had a rather poor track record in the past when it comes to supporting victims of domestic violence. There have been cases of women being told by their priest that it's their duty to go back to abusive husbands. And even now, a lot of families feel that it's a bit of a disgrace to get divorced. I remember when my cousin Joey got married, Ruth's father saying to her, "You've made your bed, my girl, and now you have to lie on it." I'm not at all sure that he'd have been willing to take her back if she'd run away from Joey.'

'But you said this Vanessa's parents are dead against her husband and think he deserved what he got,' Lucy pointed out. 'So they must've been willing to take her.'

'Yes,' Bernie admitted, smiling at her daughter's tenacity. 'But that's now that they've seen the damage that he'd been doing to her. I'm talking about before that – about the whole ethos when she was growing up. She'll have been surrounded by people passing judgment on the way so many marriages end in divorce these days and perhaps talking about how glad they are that they don't have any of that sort of thing in *their* family. And it will have made her feel, subconsciously, that it would be better to let her husband beat her to death than to desert him and have to admit that she's failed as a wife.'

'But that's stupid!' Lucy insisted. 'He's the one who's made their marriage fail.'

'I agree, love.' Bernie finished her toast and got up to take her plate to the sink. 'I'm not saying it isn't. I'm just saying that's probably a factor in why she didn't feel able to leave him. Now, we ought to be getting ready to go. Is there anything else you've remembered you need to take, since we packed the car last night?'

'I don't think so.' Lucy also got to her feet. 'I'll just get my list and double-check.'

Twenty minutes later, the moment of departure had come. Bernie sat in the driver's seat, waiting while Lucy said goodbye to Peter and Jonah. This was the first time that she would be separated for more than a few days from her much-loved stepfather and the friend whom she had helped to care for since his disabling injury more than nine years previously. She put her arms around Peter's chest and he hugged her close.

'Enjoy yourself at uni,' he said, forcing himself to sound more cheerful than he felt, and silently cursing the Oxford tutor who had rejected Lucy's application for a place there, which would have allowed her to pursue her studies while continuing to live at home, 'and be sure and keep in touch.'

'Of course I will,' Lucy promised. 'We've got broadband at the house, so I can skype you every day.'

She stretched up to kiss Peter on the cheek, before turning her attention to Jonah. She went round behind his wheelchair so that she could put her arms around his shoulders, which were the lowest point on his body where he could still feel her touch. She hugged and kissed him, murmuring in his ear, 'good bye, Jonah. I'm going to miss you.'

'Not as much as I'll miss you,' he countered. 'Now I'm going to be at the mercy of these two clowns, and no beautiful young girlfriend to turn to when I need a bit of pampering!'

Lucy laughed. 'Well, just mind you behave yourself, like a good boy,' she teased. 'I'll be checking up on you and if I get reports that you're over-doing it or not doing your physio properly, I'll be on the train and back here to give you what-for!'

She gave him a final hug resting her cheek on the top of his head. Then, taking a deep breath, she straightened up and walked over to the car.

'Bye then!' she called out, as she opened it and got in. She wound the window down before fastening her seatbelt, and leaned out, gazing up at the home where she had lived all her life, first alone with her mother, with the addition of Peter from the age of three and latterly with Jonah as a permanent guest and much-loved companion.

Bernie let in the clutch and released the handbrake. They were off!

'Give my love to Aunty Dot!' Jonah called after them, as the car started to move off.

'I will!' Lucy shouted back through the open window, waving her hand vigorously, her long golden curls blowing about her face.

The two men watched until the car turned out of the drive and was hidden by the tall copper beech hedge separating the garden from the road.

'It's going to be strange without her,' Peter sighed, turning to go back into the house.

'Yes,' Jonah agreed as he followed Peter inside. For once, he was lost for words to add to this simple statement.

'When Hannah went off to Leeds,' Peter continued, remembering the day when his own older child had left home for university, 'I thought it would be three years and then she'd come back to work in Oxford. It never occurred to me she'd settle there permanently. I know you have to let them go but ...I'd rather it was somewhere close enough to visit in a day.'

'You should be glad Hannah's up there,' Jonah joked. 'You've got your hands full with Eddie's kids. If Hannah lived locally, you'd be expected to look after hers too. It's a tough life being a grandparent these days!'

'Yes, I know,' Peter smiled. 'And, after all, Eddie came back eventually – even after he seemed to be making a life for himself in Jamaica.'

'At least we know that Lucy'll be safe in Liverpool,' Jonah said, trying to think of something positive to say about her decision to study in a city nearly two hundred miles away. 'Bernie's cousin Joey will see to that.'

Bernie was a native of Liverpool herself – a fact that she was fond of mentioning at any opportunity – and she still had a few relatives living there.

'Yes.' Peter stood in the hall, wondering what to do next. The excitement of Lucy's send-off had left him with a feeling of anti-climax.

'Now, unless you've got other plans,' he heard Jonah saying behind him, 'I'd like to make a start on figuring out the next steps in this murder mystery you've taken on. Come and have a look at the notes I've made, summarising what we know from the newspaper reports and stuff.'

While Peter had been engaged in helping Lucy with packing and taking her on a last minute shopping expedition for items that were suddenly essential but had until now been forgotten about, Jonah had spent the previous day trawling the internet for anything he could find about the murder victim and the circumstances surrounding his death. Now, he was eager to share his findings and to make plans for the next steps in their investigation.

Peter followed Jonah into the ground floor room, which served as his study and private sitting room. He sat down in front of a desk, upon which stood a large computer screen. A wireless connection enabled Jonah to display the information that he had been collating. The first page was headed, 'Victim: Christopher Nigel Wellesley.'

'He was born in 1978, which makes him fifteen years older than Vanessa,' Jonah commented. 'She was only twenty-one and fresh from college when they married. It's no wonder he was able to dominate her.'

'Mmm,' Peter agreed, scanning down the information displayed on the screen. 'And then Leah was born two years later – so not a shotgun wedding, then. I had wondered if that could've been why she married him. Or -

,' he paused in thought for a moment. 'Hang on! Didn't her sister say something about her losing a baby? Could that have been an earlier pregnancy, before Leah was born?'

'No.' Jonah shook his head. 'I've found out about all that. She gave birth prematurely to a stillborn baby girl in April of this year.'

'So, she lost a baby in April and then her husband is killed on … what was it? … the twelfth of May. That can only have been a few weeks later,' Peter mused. 'No wonder everyone thinks she did it! Young mother, distraught with grief at the loss of a baby, struggling to cope with her husband's demands and her other child – and we all know what a difficult age two is …'

'And, as you say, her sister is on record as blaming Christopher for the baby's death,' Jonah agreed, 'but I haven't found any corroborating evidence.'

'Gerry reckoned there was,' Peter recalled. 'I'd forgotten all about it, but he told me that was one of the reasons everyone was so confident that Vanessa would get away with manslaughter if only she would admit that she killed him. He said something about it looking as if she'd been kicked in the stomach. I suppose the police will have seen her medical records. Paul may be able to tell us if he was really suspected of anything.'

'He studied law at Southampton and then went into his father's solicitor's firm.' Jonah continued, scrolling down the page. 'Not a very imaginative career choice.'

'It may not have been a choice at all,' Peter observed. 'It was probably just what was expected of him. If he was the only son – which presumably he was, seeing as he inherited the family home – his father may well have just assumed that he would carry on the family law business.'

'Anyway, by the time he died, he was a partner in *Wellesley, Bracknell & Wellesley*, which has offices in the centre of Evesham. The other partner is Anthony Bracknell. He could be a good person to talk to, because, as far as I can see, he's been with the firm since before Christopher's father died. He may be able to tell us more about the family dynamics – what happened between Christopher and his sister, for example.'

'And what sort of person Christopher was,' Peter suggested. 'Except that he's unlikely to want to tell *us* anything, seeing as we're on the other side, so-to-speak.'

'No we're not!' Jonah objected. 'We're on the side of justice. He should want us to find out who killed his partner.'

'Only, he probably thinks he knows that already and that we're just trying to get her off the hook.'

The argument was interrupted by a ring on the doorbell.

'That'll be Gerry and Damien,' Jonah said eagerly. 'That's good – they've arrived early.'

Peter went to answer the door. Sure enough, the two priests were standing together at the top of the slope that led up to the front door. He took their coats and ushered them into Jonah's study.

'Go in and sit down. I'll be with you in a minute – I just need to get another chair from the kitchen.'

'Come in!' Jonah called out, evidently pleased to see the visitors. 'We've made a start, but no major breakthroughs yet.'

'We could do with a bit of help from you,' Peter added, coming in with the extra chair and putting it down between Damien and Gerry. 'We need to get a picture of what the victim – Christopher Wellesley – was like.'

'Go on Gerry!' Damien urged his friend. 'Tell them what you told me about when you were preparing him for baptism.'

'Well …,' Gerry hesitated. He thought for a moment or two, and then started again. 'Well, it was like this.' Another long pause and a short sigh. 'As I told you, Vanessa was a cradle Catholic. She wanted to get married in church. They came to me and we talked it through and it turned out that

Christopher knew nothing at all about the faith, beyond what he'd picked up through school assemblies and RE lessons; and he'd never been baptised. But he said that he wanted Vanessa to have everything she wanted and that he was willing to learn.'

'Yes – go on,' Jonah prompted, as the priest paused in thought again.

'At first, I thought he was sincere – at least in wanting to do everything to make his fiancée happy. He was very interested in Catholic teaching on marriage – especially the idea that it was for life and …'

'Yes?' Jonah said again, a little impatiently.

'I suppose, in retrospect, the alarm bells ought to have started ringing right back then,' Gerry answered slowly, 'but I thought he was just interested in knowing more about his prospective wife's faith and …'

'Oh buck up, Gerry!' Damien broke in as his friend once more tailed off into silence. 'Cut to the chase, can't you?'

'He seemed very taken with the idea of the husband being the head of the household, and he was surprised that the wedding vows don't include the bride promising to obey her husband.'

'Don't they?' Jonah asked, momentarily diverted from consideration of Christopher Wellesley's character by what was to him a surprising statement. 'I always assumed the Catholic service would use the traditional vows.'

'Oh no,' Damien told him, a small note of triumph in his voice. 'That was introduced by the Church of England. In the Catholic church, both bride and groom just promise to love and honour the other.'

'I bet Margaret didn't promise to obey you!' Peter joked, looking towards Jonah and thinking of his late wife, who had been a no-nonsense motor-cycle-riding trauma surgeon from East Lancashire.

'Of course not!' came Jonah's laughing rejoinder. 'And I'm damn' sure Bernie didn't say "obey" either!'

'No – and neither did Angie,' Peter replied, becoming more serious at the memory of his first wife, who remained the love of his life. 'It wasn't in the Methodist service that we used, any more than in the Catholic one.'

'That Thomas Cranmer has a lot to answer for,' Jonah observed. 'I'm sure a lot of trouble could have been avoided over the years, if he hadn't included that little phrase.'

'But to get back to Christopher Wellesley,' Peter said, turning back to Gerry. 'You were telling us about how he liked the idea of wives being subject to their husbands.'

'Yes.' Gerry thought for a few moments. 'At least – no, it wasn't quite like that. I mean … at the time, I thought he was just interested in the Church's teaching on marriage and in the fact that the marriage vows weren't quite what popular belief has them to be. It was only much later that I started to wonder …'

'Wonder what?' asked Jonah sharply.

'I started to wonder whether he was using Catholic teaching on marriage to … to keep Vanessa under his thumb; whether he became so keen to …,' he trailed off and sat in silent thought.

'So keen to what?' demanded Jonah impatiently.

'He decided he wanted to become a Catholic,' Gerry answered, a little reluctantly. 'It was when I told them that we'd have to get permission from the bishop for them to have a catholic marriage, because he wasn't baptised – and that it wouldn't be a sacrament if both parties weren't Christians. He straightaway said why shouldn't he be baptised first?'

'And you baptised him?' Jonah asked.

'Not right away, of course,' Gerry replied hastily. 'I explained that it wasn't just a matter of going through a ceremony. Since he was an adult and able to speak for himself, he'd have to be instructed in the Catholic faith, and make solemn vows committing himself to God. Baptism isn't just a naming ceremony, you know,' he added, looking towards Jonah, who smiled back.

'I understand that,' he assured the priest quietly. 'My father was a Baptist minister. I've seen plenty of believer's baptisms in my time.'

'Then you'll appreciate my concern that his determination to become a Catholic seemed to be more because of wanting to please his fiancée than any faith of his own.' Gerry paused in thought again. 'He was very quick learning his catechism, but somehow I never got the impression that it meant anything to him. It was just a means to an end.'

'But you could never be sure of that,' Damien intervened. 'So you had no choice.'

'It was very difficult for me to know what the right thing to do was,' Gerry went on. 'I couldn't refuse to instruct him in the faith – there was always the chance that he was sincere. And anyway, plenty of people have become Catholics in order to please their spouse and then found real faith later – perhaps when their children took their first communion. And it clearly made Vanessa happy to think that they would be able to take communion together on their wedding day. So I went ahead, and he was baptised and confirmed a few weeks before they were married.'

'And then afterwards?' Jonah asked. 'Did he continue to take an interest in the church? Or did he consider he'd done his duty by his wife and nothing more was required?'

'Oh no,' Gerry shook his head. 'He was a regular attender at Mass – much better than a lot of men who were born into the church, I have to admit. But … but, after a while, even that seemed a bit … well, I got the impression that he came to church with Vanessa every Sunday at least in part because he didn't like to allow her out on her own. Or maybe it was more that he didn't want her talking to her family and her old friends when he wasn't there.'

'Typical controlling behaviour,' Peter observed,

nodding his head.

'But I didn't think about it at the time,' Gerry added hastily. 'It was only afterwards that I started to put two and two together and work out that the signs had been there from much earlier.'

'That's always the way,' Damien agreed. 'All the little things … the odd words and gestures … the evasive answers … you see them all in a new light, once you know.'

'And when exactly did you start to suspect that all was not right in the Wellesleys' marriage?' Jonah asked Gerry.

'I suppose I first started to wonder about it after Leah was born. Vanessa's mother came to see me, very distressed that he wouldn't let them see as much of their granddaughter as she would have liked. I tried to reassure her by saying that he was probably just anxious that too many visitors would be tiring for his wife, and that being a new parent was a stressful business.' Gerry paused to reflect. 'I suppose I hoped things would just sort themselves out after a while.'

'But they didn't?' Peter asked.

'No. Deborah came to ask my advice again some months later. She was anxious because Vanessa wouldn't let them call round during the day – only in the evening when Christopher was there too. Apparently, she made all sorts of different excuses, but Deborah was convinced it was that Christopher had told her that she wasn't to talk to her family when he wasn't present. I spoke to Vanessa about it, but she denied it all and claimed that it was just bad luck that her parents always seemed to choose inconvenient times to call round.'

'Did you speak to Christopher about it?' Jonah asked.

'No. Vanessa begged me not to. I … I was very uneasy about it, but I was afraid that anything I did would only make things worse – and Vanessa insisted that everything was fine and she was happy with Christopher. She said it was just rather tiring coping with Leah all day, especially now that there was another baby on the way.'

'Ah yes,' Jonah smiled. 'Another classic technique used by controlling men to keep their womenfolk in a state of dependency – make sure they're permanently pregnant. I bet Christopher was all in favour of Catholic teaching on contraception!'

'I don't know,' Gerry muttered, rather shamefaced. 'We sort of skimmed over that rather. It's usually rather a tricky subject with new converts, and it's quite clear that most Catholics adopt a more liberal attitude to birth control in practice, so …'

'And was this the baby that was stillborn and that Vanessa's sister blamed Christopher for?' Peter cut in, trying to get the conversation back on track.

'That's right. Vanessa went into labour five weeks early, after a fall in the house. She claimed that she tripped over the cat, but after Christopher died, she admitted that actually he'd hit her as a punishment for letting Leah disturb him when he was reading and he'd caught her off balance. According to Deborah, the doctors actually thought she'd been punched in the stomach – probably more than once and possibly over a period of time. They called me to the hos-'

'Did you say *five weeks*?' Jonah cut across him. 'The baby was born *five weeks* early on the sixth of April?'

'That's right,' Gerry answered in a puzzled voice. 'What's so significant about that?'

'And Christopher was killed on the twelfth of May?'

'Ye-e-es.'

'There must be more or less exactly five weeks between the sixth of April and the twelfth of May,' Jonah explained. 'Christopher must've been killed more or less on the day the baby was due.'

'What of it?' Damien asked.

'When you're expecting a baby, the due date is something that is constantly in your mind,' Jonah told him. 'Everyone's always asking for it – at ante-natal clinics and doctor's appointments and even just friends showing an interest.'

'Jonah's right,' Peter broke in. 'That's a date that would have been impressed on Vanessa's mind, and a day when she'd have been thinking about the baby that she lost and …'

'If she was going to lose control and try to make her husband pay for being the cause of her losing it,' Jonah continued, 'that might be the day she'd do it.'

'I'm sorry,' Peter said, looking at Gerry and then at Damien. 'I know this isn't what you want to hear, but you do see …?'

'Yes,' Gerry answered quietly. 'I do see. And I know it looks bad for Vanessa. I just *know* she didn't do it.'

'And we're going to find out who did,' Jonah declared decisively. 'So go on – you were called to the hospital when the baby was born …?'

'Yes. Deborah rang when she heard Vanessa had gone into labour. She was worried in case something went wrong, with it being so early. I was there when Ruth was born. It was a girl – they called her Ruth. I gave her conditional baptism, although, if I'm honest, I knew she was already dead. I just thought it would help to reassure Vanessa – and maybe more her parents, who were a bit old-school and might have worried …'

Gerry tailed off into silence and sat there with his eyes lowered.

'Traditional Catholic teaching was that unbaptised babies can't go to heaven,' Damien explained to Jonah. 'There was supposed to be another place, called Limbo, where they spend eternity – a sort of half-way house between heaven and hell.'

'I've heard of it,' Jonah nodded, 'but I can't say I understood where the idea came from.'

'Mediaeval theologians came up with it as a way of squaring the necessity for baptism in order to purge original sin and enable the soul to enter heaven, and the injustice of innocent children – albeit born in original sin, but not having committed any personal sin – being condemned to eternal punishment in hell,' Damien continued. 'The way it was described was that they weren't being punished, but they were deprived of being with God in heaven. Anyway, in 2007, Pope Benedict confirmed the results of a theological commission, which said that there was no basis in scripture for the doctrine and that there was every reason to hope that there is a path to salvation for unbaptised infants.'

'So technically, what I ought to have done,' Gerry added, 'was to have refused baptism, but to have provided some sort of alternative blessing for the child. It just seemed simpler to stick to what they were familiar with and avoid having to deal with awkward theological questions at such a difficult time.'

'I'm sure you did the right thing,' Damien said firmly. 'I'd have done the same.'

'I have to say, I can't see that it matters,' Jonah said briskly, eager to get on. 'It's all just symbolic anyhow. But, can we get back to Christopher Wellesley? What we could really do with is some pointers to other people who might have had a grudge against him – something bad enough to make them pick up a screwdriver and stab him with it, and then leave him for dead. Any ideas?'

'No.' Gerry stared round at them blankly. 'To be honest, I don't think he knew a lot of people well enough for that. He never seemed to do much outside his home and work. In many ways he was a model family man: earning good money in a nine-to-five job and back home in the bosom of his family the rest of the time.'

'So no chance he was having an affair?' Jonah asked. 'There couldn't be a resentful *other woman* in the background anywhere? Or a jealous partner wanting to kill her lover?'

'No – I'm sure he wasn't!' Gerry sounded shocked. 'He was totally devoted to Vanessa. That was the problem: he was insanely jealous and didn't like anyone else so much as speaking to her.'

'What about male friends then?' Jonah persisted. 'Did he have any of those?'

'I don't think so,' Gerry shrugged. 'He got his business partner to be Best Man at the wedding – a chap called Anthony Bracknell. He and his wife were the only guests from the groom's side, with Christopher not having any family.'

'Who did they have as godparents for Leah?' Peter asked, latching on to another occasion when the priest might have come across Christopher's friends.

'Vanessa's sister, Louise, is her godmother,' Gerry answered a little evasively.

'And?' Jonah prompted. 'Aren't you supposed to have more than that? When we had our boys done in the C of E, we had to have two godfathers and one godmother.'

'No. You can just have one godparent,' Gerry told him, 'but most people do have at least two: one of each. They couldn't think of anyone to be godfather, so in the end they asked me. It was all a bit awkward, but I didn't like to refuse.'

'Which, of course, is another reason why Gerry feels a responsibility to try to keep Vanessa out of jail,' Damien put in. 'As Leah's godfather, he's obliged to do his best for her, and she'll suffer more than anyone if her mother gets a life sentence.'

'Wasn't there anyone else in the church they could have asked?' Peter persisted. 'If Vanessa has been going there all her life, she must've know *someone* who could have done it.'

'Like I said, Christopher always kept himself to himself – and once they were married, so did Vanessa.'

'And you didn't manage to persuade him to get more involved?' Jonah queried. 'Based on my experience of churches, I'd have thought someone with his legal background would have ended up being appointed treasurer or being put in charge of health and safety or-'

'Or safeguarding,' Peter added with a grim smile.

'We have quite a few professional people in our congregation,' Gerry replied. 'So we didn't need to ask him and he didn't volunteer.'

'So basically, you're telling us that Christopher Wellesley didn't have any dealings with anyone apart from his wife and daughter and his work colleagues,' Jonah summarised. 'You do realise,' he went on with irony in his voice, 'that this is not at all helpful for Vanessa. If she's telling the truth, then someone must have gained entry to their house while she was out shopping, confronted Christopher in his workshop and stabbed him to death. The way you're talking, about the only people who would have had any reason to call at the house are the postman and the milkman! Was he in dispute with the dairy over his bill? Or had he had an argument over mail deliveries?'

'Could it have been a burglary that went wrong?' Damien suggested tentatively.

'No,' Jonah said firmly. 'If there'd been any sign of a break-in the police would have had to tell the defence about it.'

'And Vanessa said there was nothing missing,' Peter pointed out.

'So, we're back to: who might have come to see Christopher and who would he have let in?' Jonah reiterated. 'And you seem to be telling us that there's no one!'

'Mmm.' Gerry bit his lip and looked round with a rather hopeless expression on his face. 'It's not looking good for Vanessa, is it?'

4. CLOUD OF WITNESSES

Therefore, since we are surrounded by so great a cloud of witnesses, let us also lay aside every weight and the sin that clings so closely, and let us run with perseverance the race that is set before us.

Hebrews 12:1, NRSV, Anglicised Edition

'Come in Paul – and Karen! It's lovely to see you both,' Bernie greeted DCI Paul Godwin and his wife as they got out of their car. She had heard it approaching up the long drive and had come out to meet them. 'You're looking well. Marriage must suit you.'

Paul and Karen were newlyweds, having tied the knot in her home town of Aberystwyth the previous May – the very same Saturday that Christopher Wellesley met his death, as it happened. Paul at forty-five, still looked young to have reached the heights of Detective Chief Inspector. Karen, fifteen years his junior, had recently taken her inspector's exams and was hopeful of eventually overtaking him in the police hierarchy – something of which Paul was well-aware and which did not worry him in the least. Like Peter, he had little personal ambition beyond a desire to use his talents to make a difference.

They followed Bernie into the hall, where Jonah was waiting for them, eager to get down to business. He looked approvingly at the box file and laptop case that Karen was carrying. It looked as if Paul must have been as good as his word and brought them information about the enquiry into Christopher Wellesley's murder.

They trooped into Jonah's study and Bernie helped

Karen to set up her computer, while Peter brought in a tea tray and distributed cups and plates. When these preliminaries were out of the way, everyone sat looking expectantly towards Paul, who leaned back in his chair with his hands resting on his head of curly brown hair.

'Well?' Jonah demanded.

'I've had a look at the file,' Paul answered, 'and I'll show you what I've found, but I have to warn you that I think you're wasting your time. It looks like an open-and-shut case to me.'

'Go on,' Jonah urged, unfazed by this remark. 'I like a challenge.'

'OK,' Paul sighed, taking a notebook out of the box file. 'Here's my summary of the investigation. There's a call to the police logged at 12.12. Two constables arrive on the scene at about twenty past. Christopher Wellesley is still alive at that time, but unconscious. One of the PCs goes with him in the ambulance to hospital, where he's pronounced dead on arrival, despite the best efforts of the paramedics. The other one stays with Mrs Wellesley until the call comes through that her husband is dead. He then accompanies her to her parents' house – with the baby as well – after securing the crime scene.'

He paused and took a sip of tea, before going on.

'The SOCOs[7] do the usual things: fingerprints, bloodstains, signs of forced entry etc. etc. and the SIO[8] instigates a house-to-house to find out if any of the neighbours saw anything.'

'And did they find anything interesting?' Jonah asked impatiently.

'In a word – no,' Paul answered, smiling at the remembrance of his ex-colleague's get-everything-done-by-

---

[7] Scene of Crime Officers: specialist police staff trained in forensic examination and evidence collection.

[8] Senior Investigating Officer: the police officer in charge of the enquiry.

yesterday attitude when they had worked together during his time with Thames Valley Police. 'The house was secure and there was no sign of anyone having attempted to break in. Access to the rear is via a side gate, which was locked and bolted from the inside. The back garden is surrounded by a six-foot high fence, which was undamaged. In any case, the only way over it would be through one of the other gardens, and none of the neighbours reported seeing any trespassers.'

'So, we can be fairly confident that, whoever did it was known to the victim and let into the house by him,' Peter murmured. 'We'd rather come to that conclusion already.'

'A woman living across the road from them did claim to have seen someone peering in at the front windows and attempting to open the side gate that morning,' Paul admitted, 'but she didn't see them actually gaining access to the house or the back garden.'

'Even so,' Jonah interrupted. 'It's interesting that there were any callers, because up to now nobody has been able to suggest that there was anyone who might have wanted to come to see Christopher Wellesley for any reason – never mind with a view to killing him. Did you find out who this visitor was?'

'No. The neighbour didn't recognise her and she could only give a very vague description: medium height, short dark hair, wearing a dark coloured jacket over trousers. An appeal in the local press and radio for her to come forward didn't produce any results.'

'And what time was this?' Peter asked.

'Again, it's a bit vague, but probably round about eleven.'

'OK. Let's put that one on the back burner,' Jonah said briskly. 'Anything from any of the other neighbours?'

Not really. Several of them seem to have been vaguely aware of Christopher's controlling behaviour towards Vanessa. A few said they felt sorry for her and one or two said they couldn't understand why she put up with it. One of them was a bit peeved that he hadn't joined the local Residents' Association and wouldn't contribute to the street party they put on to celebrate the royal wedding.' Paul flicked through his notes. 'Oh! There was just one other thing. His next-door-neighbour on the left-hand side complained that he'd turned the hose on his cat when it ventured over the wall into the Wellesley back garden. The local police confirmed that he'd reported the incident to them and to the RSPCA, and he was annoyed that they declined to take it any further.'

'A motive for murder?' suggested Bernie.

'Hardly!' Karen laughed. 'It's not even as if the cat was seriously injured.'

'I know it sounds ridiculous,' Jonah agreed, 'but some animal lovers do seem to get these things out of proportion. I don't suppose for a minute that he went round with the intention of killing Christopher Wellesley, but suppose he called to make another complaint and Wellesley didn't seem to be taking it seriously enough? Maybe he'd had another go at the cat, and the neighbour was demanding an apology or some sort of compensation, and Wellesley laughs in his face. If they were together in the workshop, mightn't he have lost his temper and grabbed the first weapon that came to hand and lunged at him with it?'

'Not meaning to kill him or even to do serious damage,' Peter chimed in. 'He could even have left, not realising how badly hurt Wellesley was.'

'And he's one person who wouldn't have needed to have been let into the house by Wellesley himself,' Bernie added excitedly. 'He could have climbed over the fence from his own back garden.'

'Perhaps in order to rescue the cat,' Peter suggested, 'if Wellesley was subjecting it to some sort of punishment for daring to come into his garden again.'

'OK,' Paul conceded. 'Let's have a look at his statement, shall we?'

He looked towards Karen who obligingly scrolled through a list of documents on her computer screen.

'Here it is!' she said a few moments later, clicking on a file to open it. 'His name is Jeremy Willard. He's thirty-nine, unmarried and lives alone – apart from the cat, who rejoices in the name of Bobby Dazzler. He says that he was at home all morning on the day of Christopher Wellesley's death. He didn't hear or see anything – not even Mrs Wellesley's car leaving – apart from some shouting, which could have come from any of the gardens in the road.'

'So he *could* have got over the fence and attacked Wellesley,' Bernie commented. 'At least, there's nobody to say that he definitely didn't.'

'But equally, there's no evidence that he did,' Paul objected. 'And no evidence that anyone had been in the house that day apart from Wellesley and his wife and baby. There were no unidentified fingermarks, no footprints by the fence, nothing disturbed at all. The wife herself, in her statement, says that everything looked just as normal.'

'OK. Has that exhausted the neighbours?' Jonah asked, keen to move on. 'What about other witnesses. Did you interview his business partner and work colleagues? What sort of picture did they paint of him?'

'They all said that he was a good solicitor and that he had no money worries,' Paul told them, looking down at his notes. 'They also said that there had never been any complaints made about him. However, one of our officers had a look in his correspondence files and found this.'

He rummaged in the box file and brought out a sheaf of photocopies clipped together at one corner.

'It's a series of letters from a client accusing him of costing her a lot of extra money through some mistake in the conveyance of a house that she was buying. It culminates in a threat to report him to the law society for negligence.'

'She?' queried Jonah. 'Could this have been the woman

that the neighbour saw knocking on his door that Saturday morning?'

'I don't know,' Paul admitted. 'There's nothing here about anyone following up on this … but even if it was the same woman,' he added defensively, seeing the accusatory look on Jonah's face, 'we know she didn't gain access to the house, so that's irrelevant.'

'Alright,' Jonah said equably. 'Just let us have her name and address and we'll do the following up.'

'In any case,' Karen argued, feeling that her West Mercia colleagues were being criticised unfairly, 'that's hardly a motive for murder, is it?'

'You'd be surprised,' Jonah smiled, 'but moving on: is there anything else from the solicitors' office that could help us?'

'Just something the receptionist said,' Paul answered, consulting his notes again. 'She's been with the firm since before Christopher Wellesley joined it. Back then, the two Wellesleys were Christopher's father, Bruce, and his uncle, Angus. Anthony Bracknell had only relatively recently been made a partner. She said tha-'

'Hang on!' Jonah interrupted. 'What's this about an uncle? I thought Christopher Wellesley didn't have any relatives.'

'He doesn't – not now,' Paul explained patiently. 'His parents died in a road traffic accident in 1999 and his uncle suffered a fatal heart attack in 2003. Angus Wellesley – the uncle – was unmarried and had no offspring. Bruce left two children: Christopher and an older sister, Paula, who was estranged from the family.'

'OK. Sorry,' Jonah smiled apologetically towards Paul. 'Go on.'

'The receptionist's name is Linda Hayes,' Paul resumed. 'The notes from the DC who interviewed her say that she was a bit cagey, but the general drift was that both Christopher Wellesley and his father before him were a bit prone to "wandering hands" when it came to the female members of staff. She seemed to accept it as just an inevitable part of office life, but, as the oldest most long-established, member of staff, she saw it as her duty to warn the younger women to take care, and she did her best to see to it that they were never left alone with Christopher.'

'So not quite the model family man that we've been led to believe,' Jonah murmured in a tone of satisfaction.

'And that opens up the field when it comes to the question of who that woman was who was trying to get to see him that morning,' Bernie observed. 'Do any of these female staff match the description?'

'There are only actually two other women,' Paul answered. 'There's an articled clerk called Zara Lambourne and a part time typist from a temping agency. I suppose the latter may well have moved on by now – that was four months ago.'

'And do either of them look like the woman the neighbour saw?' Jonah asked impatiently.

'I don't know,' Paul admitted. 'There's nothing in the file about their appearance.'

'Oh well!' Jonah responded cheerfully. 'That's something else we can look into. Now, can we move on to Christopher's sister? She sounds like a very intriguing personality. I assume that they did question her, seeing as she was well-known for having fallen out with the victim big-time?'

'Yes, I was coming to her,' Paul answered, making an effort not to show his irritation at Jonah's apparent lack of faith in the investigation which had been carried out by colleagues whom he respected. 'She's a university professor and a tutorial fellow at Lichfield College, here in Oxford. She-'

'Lichfield? Really?' Bernie broke in. 'I know a few people there. What's her subject?'

Before taking early retirement in order to act as Jonah's Personal Assistant full-time, Bernie had been Applied Mathematics Fellow at another of Oxford University's colleges. She was, therefore, familiar with the university and had many friends and acquaintances there.

'I'm not sure …,' Paul began, scanning through his notes.

'It's OK – I've got it!' Jonah called out, looking up from the computer screen attached to the arm of his special chair. 'I Googled her. She's a particle physicist.'

'That's good,' Bernie said with satisfaction in her voice. 'I've got plenty of contacts in the Physics Department as well as Martin and Tom at Lichfield.'

'But let's hear what West Mercia found out about her first,' Peter suggested mildly. 'Carry on Paul.'

'There's not much to say,' Paul answered, after consulting his notes again. 'She's unmarried and lives in college. She said that she hasn't so much as set eyes on her brother since their parents' funeral in '99. When asked why, she just said, and I quote: "he wasn't interested in me, so I wasn't interested in him." According to her, she was in Oxford the day he died … but there doesn't appear to be any corroborating evidence for that,' he admitted after a short pause.

'That leaves us plenty of scope for further investigation,' Jonah said with satisfaction in his voice. 'What was this family feud that kept the siblings apart, even to the extent of not inviting his own sister to see him married and her not being interested in seeing her new niece? All very promising!'

'I don't know,' Karen objected. 'It's not that unusual for siblings not to get on. It doesn't mean they're likely to kill one another – especially if they've been out of contact for the best part of twenty years! If they haven't even met for all that time, what could have happened to make her suddenly snap now?'

'That's what we're going to find out,' Jonah declared cheerfully. 'Or else we'll establish that she's innocent. Either way, we'll have a better idea about what really happened.'

'Which is most probably that the wife did it,' Paul pointed out. 'She's the one with motive, means and opportunity, and nobody would blame her for it, if only she would come clean and admit she did it.'

'Which is why it's so strange that she won't,' Peter pointed out quietly.

'Could it be that she's blotted it out from her memory?' Karen suggested cautiously. 'Don't you think it's possible that she genuinely doesn't remember doing it, because it's just too horrific?'

'I suppose it's possible,' Bernie began.

'But she remembered all about finding him there, unconscious, and pulling the screwdriver out of his chest,' Peter objected. 'That must have been just as horrific as the stabbing – more so, in fact, because that was when he started bleeding everywhere.'

'And presumably, by that reckoning, she'd have to have stabbed him *before* going out to do the shopping,' Bernie added, 'otherwise, surely she'd either remember both stabbing him *and* pulling the screwdriver back out or else neither.'

'It's difficult to imagine her stabbing her husband fatally and then calmly going off to do the weekend shopping,' Jonah agreed.

'What you say about the bleeding being caused by her pulling the screwdriver *out* of the wound, is another interesting point,' Paul put in. 'I'm no medical expert, but mightn't that mean that she killed him, even if she didn't stab him in the first place?'

'What did the pathologist's report say about it?' Jonah asked sharply.

'Dunno,' Paul shrugged. 'I'm afraid I didn't bother reading it. It seemed obvious how he died – and to be honest, it still looks obvious to me who killed him. Look – if you really want to help this woman, it seems to me that the thing to do is to persuade her to plead guilty to manslaughter with the mitigation that she was acting in self-defence and off her head following the stillbirth. The doctors will confirm that it was most likely an assault by her husband that caused the premature birth; and there are plenty of people who will back her up when she says that he was frequently violent and constantly controlling and manipulative. If she shows remorse, any jury is going to be sympathetic and the judge will probably let her off with a suspended sentence.'

'Yes, Paul,' Peter said quietly in the silence that followed. 'We know all that – and so does she. It's just that she isn't prepared to lie under oath.'

5. BROTHER, SISTER, PARENT, CHILD

For the joy of human love,
brother, sister, parent, child,
friends on earth, and friends above,
for all gentle thoughts and mild,
Christ our God, to Thee we raise
This our sacrifice of praise.

Folliott Sandford Pierpoint
Hymn "For the Beauty of the Earth"

'Right! Now let's do this systematically,' Jonah said the following morning, calling to order the case conference that they had convened in his study. Nominally, Peter was in charge but, as usual, he was taking the line of least resistance and allowing Jonah to call the shots. 'Who are our suspects – apart from Vanessa, that is?'

'Paula Wellesley would be top of my list,' Peter suggested. 'We know that she'd had some sort of falling-out with her brother, and we also know that he inherited the family home, which may have rankled with her.'

'I agree,' Bernie chipped in. 'And we only have her word for it that there hadn't been any communication between them more recently. They could have had a fresh quarrel, or one or other of them could have dredged up whatever the original one was about.'

'I rang Vanessa,' Peter added, 'and she says that she's

seen an old photograph of Christopher and Paula as children, and they both had dark hair, which fits in with her being the woman the neighbour saw.'

'OK. Let's put her down,' Jonah agreed. 'Anyone else?'

'Well …,' Bernie hesitated. 'I know you won't like this, Peter, but it did strike me that one person who seems to be very angry with Christopher Wellesley is Patrick O'Shea.'

'I know,' Peter agreed, 'but surely if *he'd* killed him, he wouldn't persist in denying it when his own daughter was accused and likely to go to jail?'

'That's what I thought too,' Bernie acknowledged, 'but … but I did wonder … He seemed to think that Vanessa ought to admit to the stabbing. Could he have been hoping that they would both be safe if she confessed?'

'I think we'd better put him down,' Jonah said. 'I don't think he'd have stuck it out so long after Vanessa was charged, but you never know. And I think we have to include Deborah and Louise too. They both seem to be angry with Christopher over his treatment of Vanessa. Now, is that all or is there anyone else?'

'There's the client who was accusing him of negligence,' Peter suggested.

'Susan Vernon,' Bernie added, checking the notes that Paul had left with them. 'And, if we're including her, then I suppose Jeremy Willard, the neighbour with the cat, ought to go on the list too. Neither of them have much in the way of a motive but …'

'But we need to remember that, whoever did it may not have intended to kill him – or even to inflict serious injury – and they may not even have known that they had,' Jonah interjected. 'So we could be looking for someone with a relatively weak motive and a hot temper.'

'Hmmm,' Peter mused. 'That could be Jeremy Willard – and he is the one person with the means of getting inside the house without having the front door opened for him.'

'I suppose Susan Vernon might have gone to talk with him to try to persuade him to give her compensation for the losses he caused her, and then grabbed the screwdriver when he made some sort of sexual advances on her,' Bernie suggested, remembering what Paul had said about "wandering hands". 'And then there are the women at the solicitor's office who might have been subject to his unwanted attention.'

'And did he confine himself to the staff?' Peter added. 'What about other female clients?'

'Those will be more difficult to track down,' Jonah murmured, looking at the list, which Bernie had been typing up on the computer. 'I think you're right, Peter: Paula Wellesley is the most likely suspect. And, if she's not guilty, she'll be able to give us valuable background information about what Christopher was really like. Let's go and talk to her.'

'I'll ring Martin and ask him to introduce us to her,' Bernie volunteered, naming one of the staff whom she knew at Lichfield College.

'Good idea!' Jonah said eagerly, 'And could you ask him to give us a bit of a briefing in private before we meet her? It may be handy to know what her colleagues think of her.'

'OK.' Bernie took out her phone and started to dial. Soon she had arranged for Dr Martin Reiss, Geology Fellow at Lichfield College, to call round at their house and then to accompany them to the college to meet Paula Wellesley.

***

'What's all this about?' the diminutive don demanded, as Bernie helped him out of his coat that afternoon. 'Why the sudden interest in Paula?'

'Come in here, and Peter will explain,' Bernie replied, opening the door to Jonah's study.

Martin Riess entered the room and took the vacant seat between Peter and Jonah. He looked round expectantly with pale blue eyes behind metal-framed glasses. His small stature, boyish features and straw-coloured hair, with no signs of greying, made him appear younger than his fifty-one years.

'I'm glad you could come, Martin,' Peter greeted him. 'We're hoping that you may be able to help us to prevent a miscarriage of justice.'

'Sounds interesting,' their friend said cautiously. He knew this family well enough to be careful not to commit himself until he understood what was involved. 'Tell me more.'

'Professor Paula Wellesley has a brother,' Peter began, 'or rather she *had* a brother until May of this year, when he was killed by means of a large screwdriver being driven into his chest. His wife is accused of his murder, but we don't think she did it.'

'And you want me to introduce you to Paula so that you can grill her about it?' Martin asked. 'But won't the police have already done all that?'

Yes,' Jonah answered, 'but we're not convinced that they asked all the right questions.'

'I'm afraid that your Paula is right at the top of our list of suspects,' Bernie said apologetically. 'You see, she fell out with her brother and hasn't spoken to him for nearly twenty years.'

'But why would she have at him with a screwdriver after all this time?'

'We don't know,' Peter told him. 'And we may well be wrong in thinking that she did. But what we do know is that nobody seems to have really known him properly – not even his wife – and it's just possible that his sister may be able to throw some light on what made him tick.'

'And, if she can tell us why *she* couldn't bear the sight of him, maybe that will give us a clue as to who else might have felt the same way,' Bernie added.'

'But first,' Jonah cut in, 'we'd like you to tell us what you know about Paula herself – and what sort of person she is.'

'I'm not sure I'm going to be able to help you much,' Martin shrugged. 'Let's see … she came to Oxford back in 2006 – from the US, I think. She was appointed to the Robert Boyle Chair of Physics for her seminal work on subatomic particles – one of the youngest people ever to hold that post. At the same time, she was given a tutorial fellowship at Lichfield. The Master expressed the opinion that she was a "considerable catch" and would attract students and researchers to the college.'

'So she's a bright lass,' Bernie commented, 'and yet her parents and brother didn't seem to think much of her.'

'Maybe they resented her success,' Martin suggested. 'What did they do? Were they academics too?'

'No,' Peter told him. 'Father and brother were small-town solicitors and her mother was a housewife, as far as we know.'

'What's she like to work with?' Bernie asked.

'Pretty easy going,' Martin shrugged again. 'Doesn't take advantage of her prestige, mucks in with open days and school visits, the students like her …'

'Is she one to bear a grudge?' Jonah asked.

'I wouldn't know. I'm not aware of anyone doing anything that she might bear a grudge about.'

'No academic rivalries? No unfair distribution of college resources?' Jonah suggested. 'No one trying to take credit for her work?'

'No,' Martin said firmly. 'I don't know about anything like that.'

'Poor Martin!' Bernie exclaimed, smiling across Jonah's chair and catching his eye. 'You're such a Mr Nice-guy you don't realise what a cut-throat world academia can be.'

'Well, as far as I'm aware, Paula is Ms Nice-guy and doesn't have any truck with that sort of thing either,' Martin retorted. 'And I can't believe that, whatever this brother of hers did, she'd be so stupid as to attack him with a screwdriver. If she wanted to kill him, she'd come up with a more efficient way of doing it.'

'Except that this appears to have turned out to be very efficient and, assuming that the wife *is* innocent, the murderer looks likely to get away with it,' Jonah pointed out drily.

'Has she really never mentioned her family at all?' Peter asked.

'No – but then I don't talk much about my family either. Why would it come up?'

There was no answer to this. They sat together in silence until, with a small movement of his left index finger, Jonah set his chair moving back away from the desk and turning towards the door.

'OK. It looks as if you've told us all you know. Let's go!'

***

The Senior Common Room[9] of Lichfield College was almost deserted when they entered it a short while later. The only occupant was an elderly emeritus fellow, dozing in a high-backed armchair in the corner closest to the open fireplace (which was empty, it being only September). A cleaner in a red and black tabard was engaged in emptying the waste bin. She nodded briefly towards Martin as she finished replacing the black liner and then left the room.

'Paula's just texted to say she'll be down in a minute,' Martin told them, looking up from his phone. 'I'll get us some coffee while we're waiting. Sit down.'

Peter and Bernie found seats at the far end of the room (just in case the elderly retired don were not as fast asleep as he appeared) and Jonah positioned his wheelchair between them.

Martin, meanwhile, filled bone china mugs bearing the college crest from a glass jug of coffee, keeping warm on a

---

[9] Usually abbreviated to SCR, this is a room where the college fellows meet for conversation or to read newspapers and journals.

table at the side of the room. He carried them over and put them down in front of Peter and Bernie, before collecting Jonah's special lidded cup from the storage space at the back of his chair. He took it back to the coffee jug, filled it, added milk and replaced the lid and drinking straw.

He brought the plastic cup back and placed it in a convenient position where Jonah could reach the straw to drink. Jonah nodded his appreciation. There were not many people whom Bernie would have permitted to perform this service for him, but Martin was an old and trusted friend and could be relied upon to help without patronising. It would be a pity if one of his colleagues – and one whom he clearly viewed with some regard – were to turn out to be a murderer.

'Hello!'

They looked up to see a tall woman in trousers and a roll-neck sweater approaching them. She had dark brown hair, cut in a pageboy style with a thick fringe that stopped just above striking dark eyebrows. Her brown eyes twinkled as she smiled round at each of them in turn. Bernie noted with approval that she included Jonah without making any distinction between him and his able-bodied companions.

'Martin said you wanted to see me,' she added. 'Something to do with the police?'

Martin made the introductions. 'These are my friends Dr Bernie Fazakerley, DI Peter Johns and DCI Jonah Porter. Peter and Jonah are retired police detectives. Bernie is Peter's wife and Jonah's right-hand-man. And this,' he continued, waving his hand in the direction of the new-arrival, 'is Professor Paula Wellesley. Sit down, Paula, and I'll fetch you some coffee while these guys explain what they're about.'

Paula sat down opposite Jonah and raised her expressive eyebrows interrogatively making them disappear beneath the thick fringe of glossy hair.

'I suppose I'd better explain,' Peter began, feeling strangely reluctant to question this self-assured and personable woman. 'We've been asked by your sister-in-law's legal team to investigate your brother's death. As you must already be aware, she's been charged with his murder, but she says she didn't do it.'

'I see.' Paula Wellesley appeared remarkably calm in the face of what should have been a surprising and perhaps distressing statement. 'And how are you expecting me to help in that endeavour?'

'We were hoping that you might be able to give us some pointers as to who else could have had a motive for harming your brother,' Jonah told her.

'If you hope *that*, you have been very badly informed,' Paula laughed. 'I haven't seen or spoken to Chris this side of the millennium!'

'Yes, we're aware of that,' Jonah acknowledged, 'but we thought that someone who obviously feels so antagonistic towards him might be able to tell us why other people might come to feel the same way.'

Paula leaned back to make room for Martin to hand her a mug of black coffee. She put it down on the small table that stood between her and Jonah and then lifted her gaze to look him in the eye.

'I'm sorry,' she continued. 'I really can't help you. I know nothing about his acquaintances or what he may have been getting up to over the last twenty-odd years. And the only person whom I know of with a motive for killing him is myself.'

'Aaah!' Jonah smiled back at her. 'I'm glad you mentioned that.'

'I suppose you need me to tell you where I was between ... what? Nine in the morning and twelve noon on Saturday the twelfth of May,' Paula suggested, poker faced. 'Well, as I told the police at the time, I was here in Oxford. I spent the whole morning in my college rooms working on a research paper. And no – there weren't any witnesses. At least, not until about eleven thirty when I went down to the porters' lodge to collect a parcel.'

She held her arms out towards Jonah, still smiling. 'Do you want to put the cuffs on me right away, or do you have some more questions first?'

'Please,' Peter intervened gently. 'If you don't mind – could you explain to us what happened between you and your brother?'

'Well!' Paula Wellesley took a deep breath and looked round at them all again. 'It's not exactly that something happened between us. That's really how it's always been. I always knew that I wasn't welcome in my family; so as soon as I had the means to do so, I got out.'

'Could you explain that a bit more?' Peter asked, looking across at her with a puzzled frown. 'What do you mean by not being welcome?'

'I was a great disappointment to my parents,' Paula expanded. 'Well, to be more precise, I was a disappointment to my father and that meant that my mother was expected to be disappointed in me too.'

'Why's that?' asked Jonah. 'I would have thought that any parent would have been proud of your achievements.'

'No. When I say "always" I *mean* "always",' Paula explained. 'I mean that I was a disappointment to them from the moment I was born, because I wasn't a son. It was made abundantly clear to me from the outset that being a girl made me into something of an encumbrance to them. For a while, when it began to look as if I might be going to be their only child, my father started to take some interest in me, but then, when Chris was born …!'

'Yes?' Jonah prompted gently.

'I was sent away to boarding school at the age of seven. When I got back at the end of the first term, I found that they've moved Chris's cot into my bedroom and I'd been consigned to the small, dark room at the side of the house that had been just a box room. Growing up, Chris always knew – we both knew! – that he was the one that mattered and that I was only there on sufferance. And he used to take advantage and do things to get me into trouble with our father, who always took his side.'

'That's dreadful!' Bernie exclaimed. 'What about your mum? Didn't she try to persuade your dad not to be so unfair?'

'I don't remember my mother ever expressing an opinion about anything in the whole of her married life. She was completely subservient to my father. What he said went. He was the head of the household and she was only there to look after him – and to produce an heir to carry on the family law firm. I made up my mind very early that I was never going to be like her – not allowed so much as to breathe without his say-so.'

'You say you escaped from your family as soon as you could,' Peter said in the silence that followed. 'When was that? And how did you … where did you go?'

'I finally broke all ties with them after I graduated in '92. I won a scholarship to do postgraduate study in America. Up until then, I didn't have anywhere else to live outside of term time, so I was pretty much stuck with them. Not that they made it exactly easy even to get that far,' she added with note of bitterness.

'Oh?' Jonah prompted.

'After I'd done my GCSEs[10], my father decided that I didn't warrant any more expenditure on my education,' Paula explained. 'I was taken out of my boarding school and brought home. He had the idea that I could get a job in a shop or as some sort of clerical assistant in an office, to mark time until he could pair me off with some suitable man who would take me off his hands and provide for me.

---

[10] General Certificate of Secondary Education: a qualification in individual subjects, taken at age 16 by school students in England, Wales and Northern Ireland, providing them with a record of their achievement similar to a leaving certificate or baccalaureate.

I didn't like that idea – why would I aspire to the sort of life that my mother was enduring? And my teachers had told me that I was good enough for uni – maybe even Oxbridge.'

'So how did you change his mind?' Bernie asked with interest. She had never come across a parent who did not want his children to succeed academically.

'I didn't. That was down to my Uncle Angus. He stuck up for me and convinced my father that it would increase the value of his asset if he allowed it to gain more qualifications.

'Angus? That's your father's brother – is that right?' Peter asked.

'Yes. He was a few years older than my father, which I suppose may have been why he had some influence over him. He was a partner in the firm, which may have had something to do with it too.'

'And he died in … 2003 – is that right?' Jonah looked up from studying his notes on the computer screen attached to his wheelchair.

'Yes, I suppose that must have been the year – it was four years after my parents.

'And did he have any children of his own?' Peter asked.

'No. He was a bachelor. He lived in a flat over the solicitor's office. He … I rather think he was probably gay, but that wasn't the sort of thing you talked about in those days.'

'So perhaps you were the daughter that he never had?' suggested Peter.

'I don't know about that!' Paula laughed. 'Anyway, he was very kind to me. He helped me with money for books and things and he got my passport back for me when I needed it to go to America.'

'How d'you mean, got your passport back?' Jonah queried.

'We all *had* passports – for family holidays in continental golf resorts and other places where my father expected to make useful contacts – but they were all kept locked up in the safe in his office. He didn't think it was appropriate for me or my mum to have access to them without his say-so.'

'And Christopher? Did the same rule apply to him,' asked Bernie sharply.

'He was only fourteen when I went to America, so I don't know if he was allowed to look after his own passport once he was an adult. I expect he was though. I don't think my father accepted that women ever became adult!'

'He'd fit in well in Saudi Arabia,' observed Bernie scathingly. 'Or perhaps in the early Victorian era.'

'Getting back to when you'd just done your GCSEs,' Peter intervened. He liked to work systematically and felt that the chronology was becoming confusing. 'What did you do then? Did your Dad send you back to boarding school?'

'No. That was far too expensive – even in order to get the benefit of my absence for thirty weeks out of the year. I enrolled myself at the local FE[11] college to do my A' levels. They were over the moon when I got into Oxford, because they'd never had anyone go to Oxbridge before.'

'Which college?' asked Bernie.

'Magdalen. I chose it because I liked the idea of a deer park in the grounds! I didn't know any other way of picking where to apply. It was only after I got there that I discovered that most schools give advice on which colleges are the best for different subjects and which are easier or more difficult to get into. Anyway, I somehow got through the interviews and was offered a place, but my father wouldn't sign the forms for me to apply for a grant. He said it was a waste of time doing a degree when I was bound to get married in a year or two.'

---

[11] Further Education colleges provide academic and vocational courses for the 16-19 age group.

She looked round at the others and smiled grimly.

'But Uncle Angus stepped in again and offered to pay the parental contribution if my father would sign the forms for me to get my fees paid[12]. He wasn't pleased about it, but he agreed in the end, on condition that it didn't cost him a penny.'

'So you went to Oxford and read Physics,' Jonah said encouragingly. 'And covered yourself with glory by all accounts, culminating in a scholarship to MIT[13], and still your father considered you to be a disappointment?'

'Yes. Not that I cared what he thought. I was just relieved to have found a way of getting out from under his thumb without tying myself to some other man.'

'Then follows an illustrious career at several top US universities,' murmured Jonah, scrolling down Paula's CV, which he had found on her university web page, 'and finally, you are offered a professorship back here in Oxford.'

'Meanwhile, your brother studies law and follows your father into the family legal business,' Peter put in. 'Did you see much of either of them – or your mother – during that period?'

'No,' Paula said concisely. Then, seeing that more was expected from her, she added, 'I didn't see anything of them at all. I stayed in America and they stayed over here. I didn't set foot on British soil again until 1999, when our parents died. I thought I ought to attend the funeral, for Mum's sake.'

'Hang on a minute!' Bernie broke in suddenly. 'Have I

---

[12] In 1989, when Paula went to university, tuition fees and a grant to cover living expenses were paid to all British students studying in UK universities, with better-off parents being expected (but not compelled) to contribute to their offspring's maintenance.

[13] Massachusetts Institute of Technology: a prestigious university in Cambridge, Massachusetts.

got this right? You didn't meet your brother at all between leaving home when he was a boy of fourteen and your parents' funeral seven years later, and yet you said that you're the only person apart from his wife who has a motive for killing him?'

'Maybe it isn't such a good motive, after all,' Paula smiled at Bernie's confusion. 'Which is convenient, because I didn't do it and I'd rather not be convicted.'

'So tell me – what exactly do you have against your brother?' Jonah asked.

'Apart from taking away what little affection my parents had for me when I was a child? And always being given his own way while I was thwarted in everything I wanted? And deliberately scheming to get me into trouble with my father, just for the fun of it? Oh! And I never wanted a penny from my father, so I don't mind, but he did inherit the house and everything our parents owned apart from a few pieces of jewellery that my mum had.'

'Yes,' Jonah said quietly. 'Apart from all that, what did you have against him?'

Paula did not reply. She sat silently drinking her coffee, waiting to see if there were any more questions.

'You can hardly have known the man,' Jonah resumed, when it became clear that Paula did not intend to add any more. 'He could have turned out quite different from that unpleasant boy that you remembered from your childhood. I find it hard to believe that an intelligent woman like you would not at least explore the possibility of that; and yet you refused even to attend his wedding, and you take no interest in your baby niece. So I ask you again: what was it about Christopher Wellesley that made you so determined to have nothing to do with him?'

'I saw quite enough of him at the funeral and at the "do" afterwards to know that he hadn't changed in the least,' Paula said at last. 'He was a nasty, manipulative little bully when he was a child, and he became a nasty, manipulative big bully when he grew up.'

'How could you tell?' Jonah enquired. 'What did he do in such a short space of time to convince you of that?'

'I suppose it wasn't really unreasonable that he completely sidelined me and hogged all the limelight,' Paula admitted. 'After all, I'd been ignoring them all for the best part of seven years. And I didn't particularly want to be given a leading role in praising our tyrannical father or our servile mother. The thing that got to me was the way he treated that girl that he brought with him – Laura I think her name was … or Lauren … or …'

'Hang about!' Jonah interrupted her musing. 'Are you telling us that he had a girlfriend back then? Someone close enough that she came to his parents' funeral?'

'Yes – didn't you know about her?' Paula looked at him in surprise. 'I would have thought the police would have found out all about that. He picked her up in … '97 it would have been, during the summer vacation at the end of his first year at uni. They lived together in the house that our father bought for him in Southampton, and then in the family home after he graduated, which was a couple of months after our parents died. It hadn't struck me until now how very convenient that was for him,' she added with a grim smile. 'Perhaps you ought to be investigating that road accident too!'

'Do you know anything more about this Lauren?' Jonah asked. 'Her surname would be helpful – or where she came from?'

'She came from Evesham. I'm not sure that I was ever told her second name … and I don't think it *was* Lauren.' Paula paused in thought. 'Lillian maybe? … No! I know! It was Leanne – and now I do remember her other name: it was Binns – Leanne Binns. She was only sixteen when they met and her father threatened to take Chris to court to get her back after she went to Southampton with him, but he gave up when he discovered the family were all lawyers.'

'What I don't understand,' Bernie said, in the silence that followed this revelation, 'is how you know so much about it when you were over in America having no dealings with your family. That can't all have come out at the funeral!'

'Uncle Angus used to write to me,' Paula explained. 'Beautiful letters on mauve writing paper, in lovely old-fashioned script, done with a fountain pen. He told me all the news – about Chris applying to Oxford and not even being invited to interview, and then going to Southampton; about his father buying him a house to live in there (as an investment property, apparently!); about this schoolgirl he was shacked up with, and her fireman father coming round to have it out with our father!'

'Do you know how long this romance lasted?' Peter asked. 'And whether there was anyone else between Leanne and Vanessa?'

'As far as I know, it was still going strong when Uncle Angus died in 2003. After that? Well, as you know, Chris and I didn't correspond.'

'What about your uncle's funeral?' Peter said suddenly. 'You told us you hadn't seen your brother since 1999, but surely you must both have been at that.'

'No.' Paula shook her head. 'After all the nonsense at our parents' funeral, I wasn't inclined to go to another of Chris's extravaganzas. All the rubbish he came out with about what a wonderful family man our father had been and how devoted Mum had been to him! I couldn't bear to hear him spouting the same sort of stuff about poor Uncle Angus. So I drank a glass of the sherry that he'd sent me the Christmas before he died and planted a tree in his memory in the grounds of the college where I was working at the time – and told Chris that I couldn't get time off to come to England at such short notice.'

'And did you keep any of your uncle's letters?' Jonah asked eagerly. 'Can we see them?'

'No. I shredded them when I came back over here. I got rid of a lot of stuff then to keep the transatlantic removal costs down.'

'I see,' Peter said thoughtfully. 'OK. So back in 2003, we've got your brother set up in the family home with his girlfriend and you over in the US. At some point between then and 2014, when he marries Vanessa, he must have split up with Leanne. You say you don't know anything about that. Did you hear about his marriage? Presumably you will have been invited?'

'No. Why would he want to invite me?'

'You were his only living relative,' Jonah pointed out.

'Well, he didn't – and I wouldn't have gone if he had.'

'So, I suppose he won't have told you about the birth of his daughter either?' Peter suggested.

'No. The first I knew about either the wife or the kid was when the police came round to talk about his death. They're both better off without him, in my opinion.'

'Except that the wife is likely to serve a life-sentence for his murder,' Jonah said drily.

'Well, she was fool enough to marry him!' Paula stopped suddenly and looked round sheepishly. 'I'm sorry, that was rather unkind, wasn't it? But I'm afraid I can't have so very much sympathy for his wife – or even for that poor Leanne girl – because if they'd got any sense, or any backbone, they'd have left him within a few months, instead of putting up with him for … how long must it have been? … four years! If this Vanessa woman did kill him, then good for her! She's done womankind a favour – and in particular, she saved her poor daughter from going through what I had to go through growing up.'

'Going back to Leanne for a moment,' Peter said, breaking the silence that had followed this outburst. 'Can you tell us any more about her? What she looked like? Her home address? Anything at all that might help us to find her?'

'No, I don't think so,' Paula shook her head. 'I only met her the twice – at the funeral and then a couple of days later when Chris called me in to clear my last few remaining possessions from my room in the house. She looked like a little weed, but then she was only eighteen, I suppose. As far as I remember, she was blond and skinny. She had a silly little nervous laugh and smoked like a chimney all the time.'

'Do you still have a key to the family home?' Jonah asked suddenly, looking up from his computer screen, where he had been studying his notes of the case. 'I presume you were entrusted with one while you were resident there?'

'I think my father was quite reluctant about that,' Paula smiled back at him, 'but even he could see that it was inconvenient to him if I couldn't let myself in when I came home from college. So yes, I did have a key back then. I don't think I still have it, but surely Chris will have changed the locks by now anyway?'

'Maybe, maybe not,' Jonah replied. 'It's not something people tend to do unless they lose the keys or have reason to believe the house is insecure. Perhaps you could have a look for your key? Then we'll be able to find out if he did or not, won't we?'

'Why would I want to find a key that proves that I could have got into the house and killed my brother?'

'Because, if it still fits the lock, then it proves that any key that Leanne Binns may have will also enable *her* to get in,' Jonah answered, smiling up at Paula and catching her eye.

'And she has a better motive than I do for wanting him dead,' Paula continued, smiling back, 'since she was first abused by Chris and then thrown over for another woman, who not only persuaded him to marry her but also has a child by him.'

'Precisely!' Jonah agreed. 'So you will have a look for that key, won't you?'

'OK.' Paula drained her mug and set it down on the table. 'Is that it? Are we done now?'

'Yes, I think that's all.' Peter looked across at Jonah who indicated acquiescence with a slight tilt of his head.

'We'll leave you in peace now. You will let us know if you find that key – or any of your uncle's letters – won't you?'

'You can tell me and I'll pass on the message,' Martin volunteered.

Paula looked at him in surprise, as if she had forgotten that he was there.

'Are you part of this attempt to exonerate the wife too?' she asked.'

'Oh no!' Martin hastened to distance himself from the investigation. 'I'm just a friend of the family.'

'This Vanessa's family you mean?' Paula sounded puzzled.

'No. I meant Bernie and the others. We go back a long way.'

'I see.' Paula still sounded puzzled, or perhaps intrigued, but said nothing further. She got up to go. 'I'd better be getting back. I've got a pile of undergraduate assignments to mark.'

***

'What do you make of her?' Peter asked, when they were safely back in the privacy of their car. 'Do you think she could be our murderer? She certainly hated her brother.'

'But, if she's telling the truth, she hadn't seen him for years,' Jonah objected. 'So why do it now?'

'I'm afraid I'm probably biased,' Bernie admitted, 'but I liked her style. I can identify with her a whole lot more than with Vanessa, if I'm honest.'

'I think this Leanne girl is much more promising,' Jonah agreed. He too had been impressed by the calm and resilient don, who reminded him of his own late wife. 'We ought to track her down and find out where she was the day Christopher Wellesley was killed.'

'I'll ring Paul and ask him to try to find her,' Peter volunteered. 'And I'll get on to Somerset House – or wherever it is they keep wills these days – and get copies of Paula's parents' and uncle's wills. I'd like to know if she was as hard-done-by as she makes out and if good old Uncle Angus did anything to redress the balance.'

***

Martin tapped nervously on the heavy oak door bearing the words "Professor Paula Wellesley, Fellow in Physical Science" and stood with head bowed, waiting for a response.

'Come in!' came Paula's voice from inside the room, after a brief pause.

Martin opened the door and went in. Paula was sitting on a low settee with a pile of papers on the coffee table in front of her. The evening light, slanting in through two gothic-style widows, fell across the room making a pattern of light and dark on the couch and table and on Paula's face as she looked to see who the caller was. She got up when she saw Martin standing nervously in the doorway.

'Hi Martin!' she greeted him. 'What brings you here?'

'I – I just wanted to check you were OK,' he stammered. 'After the inquisition this afternoon, I mean.'

'I'd hardly call it that!' Paula laughed. 'It was just a friendly chat – nothing like as bad as my PhD viva!'

'Still …,' Martin continued tentatively, 'I thought … I was afraid it might have … wakened up memories that were best left alone,' he finished at last.

'Ah!' Paula nodded. She got up and walked over to a tall, carved oak cupboard built into the corner of the room between the chimney-breast and the wall containing the windows. 'I was just going to have a pre-dinner sherry. Will you join me in a toast to my Uncle Angus?'

'Thanks.' Martin closed the door behind him and crossed the room to sit down on the settee.

Paula poured the drinks and placed the glasses on the coffee table before sitting down next to him.

'I can't stay long,' Martin told her. 'My mother will worry if I'm late for dinner.'

'You still live with your mother?' Paula queried. Martin

thought that he detected a hint of amusement – possibly even derision – in her voice.

'Well, it's not so much "still" as "again",' he explained. 'Like you, I spent a few years in the States before I got my fellowship here. When I moved back, it seemed convenient for us to pool our resources to buy a house we could share – with Oxford prices being what they are.'

'And what about your father?'

'He … he died a long time ago.'

'Oh.' Paula paused, before asking, 'Is that a cause for regret?'

For a moment or two, Martin was nonplussed. This question was so different from the usual embarrassed expression of sympathy, which was the normal response when the death of a parent was mentioned, that he did not know what to say. He looked at Paula, sipping her sherry and waiting for his reply as if her question was the most natural thing in the world. He looked down at his own glass, desperately trying to gather his thoughts.

'When I was coming up to eight years old, my mother brought me to England from East Germany,' he began at last. 'Before my father could try to follow us, the Stasi arrested him. He was still in custody when he died two years later.'

'I'm sorry. I had no idea,' Paula sounded uncertain of herself for the first time that day. 'I always assumed you were English. I hadn't realised you were a refugee.'

'I always blamed myself for his death,' Martin continued. 'I knew that they only tried to escape to the West in order to give me a better life.'

'But that's ridiculous! How could it be your fault? You were only eight.'

'I didn't say I thought it was my fault,' Martin argued quietly. 'I just said that I felt guilty. Things that happen when you're a child can have a lasting effect … Things like being displaced by a younger sibling, for example.'

6. LAST WILL AND TESTAMENT

Once when Jacob was cooking a stew, Esau came in from the field, and he was famished. Esau said to Jacob, 'Let me eat some of that red stuff, for I am famished!' (Therefore he was called Edom.) Jacob said, 'First sell me your birthright.' Esau said, 'I am about to die; of what use is a birthright to me?' Jacob said, 'Swear to me first.' So he swore to him, and sold his birthright to Jacob. Then Jacob gave Esau bread and lentil stew, and he ate and drank, and rose and went his way. Thus Esau despised his birthright.

Genesis 25:29-34 NRSV, Anglicised Edition

It took Paul three days to track down Leanne Binns. His call came through to Peter's mobile phone while they were on their way back to Evesham to speak again with Vanessa and her parents and to visit *Wellesley, Bracknell & Wellesley*, solicitors. Fortunately, Bernie was driving, so Peter took the call. He switched the phone to loudspeaker so that Bernie and Jonah could also hear what their friend had to say.

'I've managed to find that girl you were after,' Paul reported. 'It was lucky you mentioned that her dad was a firefighter. That gave me somewhere to start. He's retired now, but some of his former colleagues remembered him. Anyway, I've got an address for her parents – which looks likely to be the same as when Christopher Wellesley knew her – and another for Leanne and her current boyfriend.'

'That's great! Can you give them to me?' Peter asked, fumbling in his pocket for a pen and snatching up a filling station receipt from the pile that lay in the well between the two front seats.

Paul dictated the address of John and Lesley Binns, Leanne's parents. Then he hesitated.

'I'm not sure you ought to interview Leanne,' he said at last. 'From what I can tell, she's in a rather fragile state mentally.'

'In what way exactly?' Peter queried.

'She's not a psychotic killer, if that's what you're thinking,' Paul added hastily, detecting a certain eagerness in Peter's voice that suggested that he thought that her illness might be of significance to the case. 'I'm not sure exactly what her diagnosis is. I just know that she was only discharged from a secure mental health unit a couple of days ago.'

'What does she look like?' Jonah called from the back of the car. 'Does she fit the description of the woman the neighbour saw?'

'I've only got an old school photograph to go on,' Paul answered. 'That confirms that she has – or had – dark hair, but that's about all.'

'Can you find out a bit more about her and her mental state?' Peter asked. 'I don't want to cause her distress any more than you do, but she *is* our most likely suspect. Can you at least find out if she has an alibi for that Saturday?'

'OK,' Paul agreed with a sigh. 'I'll do my best.'

'Thanks. We'll have to go now – I think we're here.' Peter terminated the call as they pulled up in front of an unostentatious office in a row of small shops. Through the window (which was adorned with promises of excellent service in the fields of conveyancing, personal injury claims, motoring offences, clinical negligence claims, probate matters and wills) Peter could see a middle-aged woman sitting behind a reception desk.

Peter got out and went round to undo the fastenings that held Jonah secure in the back of the car. Bernie, meanwhile set up the ramp to enable him to drive his wheelchair down on to the pavement. Jonah had arranged an appointment with Anthony Bracknell, ostensibly to discuss the drawing-up of his will, and Bernie was to accompany him in her role as his personal assistant.

'I'll browse around the shops and see if I can pick up any gossip about the firm,' Peter told the others. 'You never know, the people from the neighbouring businesses may know about any strains there may have been between the partners.'

'OK,' Bernie agreed. 'If you're not in the car when we get out, I'll give you a ring.'

***

Over a lunch of fish and chips, which they ate in the car on the roadside overlooking the river, they compared notes.

The greengrocer, who occupied the shop on the right of the solicitors' office, had told Peter that both Wellesley and Bracknell got on well with their neighbours and the business appeared to be doing well.

The hairdresser on the other side provided him with some slightly more promising information. To promote goodwill among neighbours, they offered a discount to the proprietors of other businesses in the road. Hence, Mrs Wellesley and several of the female members of staff at *Wellesley, Bracknell & Wellesley* were customers of theirs. Senior stylist, Wendy Balding, expressed the opinion that Vanessa "didn't even dare to breath without asking her husband's permission first". She also hinted at stories of inappropriate touching of female colleagues by senior people in the solicitors' firm.

The flat over the office, which had once been occupied by Mr Angus Wellesley, was now let to a young man who worked in one of the estate agents a few doors further down the road. He happily confirmed that he was content with his landlords and was unaware of any tension between the two partners. He had never met Vanessa, which struck him as "odd, now you mention it", since he had been to several social functions at which Christopher had been present. But perhaps she didn't like that sort of thing, he suggested, or maybe it was because they had a young child.

Anthony Bracknell had reacted angrily at first, when he found that Jonah had obtained an interview with him under false pretences. However, Jonah's disability, together with his charming lop-sided smile, soon disarmed him and when he heard that there was a possibility of clearing Vanessa's name, he appeared genuinely eager to help.

'Anthony told me he only met Vanessa a few times,' Jonah related to his friends through a mouthful of battered haddock. 'At the wedding, of course, and then once or twice at the office. He said she always seemed very timid and withdrawn. The thing that surprised him about the murder was not so much that she'd wanted to do it, as that she would have the nerve to pick up a screwdriver and stab someone in the chest with it. *Couldn't say "boo" to a goose* was how he characterised her.'

'Hmmmph!' Peter snorted sceptically. 'I've seen plenty of timid little mice who suddenly turn on their tormentors when they can't stand it any longer. We're going to need more than that to convince a jury.'

'I don't think Anthony really liked Christopher very much,' Jonah continued. 'Obviously he couldn't exactly tell me that, but I got the impression that he didn't have much time for either Christopher or his father. Anthony was articled[14] to Angus Wellesley when it was just the two brothers working together, and went on to become a partner before Christopher joined them.'

'Angus definitely seems to be the most likeable member of the family,' Bernie agreed. 'Linda Hayes, the receptionist, told me that things ain't what they used to be

---

[14] Trainee solicitors are known as articled clerks. They are contracted to work for a qualified solicitor, who is responsible for instructing them in the profession.

in the firm since he died.'

'Anyway,' Jonah resumed. 'Anthony's opinion is that Christopher was a narcissist, and his father and uncle indulged him. If it had been up to him, he'd never have given him a partnership, but he was junior to the others, so he didn't like to raise any objections. He reckons Christopher was none-too-bright and lazy with it.'

'The more I hear of this Christopher, the more I think that whoever killed him was doing the world a service,' Bernie observed.

'That's all very well if we're trying to get Vanessa a lighter sentence,' Peter pointed out, 'but it doesn't help us to clear her – rather the opposite, because the more of a bastard he was, the more motive she had for killing him.'

'Anthony showed me a copy of Christopher's will,' Jonah told them. 'It leaves everything in trust to his offspring, favouring males over females-'

'How d'you mean?' cut in Bernie.

'If he and Vanessa had had another child and it had been a boy, then he would have inherited everything, apart from the proceeds of a life insurance policy that Christopher took out when Leah was born.'

'And what if their second child had lived?' Peter asked. 'The baby that died was a girl, wasn't she?'

'I assume that either Christopher would have taken out another insurance policy to cover her expenses until she came of age or the two girls would have had to share the existing one,' Jonah surmised. 'But only if they subsequently had a brother. If there were *only* girls then they would inherit.'

'And what about Vanessa?' asked Bernie. 'Didn't she get anything? I mean, usually the whole estate passes to the wife – to avoid paying inheritance tax, if for no other reason.'

'She gets a life-interest in the house, conditional upon her continuing to live in it and not re-marrying or co-habiting, and a small pension, which passes to the children if she re-marries.'

'I suppose at least that removes any financial motive for her killing him,' Peter observed.

'And it's further evidence of the contempt in which Christopher held women in general and his wife in particular,' Bernie added.

'Anthony expressed the opinion that, if Vanessa does manage to prove her innocence, she ought to contest the will,' Jonah said, with a note if satisfaction in his voice. 'He agrees that it's monstrous not to leave her anything when she's given up her career to look after him and his offspring. He pointed out that she'd have got considerably more in a divorce settlement.'

'Now that's an interesting point!' Peter exclaimed. 'You're right. If Vanessa wanted to get away from Christopher and start a new life, she'd have done much better filing for divorce on the grounds of *unreasonable behaviour.*'

'Hmm!' Jonah grunted. 'That's all very well, but the current defence case is that she acted on impulse having lost control as a result of his intolerable behaviour. That means it's not really relevant that her actions aren't the most advantageous option for her. The whole point is that she's supposed to be not thinking straight!'

'And it's well-known that people in abusive relationships find it very hard to psych themselves up to getting out of them,' Bernie added. 'With her husband being a lawyer as well, what chance is there that she would have believed that she'd be able to divorce him and keep custody of Leah?'

'Getting back to Christopher,' Jonah said, sucking up a mouthful of water from his lidded cup. 'Anthony also showed me his father's will. It was very similar to Christopher's, which is interesting in itself. As Paula told us, it leaves everything to Christopher. Their parents were killed together as it happens, but if their mother had survived him by thirty days, she would have got a life-interest in the family home (which was entirely in Bruce Wellesley's – that's Christopher's Dad's – name) with the same strings attached about not re-marrying. Her will leaves her clothes and jewellery to Paula and everything else to her husband, or, in the case that he did not survive, to Christopher.'

'Women's liberation and gender equality seem to have passed the Wellesley family by,' Bernie observed drily.

'Did Anthony give you any indication of what "everything else" comprised?' Peter asked.

'He thought, not much. She'd had a small legacy from her parents, but that had gone into a joint bank account and her husband had syphoned it off and invested it in shares in his sole name.'

'I'm liking Christopher and his father less and less every minute!' Bernie declared.

'Anthony is executor of Christopher's will and trustee for Leah's inheritance, until she reaches twenty-one,' Jonah resumed.

'Not eighteen?' queried Peter.

'In keeping with their early-Victorian attitudes, the Wellesley's don't seem to have considered that anyone can be trusted with money until they are over twenty,' Jonah confirmed. 'It won't surprise you to know that Anthony does have discretion to release the funds if Leah were to make a "suitable" marriage before that age.'

'I don't believe it!' Bernie shook her head in amazement.

'I think Anthony Bracknell is rather uncomfortable with being expected to administer it all,' Jonah nodded. 'As I said, he'd be all for Vanessa contesting the will, if only she wasn't charged with Christopher's murder.'

'OK, so we've established that Christopher was a misogynist from a family of misogynists,' Peter summarised, 'and that Vanessa had every reason to want to get away from him. But this isn't really anything more than we knew already – and it certainly doesn't help us to find the person who really killed him!'

'I may have a few possibilities to add to our list of suspects,' Bernie volunteered. 'I stayed outside at reception while Jonah had his consultation with Anthony. I managed to get into conversation with Linda Hayes, the receptionist and Zara Lambourne, who is an articled clerk with the firm. Articled to Anthony I imagine – I can't see Christopher taking on a mere woman! Or maybe …,' she paused in thought.

'Maybe?' prompted Jonah.

'It just occurred to me that he might quite like having a woman training under him, even though he doesn't rate them. He does seem to enjoy exercising power over women, and having one as his clerk might suit him very well.' Bernie paused again. 'Anyway, what I was going to tell you was that Linda confirmed what she'd already told the police about Christopher being known as something of a sex-pest within the practice, and Zara backed her up. She – Zara that is – said that she'd been putting up with it because she didn't want to jeopardise her training, but as soon as she qualified, she was going to sue him for sexual harassment.'

'Hmm!' Jonah murmured. 'That's all very well as evidence that he was a nuisance to women and that they didn't like him, but this Zara is hardly going to kill him, when she could wait and take him to the cleaners for compensation.'

'He could have gone too far and she lashed out in self-defence,' Peter suggested tentatively. 'Say she *is* his trainee and he asked her to go to his house that morning – ostensibly to work, but really so that he could get her alone with him. She might have gone because she doesn't want to risk losing her place before she qualifies, and then …'

'I'm not sure she'd have done that.' Bernie shook her head. 'She seemed far too level-headed and strong-minded to fall for it. And Linda would have backed her up in saying that it was inappropriate for her to visit him at home. I was more thinking about some of the other staff – the more junior ones, who might be more vulnerable and more easily taken-in.'

'Such as?' Jonah asked quickly.

'There's an agency typist called Kelly Phillips,' Bernie told them. 'Or at least there was. According to Linda, she came to them in April and worked for three weeks and then on the Monday after Christopher was killed, she just didn't turn up for work. Eventually – a few days later – the agency rang to say that she wasn't available anymore and they would send a replacement. No explanation, but Linda put two and two together and concluded that she'd probably asked not to come again in order to get away from Christopher. She became all the more convinced of this when the replacement was a young man.'

'I think you could have something there,' Jonah said excitedly. 'I wonder why the police didn't pick up on it before.'

'Too confident that they already knew who the murderer was,' Peter said dismally.

'No. I don't think they'll have known about her,' Bernie explained. 'They interviewed Linda that Monday – before she realised that the girl wasn't coming in again.'

'OK,' Jonah acknowledged. 'We'd better add her to the list of suspects. Did your friend Linda give you any indication where we might find her?'

'I've got the name and address of the agency,' Bernie nodded. 'Linda was very obliging. I think she feels sorry for Vanessa and wants to help her. I let her think that we're just looking for more evidence of Christopher's appalling behaviour, rather than any suggestion that Kelly might be a suspect. I'm not so sure she'd be so co-operative in that case.'

'Good! That gives us something to work on,' Jonah said briskly. 'Now, is that all, or is there anything else?'

'Yes,' Bernie confirmed, smiling round at them both. She was feeling rather pleased with herself. Unlike when

Jonah had been a serving police officer and she had been acting as his personal assistant, she was now an equal partner in the investigation, and she was enjoying her new role. 'Linda Hayes has been with the firm since the year dot. I asked her if she knew anything about Leanne Binns. She remembered there being a lot of fuss about a live-in girlfriend of Christopher's when he was at university. She overheard Christopher's father talking to Uncle Angus about "paying her off".'

'Now that *is* interesting!' Jonah exclaimed. 'Do you think Leanne was pregnant and trying to force him to marry her or demanding maintenance?'

'Linda didn't know. She said it all quietened down after a while and Christopher got his degree and then joined the firm, first as an articled clerk and then as a solicitor. She doesn't know what happened to the girl.'

'According to Paula, Leanne was still living with Christopher when their parents died – in fact, right up to when Uncle Angus died four years later,' Peter commented. 'But does this girlfriend have to be Leanne? Could he have had more than one? Could the fuss that Linda remembers have been to do with him chucking one and taking up with another?'

'It seems to me we've *got* to speak to Leanne Binns,' Jonah said decisively. 'Let's give Paul a couple of days to find out some more about her and then, if he won't give us her address, I vote we call on her parents. We can't afford to hang about – the trial starts a week on Monday!'

They finished their meal and then made their way to the O'Sheas' house. Deborah greeted them warmly and brought them tea and ginger cake. Patrick hastened to move furniture to make room for Jonah's wheelchair in their cluttered front room. Vanessa looked up at them rather listlessly from the floor, where she was playing with Leah and a variety of soft toys, who appeared to be having a picnic.

'We've made a bit of progress,' Peter told her, 'but now

we need to ask you some more questions.'

Vanessa nodded, and then reached out across the check-patterned tablecloth spread out on the floor in front of her and pretended to cut up a large plastic pizza, which was lying at its centre.

'Go ahead,' she murmured, as she handed round pieces of the toy food to a large brown teddy bear, a pink rabbit and two dolls. 'What do you want to know?'

Leah, sitting between the bear and one of the dolls, picked up a piece of pizza and held it to the bear's mouth.

'Eat up Teddy!'

'Did your husband ever talk about his previous girlfriends?' Jonah asked, coming straight to the point. 'In particular, did he ever mention one called Leanne?'

'No.' Vanessa shook her head. 'Of course, I knew he'd had girlfriends before me, but he never talked about them.'

'This Leanne seems to have been in quite a long-term relationship with him,' Jonah persisted. 'According to his sister, she lived with him while he was at uni and then here in Evesham after he graduated. Are you sure he never mentioned her at all?'

'Yes. I'm quite sure. He always used to say that he was sorry I wasn't the first, but now he'd met me, he knew that I would definitely be the last. He always made out that none of the others meant anything to him.'

'OK. Let's leave that.' Peter took over the questioning. 'Do you mind if we go over again the sequence of events that morning when you found Chris? Can you-'

'Christopher, please!' Vanessa interrupted with surprising vigour. 'He always hated it when people called him Chris.'

'Sorry,' Peter apologised. 'Christopher. Can you describe what you saw exactly when you came home and found Christopher?'

'No, I don't think I can – sorry.' Vanessa smiled up at him regretfully. 'It's all a bit of a blur really. I just remember seeing him lying there on the floor and then hearing Leah crying behind me and taking her upstairs to quieten her down so he wouldn't be angry with us.'

'And you're sure there was nothing else unusual?' Jonah pressed her. 'Nothing out of place? Nothing there that you weren't expecting – or anything missing?'

'No. Nothing.' Vanessa shook her head.

'What about your green waterproof?' Deborah said suddenly. 'Don't you remember? We couldn't find it when we went back for your things.'

'Vanessa?' Jonah looked down at her eagerly awaiting her confirmation of this small piece of evidence suggesting that someone else could have been in the house that day.

'Yes. Mum's right. My long green coat was hanging up in the hall – only it wasn't there when she went back with Dad to get our things.'

'Are you saying it disappeared between when you got home that day and when they went back?' asked Peter. 'Or did you mean it had already gone then?'

Vanessa looked up at him blankly, not understanding the question.

'What Peter's asking,' Jonah explained, 'is: could it have been taken by someone who came to the house while you were out shopping? When did you see it last?'

'It was there when we set out for the shops,' Vanessa said, more confidently than before. 'I'm sure about that, because Leah was playing peek-a-boo behind it and didn't want to come out and get in her car seat.'

'Good,' Jonah said encouragingly. 'So, it was there in the hall while you were out and then later it was gone. Did you see it when you came in with the shopping?'

'I don't remember seeing it – but I can't honestly say I noticed it was gone,' Vanessa answered, appearing a little less languid than before. 'Do you really think it's got something to do with whoever killed Christopher?'

'It's the first evidence we've found that there was anyone else in the house that morning,' Peter told her. 'Which has to be good. I'm just not sure what it tells us about them or how it's going to help us to prove that they killed him and not you.'

'Can you describe the coat to me?' Jonah asked.

'It was just a long green waterproof,' Vanessa shrugged. 'I kept it there, by the front door in case it was raining when I was getting things out of the car and that sort of thing. It was a bit big, so I could put it on over my other coat if I needed to. It had a hood and zipped up at the front.'

Jonah opened his mouth to ask another question, but he was interrupted by Leah who, leaning across to feed the pink rabbit, suddenly pitched forwards and fell face down on the floor. She burst into tears. Vanessa quickly picked her up in her arms and held her to her, rocking her gently.

'There, there. Don't cry darling,' she crooned softly. Then she looked up at the others and smiled apologetically. 'She's tired. I'd better take her for her nap.'

Still murmuring gentle reassurances to her daughter, she scrambled to her feet and left the room.

'Do you really think that coat is an important clue?' asked Deborah eagerly.

'Potentially,' Peter answered cautiously.

'But only really if it helps us to find out who came to the house while Vanessa was out,' Jonah added.

'But doesn't it at least prove that there was someone there?' Deborah persisted.

'I'm afraid that's not how the prosecuting counsel will see it,' Jonah replied drily. 'I imagine that they will point out that it was *you* who noticed that the coat was missing, not Vanessa.'

'What difference does that make?'

'They will go on to suggest that it was Vanessa herself who removed the coat from the house,' Jonah explained. 'If I were prosecuting, this is the picture that I would paint. Vanessa gets ready go out. She puts Leah in the car. It looks like rain, so she goes back for her coat. She puts it on. Then she remembers something she wants to say to

Christopher, so she goes into his workshop to see him – or maybe just to say goodbye. They argue. She loses her temper and snatches up a screwdriver from the bench and …'

'Christopher slumps to the floor.' Peter took up the tale. 'Vanessa thinks he's dead – or maybe she doesn't think about it at all. She looks down at her coat and realises that there are spatters of blood on it. All she can think of is getting rid of the coat and with it the evidence that she killed her husband. So she takes it off and folds it over inside out. Then she goes off to the shops as normal, taking the coat with her. She dumps it somewhere in a litterbin or in the river, or …'

'And then she does her shopping and comes home,' finished Bernie.

'But when the police came, she had blood all over her,' Patrick objected. 'Why bother getting rid of a coat with a few drops on it and then coming back and kneeling in it and holding the body and all that?'

'What the prosecution will say is that, when she got back, she discovered that he wasn't dead after all. She didn't want him to be able to accuse her, so she pulled out the screwdriver from his chest to make sure that he bled to death,' Jonah answered promptly. 'I'm sorry, but this evidence doesn't prove that Vanessa didn't kill her husband; all it does is to give us another clue to follow up to see if we can find out who did.'

'Aaaah!' Patrick sighed. 'For a moment I thought … I can't help thinking it might be better if she just pleaded guilty to manslaughter like the lawyers say she should.'

'Do you think she might have done it?' Deborah added hesitatingly. 'And then blotted it out from her mind, so she doesn't remember? She's been wandering around in a daze for months – ever since she lost the baby – and even before that … Well, she hadn't been the Vanessa that we knew for a long time.'

'She should never have married him,' Patrick declared.

'I always said he was too old for her. She was only eighteen when they started going out, and he was over thirty.'

'She'd just finished her degree when they got married,' Deborah added. 'She was planning to go on to teach, but he made her give it up. He said there was no need for her to work when he earned enough to keep them both.'

'I was taken in,' Patrick continued. 'I should've put my foot down and told her she mustn't marry him, but when he said he was becoming a Catholic, I started to think maybe I'd got him wrong.'

'To be fair, they did seem very happy at first,' Deborah conceded.

'The rot really set in when she was expecting Leah,' Patrick went on. 'I reckon he was jealous of the baby and thought Vanessa might start caring more for her than for him.'

'He was just a selfish spoilt brat who couldn't bear not being the centre of attention,' Deborah agreed scornfully.

'I'd happily have stuck that screwdriver in him myself!' Patrick declared. 'And I'd go into court and swear that I did, if I thought it would get Vanessa off, but Debs and I were at home together that day, so I couldn't do that without implicating her too!'

7. LEGAL DEFENCE

And earthly power doth then show likest God's
When mercy seasons justice.

William Shakespeare
The Merchant of Venice

Vanessa's legal team comprised her solicitor, Yasmeen Jamali, her barrister, Christabel Bagshott-White QC[15], and Christabel's pupil, Justin Holder. Peter, Jonah, Bernie and Father Gerry met them in Yasmeen's office in a large Victorian house near Evesham railway station. They were polite, and agreed to appoint Peter and Jonah as official members of the defence team; but it was very clear that their advice to Vanessa was to plead guilty to manslaughter at the earliest opportunity, preferably before the trial date. They appeared flummoxed when Peter asked simply, 'but what if she didn't do it?'

'Do you honestly think there was some sort of intruder who got in and stabbed him?' Yasmeen asked after a long uncomfortable silence.

'Vanessa says it wasn't her, and I believe her,' Gerry said firmly. 'Which only seems to leave one other option, doesn't it?'

'We may not be able to find whoever it was,' Jonah added, 'but we're going to have a jolly good try. We've

---

[15] Queen's Counsel: a title bestowed on senior lawyers in Great Britain and many Commonwealth countries.

already got a list of suspects, but we need you to give us access to the defence witnesses and to show us the files that the police handed over to you under the disclosure rules.

'That shouldn't be a problem,' Yasmeen assured them. 'My client has indicated that she wants you to be given every assistance. However,' she went on, looking Jonah directly in the eye, 'I do have to warn you that I advised her against any further investigation and that I am very concerned that you may be raising false hopes.'

'You may also be damaging her chances of a lenient sentence by encouraging her to enter a *not guilty* plea,' Christabel added.

'But she's already determined to do that,' Gerry argued, 'because she refuses to lie under oath.'

'OK.' Yasmeen leaned back in her chair and looked round at them all. 'I've said my bit. Now tell me who these suspects of yours are.'

Jonah brought up a table on his computer screen, which he rotated so that Yasmeen could see it.

'Top of our list,' he told her, 'is Leanne Binns. She lived with Christopher Wellesley as his lover from 1997 to at least as recently as 2003. According to Wellesley's sister, Paula, he treated her pretty badly – much the same as he did his wife later. She's still living in Evesham, and has recently been discharged from a secure mental health unit. We haven't been able to follow up on her yet, but we will.'

'That does sound interesting,' Christabel agreed. '2003 is rather a long time ago, but an unstable ex-girlfriend would certainly raise questions in a jury's mind.'

'Then there's Paula herself,' Jonah continued. 'She has ample reason to be resentful of her brother: he was the apple of her parents' eye, while they pretty much ignored her; and he inherited everything while she was cut off with – well, not exactly the proverbial shilling, but not much more.'

'And she doesn't have an alibi,' Peter added.

'Although, personally, I think she's far too sensible to go round stabbing people to death for the sake of some old family feud,' Bernie put in. 'To my mind, Leanne is a much better bet.'

'Those are the main contenders,' Jonah continued, 'but we also have the next-door-neighbour who was in dispute over Wellesley's treatment of his cat, a temporary secretary who may have been sexually assaulted by him, a client who was threatening to report him to the Law society, and …,' he hesitated. 'And there's also Vanessa's parents. They've been very outspoken about his treatment of her and, unless you can tell me otherwise, their only alibis are one another.'

'Yes,' Yasmeen agreed, 'I have to admit I did wonder about Patrick O'Shea … and there's also Louise – Vanessa's sister. She was very unwise to give that newspaper interview. If you'd like to meet her, I could go over to Swindon with you and introduce you,' she added, beginning to sound rather more enthusiastic about the prospect of an investigation.

'Thanks,' Peter said eagerly. 'That would be great.'

'As soon as possible,' Jonah added. 'As you are aware, we don't have much time to waste.'

Yasmeen telephoned Louise O'Shea and arranged for them to meet with her the following day. Then she turned back to Peter and Jonah. 'What next?'

'I think we ought to take away all these witness statements that you've got for us and go through them,' Peter said, always meticulous in checking every piece of evidence thoroughly.

'And I'm going to get on to West Mercia Police to let them know that we're working on this case in an official capacity and to check with them that there isn't anything else that they haven't got round to sharing yet,' Jonah added. 'In particular, I want them to give us a list of any items that they took away from the crime scene. We're going to look like complete idiots if it turns out that *they* took that coat for some reason.'

'And while you're doing that, do you think you could get us permission to have a look round the house for ourselves?' Bernie asked. 'I'd like to see how difficult it would really have been for someone to get into the back garden and then into the workshop.'

8. CHERCHEZ LA FEMME

Il y a une femme dans toutes les affaires; aussitôt qu'on me fait un rapport, je dis: « Cherchez la femme! »

(There is a woman in every case; as soon as someone brings me a report, I say, "Look for the woman!")

Alexandre Dumas (Père)
The Mohicans of Paris (1864 theatrical adaptation)

'OK. What is it you want to know?' asked Louise O'Shea, looking across the table at Yasmeen. 'And what've you brought in these private eyes for?'

She had agreed, somewhat reluctantly, to meet them during her lunch break. Now they were sitting in a café in the centre of Swindon with sandwiches and mugs of coffee in front of them.

'We think that your sister didn't kill her husband,' Peter explained. 'And we're hoping that we can prove it by finding out who did.'

'I thought you said Vanessa ought to plead guilty,' Louise retorted, still looking towards Yasmeen. 'Isn't it a bit late to start changing tack now?'

'Yes,' Yasmeen admitted. 'That is what I advised her; but I can't go further than to offer advice. If a client insists on a *not guilty* plea, then I have to work with that as best I can. Vanessa has asked these people to investigate what happened and, since she is adamant that whatever happens she is unprepared to enter a guilty plea, it seems to me that it's worth giving it a go.'

'Well, I think you're wasting your time!' Louise was unconvinced. 'I'm sure poor Vanny must've done it – and I don't blame her! She must have been absolutely desperate after the way he'd been treating her. It was sickening. The number of times I'd begged her to leave him! But she wouldn't listen. She was determined that marriage was for life, come what may. She always did take everything far too seriously – especially when it had anything to do with the church.'

'You don't share her views then?' Jonah asked when Louise's tirade abated. 'Father Gerard seemed to think the whole family were staunch Catholics.'

'Father Gerry sees what he wants to see,' Louise replied a little scornfully. 'And I know that Mum and Dad like to think they brought us both up to be good Catholics, so I don't go out of my way to disillusion them. But you won't find me walking down the aisle with any man and vowing to stick with them "till death do us part".'

'Interestingly, Christopher Wellesley appears to have shared your opinion of marriage until he met Vanessa,' Jonah said, conversationally. 'We've heard that he had a live-in girlfriend for years when he was younger. We're trying to find her. Presumably you don't know anything about her? Her name was Leanne Binns.'

'No.' Louise shook her head. Her face took on a slightly less hostile expression. 'I never knew him to talk about his life before he knew Vanny. Why are you looking for this Leanne?' she added, evidently interested now. 'You don't think *she* killed Chris do you?'

'We don't know,' Peter told her quietly. 'That's why we need to speak to her.'

Louise turned towards Peter and looked him up and down as if she had not noticed his presence until this moment.

'You really do think that Vanny didn't do it, don't you?' she said at last.

'Yes.' Peter said simply. Louise sat looking at him in

silence for several seconds before replying.

'OK. How can I help you?'

'Well, just for the record, can we start with where you were and what you were doing on Saturday the twelfth of May?' Jonah jumped in immediately.

'I was out shopping all morning. We'd planned a dinner party that evening and I needed to get stuff for it.'

'We?' Jonah queried.

'Me and my partner, Tom.'

'You live together?' Jonah asked. 'Just for the record,' he added with a smile. 'I won't be reporting back to your mum – or Father Gerard!'

'Yes. We live together. We also work together. We're both mechanical engineers. We met at uni and now we both work for Honda. Is that enough of the bio? Can we get on?'

'In a minute.' Jonah smiled at her again. 'First, please indulge me while I get the sequence of events right in my head. You were out shopping all morning – alone I take it?'

'Yes. I can probably find the till receipt from the supermarket if you like –with the time stamp on it to prove I'm telling the truth.' Louise was starting to sound aggressive again.

'That would be helpful,' Jonah said, continuing to smile. 'Although, it wouldn't actually prove anything, since you could easily have got your partner to do the shopping while you popped over to Evesham to see your sister.'

'When did you hear about your brother-in-law's death,' Peter asked, hoping to pacify Louise by steering the conversation on to less contentious ground.

'Mum rang me that afternoon. I cancelled the dinner and went over there right away.'

'You're very close to your sister?' Peter suggested.

'Yes.' Louise hesitated, watching Peter closely as if she were not sure whether she trusted him. After a few moments, she continued. 'I always used to feel responsible for her. When we were kids, I mean. I'm three years older than her and … well, she was never what you'd call assertive. She always had a tendency to let people turn her into a doormat. I suppose that was probably one of the things that Chris found attractive about her.'

'When was the last time you spoke to her?' Peter asked. 'Before Christopher's death, I mean?'

'The night before – on the phone. He doesn't approve of her speaking to me. He thinks I fill her head with ideas, which I do try to do,' she laughed mirthlessly, 'but it never has any effect. He won't let her have a mobile and he always checks the outgoing calls on the landline, so I rang her. He was in the shower, so we were able to talk for a few minutes. Then he came out and she put the phone down. You see the sort of man he was!'

Louise looked round at them all, as if daring them to disagree with her assessment of her brother-in-law's egregious nature.

'What did you talk about?' Jonah asked after a short pause.

'The usual,' Louise shrugged. 'I tried to persuade her to leave him – to come to stay with us, or else to go back to Mum and Dad. She said she couldn't and that Chris wasn't really as bad as I thought and that she didn't want her daughter to have a broken home.'

'You weren't tempted to try to finish the conversation the next day?' Jonah suggested. 'After it was interrupted, I mean. You didn't consider going over to Evesham and trying to meet up with your sister when she came out of the house to go shopping?'

'No! And neither did I go round while she was out and stab her husband with a screwdriver,' Louise said angrily. 'I don't deny I'd have liked to, but I knew Vanny would never forgive me if I did serious damage to the toe-rag; and I also knew that whatever I did or said to him, he'd take it out on her later.'

'Vanessa told us that a green coat of hers went missing

from the hall while she was out that morning,' Peter said, once more trying to direct the conversation on to safer ground. 'Do you happen to remember it? She said it was a waterproof with a hood.'

'I think maybe I have seen her wearing it once or twice on the way to Mass – over her Sunday coat to keep dry when it was really chucking it down.'

'You still go to Mass at St Monica's then?' Bernie asked in surprise.

'Only very occasionally – when I can't think of any more excuses why I can't go over to Sunday lunch at Mum's! No, that's not fair. I don't mind spending time with Mum and Dad; it's just awkward with Tom not being a Catholic and with them not realising that we're living together.' Louise paused for a moment in thought. 'But what's so important about Vanny's coat?'

'It's the one piece of hard evidence to suggest that someone else was in the house that morning,' Peter told her.

'That – and the neighbour who told the police that she saw a woman answering your description trying to gain entry,' Jonah added.

'Well, it wasn't me!' Louise retorted angrily. 'But if someone saw this woman, why aren't the police looking for her? Why are they leaving it to you lot?'

'Because the witness didn't see her actually enter the house, and because there was already ample evidence to charge your sister,' Jonah replied. 'Also, your mother only remembered about the coat going missing a few days ago.'

'I still don't see the significance of the coat,' Louise admitted.

'*We* think that whoever killed Christopher may have taken it to put on over their clothes to hide any blood spatter they got on them when they did it,' Peter explained. 'According to Vanessa, it was hanging up in a prominent position close to the front door. They could have grabbed it on their way out.'

'And you think it must've been this woman that you say the neighbour saw – the one who allegedly looks like me?'

'I said, "answering your description",' Jonah corrected her with a smile. 'That only means dark hair, neither very short nor very tall – could be almost anyone actually!'

'Can you think of anyone who might have wanted to call on your brother-in-law that morning?' Peter asked. 'Or on your sister, I suppose?'

'No.' Louise shook her head. 'I wasn't aware of him having any friends to speak of – or any enemies! He kept himself to himself and insisted that Vanny did too.'

'Oh well!' Peter looked at his watch. 'We'd better let you get back to work. Thank you for your time.'

He got up to go. Bernie put away the laptop computer on which she had been taking notes, while Jonah turned his wheelchair to face the way out. Louise watched them go. Then, just as Bernie put her hand on the door to open it for Jonah to go through, she called after them.

'Do you really think you can stop Vanny going to prison?'

Peter turned and looked at her.

'I don't know,' he said quietly, 'but we are going to do our best.'

***

Back home, over mugs of strong tea and a plate of Peter's home-made scones, they held a case conference to assess what they had found out so far.

'I'd say we must be looking at the murderer being a woman,' Jonah declared. 'We know there was a woman noseying about outside the house that morning. And only a woman could have worn the coat – especially if it was put on over her outside things.'

'I don't know,' Bernie argued. 'It could be a small man – or they may have taken the coat for some other reason, not to wear at all.'

'Most of our main suspects are women, in any case,'

Peter pointed out. 'And unfortunately, most of them have dark hair, like the woman that Jacqueline Lindhurst saw.'

'Louise's hair's long – not short like Mrs Lindhurst's description,' Jonah pointed out. He had liked Louise and admired her spirit and family loyalty.

'But it was tied back in a sort of bun thing on her neck,' Bernie countered. 'From across the road, it could easily have looked like short hair.'

'I make it seven, so far,' Peter continued. 'Leanne Binns – she must be top of any list – Louise O'Shea, Paula Wellesley, Deborah O'Shea-'

'Only if you assume that Patrick is lying when he says they were together that morning,' Bernie put in quickly.

'Deborah O'Shea – possibly working with her husband,' Peter resumed, 'Susan Vernon, Kelly Phillips, and Zara Lambourne. Not to mention any other clients or staff members whom Christopher touched up at work!'

'We can rule out Zara,' Bernie said decisively. 'She's black. I'm quite sure that the neighbour would have noticed that.'

'Yes,' agreed Jonah. 'It would be the first thing she would have noticed in a place like Evesham. I can't imagine they have a very large ethnic minority community there.'

'Presumably we don't know what Susan Vernon or Kelly Phillips looked like?' asked Jonah, looking towards Bernie.

'No. I didn't think to ask.'

'Never mind. They're not very likely suspects anyway. I reckon we ought to be concentrating on Leanne. She has by far the best motive, in my opinion.'

'Apart from Vanessa,' Peter pointed out morosely, 'and her parents and sister!'

'And Paula,' Bernie added. 'I can't imagine her doing anything so stupid, but her motive is undeniable.'

'Can we at least dismiss the next-door neighbour?' Peter asked, looking at the list of names on the computer screen. 'If the disappearing coat has anything to do with the murder, it's not likely to have been him.'

'Because he wouldn't have taken a woman's coat?' queried Bernie.

'No – more because he'd have had no reason to go near the front door. Even if he came in through the front, he'd surely have left over the garden fence, so that nobody would see him after he'd killed Christopher. And he wouldn't need a coat to cover bloodstains because he could just go home and change his clothes'

'So – what next?' Asked Bernie, looking round at the others.

'We wait for tomorrow when Karen's going to take us to the crime scene to have a look for ourselves,' Jonah declared. 'That may tell us whether the man-with-the-cat could've got over the fence, and how much the neighbour-from-over-the-road could actually have seen of the woman who came calling.'

'And meanwhile,' Peter added, 'I'm going through all the statements from the house-to-house, in case anyone mentioned something that the police didn't pick up on.'

9. CRIME SCENE

It is a capital mistake to theorize before one has data.
Sir Arthur Conan Doyle
The Adventures of Sherlock Holmes (1892)

'That's the house!' Karen called out over Bernie's shoulder. 'There, on the left – the one with the big rhododendron bush in the front garden.'

Bernie pulled up in front of a large detached house, built in mock-Tudor style with white-painted walls and contrasting black beams. To the left of the front door there was a curved bay window with green curtains drawn across it to prevent sightseers looking in. A smaller window on the right had vertical blinds, also closed.

They got out and looked around, noting that the gable end on the left-hand side of the house was on the boundary with the next-door property, while at the right, there was space for a carport at the side of the house, in front of a high close-board fence with a gate in it leading to the back garden.

'Which side does Jeremy Willard live?' asked Peter. 'The neighbour with the cat.'

Karen consulted her notes. 'On the left,' she answered, pointing. 'Number twenty-four.'

'And the Wellesleys are number twenty-six,' Peter mused. 'What about Jacqueline Lindhurst? – the neighbour who saw the woman trying to get in.'

'Across the road at number twenty-three,' Karen said, turning round to look at the other side of the road. 'That's twenty-seven over there … so it must be that one two doors further down.'

'And it said in her statement that she was in her front room when she saw the woman,' Peter said thoughtfully. 'Hang on while I check that out.'

He walked across the road and positioned himself in front of another imposing house. The others watched as he leaned from side to side, peering towards the Wellesleys' home. Intrigued by this performance, Bernie ran across to join him.

'What is it?' she asked.

'Well, you have a look,' Peter replied, pointing across the road towards Karen and Jonah, who were standing together on the pavement outside number twenty-six. 'Can you see the back gate from here?'

'No,' Bernie admitted, after checking for herself. 'It's too far down the side of the house. And I can't even see the front door very well, because of that rhodo. I'm starting to think that our Jacqueline has a rather vivid imagination!'

'That's exactly what I was thinking,' Peter agreed. 'I suppose the angle may be a bit different from inside the house, but I'd say that when she says she saw the woman trying the back gate, she actually means that she saw her going round the side of the house and then coming back again.'

'So she could have been doing something quite different,' Bernie said excitedly. 'Looking for a side window, maybe – or for a key to the front door! It always amazes me how many people still keep a key hidden somewhere, in case they lock themselves out. Perhaps the Wellesleys kept one in the carport and she knew about it!'

'And then, she could have come back and let herself in at the front door,' Peter continued. 'And the neighbour wouldn't have been able to see because of that bush.'

They went back across the road and explained this new theory to Jonah and Karen. Karen was sceptical.

'The SOCOs went over the house and garden with a toothcomb,' she said. 'They'd have found a key if one had been left anywhere.'

'Not if this mystery woman took it away with her,' Bernie pointed out. 'That's what I would've done if I'd used it to get in and kill someone. I wouldn't want the police knowing that just anyone could have got in.'

'On the other hand, if Vanessa told them about the key and then they found it was gone, that would suggest exactly that,' Jonah pointed out. 'So it might be better to put it back where you found it.'

'If *I'd* just stabbed someone with a screwdriver, I don't think I'd have been thinking things through as logically as that,' Peter commented. 'I'd just want to get away as fast as I could. I think she might very well have put the key in her pocket after she got in and then walked off with it.'

'And if she *had* been thinking things through, she'd want to take it away in case it had her fingerprints on it,' Bernie added.

'Shall we go inside?' Karen asked. 'If you've all finished out here?'

'Yes,' Jonah nodded. 'Let's have a look at this famous workshop, where the dirty deed was done!'

Karen unlocked the door and stepped inside. Bernie set up the portable ramp and stood back while Jonah drove his wheelchair up and over the step. Soon they were all standing in the hall, looking round at cream-painted walls and an expensive-looking brown Axminster carpet. The front door opened against the wall on their right. Beyond that, an alcove housed a row of hooks, most of which had coats hanging on them. Further on, two doors led off the hall. Both were firmly closed.

'The green coat that went missing must have been hanging on one of those,' Jonah said, inclining his head towards the row of hooks. 'You can see how someone might have grabbed it as they were heading for the door.'

'Especially if they were coming from the workshop,'

Karen agreed, looking up from the plan of the house, which she had brought with her. 'That second door on the right leads to the kitchen and then the utility room and workshop are beyond that.'

'And this other door?' asked Peter.

'The dining room – and then, across the way, that door is for the lounge.'

'OK. Let's go on through,' Jonah said, looking to Bernie to open the kitchen door. She did so, and they all followed him into a large room fitted with marble-effect worktop over white-fronted cupboards. There was a small window at the back of the house over a sink unit.

'The utility room is through there,' Karen said, pointing towards a door in the back wall to the right of the sink. It's in an outrigger that doesn't go the full width of the house, and the workshop is beyond that.

They followed her through the kitchen and utility room and stood looking down at a brown stain on the bare concrete floor of the workshop.

'That's where he was lying, I take it?' Peter asked.

'Yes,' Karen confirmed, holding out a photograph of the crime scene, which she had taken out of her file of notes. 'One of the ambulance crew took this, before they moved him. You can see the screwdriver lying next to him – where his wife dropped it after she pulled it out of his chest.'

'There are plenty of potential murder weapons here,' Peter commented, looking round at an array of saws, screwdrivers and chisels all hanging tidily along the wall above a wide bench on which there lay several boxes of nails and screws, a Stanley knife and a packet of spare blades, a large claw hammer, and an electric drill.

'That window,' Jonah said suddenly, looking up at a large window on the left-hand wall of the workshop. 'That must face towards number twenty-four, mustn't it? Would Jeremy Willard be able to see Christopher in here from his garden?'

Peter went over to the window and peered out, craning his neck to look in all directions.

'I shouldn't think so,' he answered. 'The fence is too high – unless he's well over six foot. But I can see his bedroom windows from here, so presumably he would be able to see the workroom from upstairs in his house.'

'At least he'd be able to see if there was a light on in the workshop,' Bernie agreed, 'and maybe the outline of someone moving about.'

'The window doesn't open,' Karen observed. 'So he couldn't have got in this way.'

'But he could have climbed over the fence and got into the utility room through the door from the garden and then from there into here,' Bernie pointed out. 'We're assuming it was the middle of the morning, remember, and the back door would be unlikely to have been locked.'

'OK then. Let's go and have a look at that fence,' Jonah said, moving back to make way for Karen to open the back door and waiting patiently while Bernie collected the ramp from the front of the house and brought it through here to enable him to follow Peter and Karen out into the garden.

'Look there!' Bernie called out excitedly. 'It's not a fence all the way. For the first few metres behind the house, there's a wall, and then the fence starts beyond that.'

She ran across the paved area between the utility room and the boundary with the adjoining property and climbed on to a wooden bench, which stood in front of the wall.

'It'd be easy-peasy to get over this wall,' she declared, stepping nimbly on to the back of the bench and hauling herself on to the top of the wall. 'Much easier than getting over a fence.'

She sat astride the wall and looked down into the garden of number twenty-four. The first thing she saw was a large ginger cat curled up asleep in the sunshine on the top of a substantial plastic water butt, which occupied the corner between the wall upon which she was sitting and the back of Jeremy Willard's garage. She crawled along the wall and bent down to speak to it.

'Hello! Are you the cat who caused all the trouble by trespassing in Christopher Wellesley's garden?' she asked.

The cat opened two large tawny eyes and stared at her sleepily. Then it got up, stretched luxuriously and put its front paws up on the wall next to Bernie. She put out her hand and scratched it behind the ears. The cat began to purr loudly.

'You're a friendly boy, aren't you,' she said in the voice that adults reserve for when they are speaking to animals or small children. 'Aren't you afraid that I'll turn the hose on you?'

'What do you think you're doing?' Peter asked from below in an anxious whisper. 'Come down off there, before Willard sees you.'

'What are the chances of him being around on a Wednesday morning?' she retorted. 'He'll be at work.'

Nevertheless, she got down off the wall and sat down on the bench, so that she was on a level with Jonah in his chair. Peter and Karen sat down beside her.

'Did you see anything interesting over there?' Jonah asked.

'Yes. Not only did I make the acquaintance of *the cat*, I was also able to see that there's a handy water butt next to the wall on Jeremy Willard's side, which he could have climbed on to get over the wall. The other interesting thing is that the garden of number twenty-four is at a higher level than number twenty-six, so it's quite possible that Willard *would've* been able to see into Christopher's workshop from there.'

'And we've already seen how easy it would have been for him to get back over the wall using this bench,' Jonah added, nodding in agreement. 'So if Willard wanted to kill Christopher, he would have had no difficulty doing it. All he had to do was to wait until Vanessa went out – which she did regularly every Saturday morning – and then have a look over the fence to see that Christopher was busy in his workshop, before climbing on to the water butt, over the wall and – Bob's your uncle! The question is: did he have enough motive? I'm fairly certain that a jury would say he didn't.'

'And there's no sign of anyone having climbed over the wall,' Karen pointed out. 'No scuff marks or moss knocked off – and the SOCOs didn't find anything of that sort either.'

'Can you see any signs that *I* just climbed up there?' Bernie challenged. 'The wall's in good condition and there's not a lot of moss, with the weather having been so dry this year.'

'Bernie's right,' Jonah backed her up. 'Someone could climb over this wall without leaving any visible traces.'

'What did Willard say in his statement to the police?' asked Bernie. 'Was he at home that morning?'

'Yes,' Peter told her promptly. 'I checked all the witness statements. 'Willard says that, at about half-past ten, he heard shouts coming from over the fence. He had a look over it, thinking it might be Christopher shouting at his cat again, but there was nobody in the garden so he went back indoors and forgot about it until the police called the next day. He assumed that it must have been coming from further down the road.'

'Which, of course, it might have been,' Karen pointed out.

'And was there anyone with him that morning?' Jonah asked, ignoring her intervention.

'No – not even the cat!' Peter smiled. 'But that's hardly evidence that he's lying, is it?'

They sat in silence for several minutes, wondering what to do next.

'I think we ought to do the rounds of the neighbours again,' Jonah said at last. 'I want to find out if anyone saw a woman in a green coat going away from number twenty-six sometime after ten that morning.'

'I agree,' Bernie said eagerly. 'It's too much of a coincidence that coat going missing the same day Christopher was murdered. The killer must have taken it, and why would they do that other than to put it on to hide their own clothes?'

'Always assuming that it *did* go missing that day,' Karen said sceptically. 'We only have Mrs Wellesley's word for it. It could be just a story she dreamed up to convince Peter that she was innocent; or she could've been mistaken. Maybe she or Christopher moved it from its peg for some reason and it's still in the house somewhere.'

'Maybe,' Jonah smiled back at her, 'but while we're here, we might as well try asking around – and you never know, someone may remember something they didn't think to tell the police first time around.'

'OK,' Peter agreed. He shared much of Karen's scepticism, but recognised firstly that Jonah would not be satisfied unless he got his way, and secondly that, with rather few other lines of enquiry open to them, it made sense to explore this one, however unlikely it seemed that it would bear fruit. 'You and Bernie take the odd numbers, and Karen and I will do the even ones.'

***

Jacqueline Lindhurst recognised Jonah immediately, from having seen him on the television news. She considered him to be something of a celebrity, and readily invited him in to discuss her witness statement. Unfortunately, despite her eagerness to be of help, she had nothing to add to her original account. She had not noticed anyone else in the street after seeing the woman with the dark hair peering in at the windows of number twenty-six. She had not looked out of her window again until alerted by the sound of the ambulance siren.

Jonah thanked her graciously and departed, leaving his card with instructions to her to ring him if she remembered anything else that could be of assistance in establishing who the mystery woman had been.

There was nobody in at number twenty-five, but they struck gold at number twenty-seven, the house immediately opposite the Wellesley family home. The door was opened by a grey-haired woman wearing an apron over black trousers. She looked suspiciously at Jonah and Bernie, but consented to answer their questions when Jonah addressed her by name and she saw that Bernie was holding a copy of the statement that she had made to the police several months earlier.

At first it appeared that she would have nothing further to add, but eventually she realised that Jonah was interested in all comings and goings in the street that morning, and not just visitors to number twenty-six.

'There was a car parked two or three doors down,' she said at last. 'I don't know how long it was there. All I saw was a woman getting in it and driving off.'

'Do you remember what time that was?' Jonah asked eagerly.

'Well, I saw it because I was on the doorstep signing for a parcel that the postman had brought. He can come any time between ten and ten forty-five.'

'Good. That's very good,' Jonah said encouragingly. 'Now, Mrs Lowndes, can you remember anything about the woman? Her appearance – what she was wearing – if she was carrying anything?'

'She had a green coat, with a hood,' the woman said at once. 'I remember that particularly, because it was a hot day and no sign of rain, so I couldn't think why she had a waterproof on – and the hood up too!'

'Thank you, Mrs Lowndes,' Jonah said, trying to suppress his excitement at hearing this news. 'That is most incredibly helpful. Now, can I ask you to have a think about the car? Can you remember what it looked like at all?'

'It was red.' Hazel Lowndes paused in thought. 'Yes, definitely red and I think it was a hatchback, but I couldn't swear to that. I'm sorry, that's all I can remember.'

***

'So now we have some solid evidence of a woman leaving the crime scene wearing a green coat like the one that went missing from Vanessa's hall,' Jonah said triumphantly, when they joined Paul for lunch at a pub close to the police station in Evesham.

Paul had been spending his morning pacifying members of the local CID, who were less than pleased at their investigation being called into question by a retired officer from another police force. He listened to this news with mixed feelings. Everything would have been much simpler for him if Peter and Jonah had become convinced of Vanessa Wellesley's guilt. Anything that cast doubt on that posed a potential threat to his colleagues who might be accused of incompetence – or worse. He felt obliged to pour a small dose of cold water on Jonah's idea.

'That's still a long way from proving that this woman killed Christopher Wellesley,' he said firmly. 'For a start, are you *sure* you didn't mention the green coat *before* this Mrs Lowndes remembered seeing a woman wearing one?'

'Absolutely sure,' Jonah retorted. 'What do you take me for?'

'I can confirm that,' Bernie backed him up. 'She came out with the description of the coat completely spontaneously.'

'It still doesn't *prove* anything,' Paul insisted.

'We know.' Peter stepped in to de-fuse the row that seemed to be brewing. 'It could perfectly well be a different coat worn by a woman who had nothing at all to do with the Wellesleys. She may have been visiting another house altogether. But it *is* a piece of evidence that warrants being followed up.'

'The woman in the green coat – if she exists at all – can't be the same as the woman Mrs Lindhurst saw looking in at the windows of number twenty-four,' Karen said, looking up from the sheaf of witness statements, which she had been studying. 'She says she saw her at round about eleven o'clock, which is *after* the woman in the green coat drove off.'

'There you are!' Paul said, exultantly. 'Are you trying to tell me there were two different women trying to call on Christopher Wellesley that morning?'

'Who knows?' Jonah responded. 'That's no more of a coincidence than your idea that a woman wearing a green waterproof with the hood up on a hot sunny day has nothing to do with the disappearance of an identical coat that same morning!'

'Well, one person who can't have been either of those women, is Leanne Binns,' Paul came back at once. 'I checked up on her, like you asked me to, and she was sectioned[16] on the ninth of May and only discharged from the secure unit last week.'

---

[16] Detained in hospital under the provisions of the Mental Health Act 1983, as stated in section 2 or 3 of the Act.

10. RACE AGAINST TIME

Yesterday is gone. Tomorrow has not yet come. We have only today.
Let us begin.

Mother Teresa of Calcutta

'Thank you for all your hard work,' Yasmeen said, looking round at Peter, Jonah and Bernie. They were back in her office, drinking cups of tea while Peter summarised the main findings of their investigation. 'I think you've uncovered a few things that may help to cast doubt on Vanessa's guilt in the eyes of the jury – don't you think so Christabel?'

'Yes,' the barrister agreed. 'You've come up with plenty of alternative people who might have had a motive for killing Christopher Wellesley. Now we need to think about how best to play this. If we tell the jury about all of them, they'll probably just get confused and think we're taking them for a ride. We need to fix on one, or at most two, really plausible suspects and work on convincing them that there's enough evidence against them to cast doubt on Vanessa's guilt.'

'We're not through yet,' Jonah told her. 'We've still got several lines of enquiry to follow up on.'

'But the trial starts on Monday,' Yasmeen reminded him. 'There's no time. It'll be much better to concentrate on making the most of the evidence that we have, rather than going out looking for more.'

'And don't forget that, if you carry on digging you may turn up something that incriminates Vanessa,' Christabel added. 'Or makes it clear that one of our alternative suspects didn't do it!'

'But surely we're trying to get to the truth, aren't we?' Peter asked quietly.

'That rather depends on what the truth is,' Christabel answered. '*My* job is to defend my client and to prevent her receiving a prison sentence.'

'Even if that leaves some other innocent person appearing, in the eyes of the jury – and of the public – as if they are a murderer?' demanded Bernie.

'If that happens then it will be for their defence counsel to prove their innocence,' answered Christabel smoothly. 'That's the way the law operates.'

'But we don't have enough evidence for a prosecution against any of them,' Peter objected. 'So, if the jury acquits Vanessa on the grounds of *reasonable doubt*, not only will she still have it hanging over her that she might be guilty, but someone else may be under that cloud too.'

'That's what happens when you start digging around in a case of this sort,' Christabel shrugged.

'Unless we can get enough evidence to *prove* that someone else did it,' Jonah put in. 'Which is why we need to carry on. Even if we aren't in time to prevent Vanessa being convicted, we may be able to demonstrate grounds for an appeal and then …'

'Well, we can't stop you,' Yasmeen sighed. 'Just take care and don't bother to tell us if you come up with anything that will be unhelpful to Vanessa's case.'

'We can definitely make use of Mrs Lindhurst as a defence witness,' Christabel added. 'Her evidence will give me scope for impressing upon the jury that someone else could have got into the house while Vanessa was out – and that at least one person attempted to do so.'

'And the missing coat presses home that point,' Peter added.

'So long as we don't allow them to find out that someone was seen wearing a similar coat some time *before* the dark-haired woman was seen trying to get in,' Christabel said drily. 'That's just the sort of thing I meant when I said that finding more evidence may be counter-productive. We have to decide whether we want the jury to believe that the mystery woman that Mrs Lindhurst saw is our murderer, or if it was the woman in green whom the other neighbour remembers. If we tell them it could be either of them, but we don't know which, it'll simply confuse them and make them all the more certain that we're trying to pull the wool over their eyes.'

'Which is precisely what you seem to be doing,' Jonah said coldly. 'I went into policing with the idea that it was all about protecting the innocent and convicting the guilty. You make it all seem like a game, in which the truth doesn't count for very much.'

'That's the way the adversarial system of justice works,' Christabel replied complacently. 'The police investigate crimes and identify the most likely perpetrator; the crown makes the case for prosecuting them and the defence counsel puts forward reasons why they might be innocent or less culpable. It's not my job to find out the truth, only to defend my client.'

'Would you defend someone whom you believed to be guilty?' asked Peter.

'Somebody has to do it,' Christabel shrugged. 'I must say, for two retired coppers, you seem very naïve and idealistic. Surely, you must realise that the criminal justice system is all about convincing people that crime doesn't pay? The law sets the boundaries of acceptable behaviour and the courts provide public assurance that anyone who oversteps the line will be caught and punished – after having been given every opportunity to establish their innocence.'

'Can I just check?' Justin asked hesitantly, looking up from the notes that he had been taking of the meeting. 'Are we agreed that we're going to call Jacqueline Lindhurst? Are there any other witnesses that I need to contact?'

All eyes turned towards Christabel's pupil whose presence everyone had almost forgotten. He looked round at them earnestly, waiting for her answer.

'Yes, Mrs Lindhurst's statement about seeing a woman trying to enter the house is certainly worth putting before the jury, Christabel ruled. 'But *not* the other neighbour – the one who saw the woman in the green coat earlier.'

'It may not have been earlier,' Bernie said suddenly. 'Don't you remember, Jonah? What she actually said was that it was when the postman called – and she said he usually came before quarter to eleven. What if he was late that day?'

'You're right!' Jonah agreed excitedly. 'And there's another thing – we ought to interview that postman. He must have been walking down the road at much the same time as Christopher was being killed. He may even have delivered letters to the Wellesleys' house – possibly even spoken to Christopher. Why isn't there anything about him in the police files?'

'Presumably nobody thought of him until now,' Peter answered. 'I'll get on to the post office and see if they can tell me who was on duty that day. With any luck, they'll have records of what time he called at Mrs Lowndes' house with her parcel.'

'Meanwhile, I'm going to have a chat with the porters at Lichfield College,' Bernie declared. 'I hope it wasn't Paula who killed her brother, but her alibi is decidedly shaky and she looks like our best bet, now that we've had to rule out Leanne Binns.'

'And I intend to ring the temp agency to see if I can find out why Kelly Phillips left *Wellesley, Bracknell & Wellesley* in such a hurry,' Jonah chimed in. 'Don't worry,' he added, smiling towards Christabel, 'we won't trouble you with our findings unless they prove your client didn't do it.'

Bernie got up and opened the door, holding it wide for

Jonah to take his wheelchair through. Then she followed him out, with Peter bringing up the rear and closing the door behind them. Christabel looked round at her colleagues.

'Are you *sure* you can't persuade Vanessa to plead guilty to manslaughter?' she asked Yasmeen. 'The evidence of her husband's appalling treatment of her is quite compelling. I would have no difficulty persuading the judge to give her a suspended sentence.'

'No,' Yasmeen shook her head. 'She absolutely refuses. I've been through the arguments time and time again, but she won't budge.'

'Maybe she really didn't do it,' Justin suggested nervously.

'Maybe,' Christabel admitted, smiling indulgently at her pupil, 'but, since there's virtually no chance of proving that, she would do better to accept that it's inevitable that the court will decide that she killed her husband, and to concentrate on explaining why she doesn't deserve to be sent to jail for it. If things had been handled properly from the start, we might even have avoided the inquest coming up with *unlawful killing*. If Vanessa had said the right things, we might have got an open verdict or even *Accidental Death*.'

'How?' asked Justin.

'Easy!' Christabel declared. 'Imagine you're the coroner. This young mother's there in front of you, distraught at having killed her husband. How did it happen? She really isn't sure. She remembers him being angry with her – he was often angry – and shouting and threatening her – or better still, threatening her little girl. He lunges towards her and she grabs hold of a screwdriver to try to fend him off. He keeps coming and she holds it out in front of her – and then the next thing she knows, he's fallen on to it and its sticking out of his chest. She panics and pulls it out, not realising that it's the worst thing she could do. And then there's blood everywhere and she's terrified and the child's screaming and she doesn't know what to do and ...'

'And then there's all the evidence of her state of mind and his history of abuse,' Yasmeen added. 'The poor woman was suffering from post-natal depression and post-traumatic stress disorder, following the still-birth of her baby.'

'Whose death was almost certainly caused by her husband's treatment of her,' Christabel continued. 'The coroner would most likely give her the benefit of the doubt and accept that she didn't mean to do him any harm, just to fend him off from hurting her, or her child. So, now can you see why it's so inconvenient that she's insisting that she wasn't even there when it happened? The jury won't believe her, and the judge won't be able to be lenient when she hasn't shown any remorse.'

***

'You don't really believe that Paula killed her brother, do you?' Martin asked Bernie, as they walked together along the narrow street that led to the great arched gateway in the honey-coloured stone front wall of Lichfield College.

'I hope not,' Bernie answered, 'but our number one suspect turns out to have the perfect alibi – she was locked up in a secure unit under the mental health act at the time, for her own protection – and your Paula is next on our list. You have to admit that she had good reason to resent her brother.'

'But not to kill him,' Martin argued. 'Why would she even think of him after all this time? She hadn't seen or spoken to him for years!'

'We've only got her word for that.'

121

'And you've only got the wife's word that she didn't do it,' Martin countered. 'And her motive is far better, because she was having to live with the bastard.'

'And Paula's alibi is extremely weak,' Bernie continued, 'if you can call it an alibi! "I was alone in my room all morning" isn't exactly evidence, is it?'

'Except that it's what most live-in dons probably do most Saturdays,' Martin replied. 'So why question it?'

'Because we need to get to the truth. If we can find someone to back up her story then we can rule Paula out and move on to number three on our list – although I'm not sure who that is: probably Vanessa's sister or mother, which isn't a big improvement on her doing it herself!'

'The truth?' Martin asked. 'What exactly do you mean by *truth*?'

'In this case, it's simple – we want to know who actually was holding the screwdriver when it entered Christopher Wellesley's chest, and why they were holding it, and whether they intended to do him serious damage with it.'

'And there's only one person in the world who knows the answer to that,' Martin pointed out. 'And they're hardly likely to tell you, are they?'

'If they think we can prove that they were there, they may well tell us all about what happened and why.'

'Well their version of it,' Martin said sceptically. 'That's what I meant – everyone's truth is different. And how can you be so sure this Vanessa is telling the truth when she says she didn't do it herself?'

'I suppose mainly because it would benefit her much more if she said she *did* do it – in self-defence or to protect her little girl. And because Father Gerry is convinced that she wouldn't endanger her immortal soul by refusing to confess, if she had done it.'

'And you think that finding the truth is going to put everything right?' Martin asked. 'Like what it says up there?'

They had reached the end of the street now and were at a T-junction with another of the cobbled streets that wound between the ancient colleges. Ahead of them, there loomed up the grand entrance to Lichfield College, founded in the closing years of the thirteenth century by the Bishop of Lichfield. Martin stopped and pointed across at the college crest, which was carved into the stonework above the great oak doors. Beneath the red and black painted shield were the words, "veritas liberabit vos".

'The truth will set you free,' Bernie translated, her convent school education enabling her to recognise these words from the Latin version of St John's Gospel. 'Well, I certainly am hoping that finding the truth will set Vanessa Wellesley free.'

'And lock someone else up,' Martin added gloomily. 'Quite possibly someone who doesn't deserve it any more than she does!'

'I'm afraid you may be right there,' Bernie sighed. 'It's looking very much as if, whoever did it, it must be someone a whole lot nicer than Christopher Wellesley! But that isn't really the point, is it? The point is that, if anyone is going to be locked up, it ought at least to be the person who committed the crime, even if we're all agreed that the world is a better place as a result. So now, you are going to introduce me to your porters in the hope that they will be able to confirm Paula's story that she stayed innocently at home on 12th May, apart from popping down to the lodge to collect her mail.'

'Fat chance of that!' Martin snorted. 'That's over four months ago. Do *you* remember everything that happened on a random day back in May?'

'Who knows? We may strike lucky.'

The mighty main doors were closed to deter tourists from wandering uninvited through the college, but the smaller door, built into the right-hand large one, was fastened open to allow staff and students to enter and leave freely. As Bernie stepped over the threshold, she reflected on the unsuitability of so many of the mediaeval buildings in Oxford for wheelchair-users such as Jonah.

The door led into a dark passage through the building. Its arched ceiling was hidden in shadows. Ahead of them lay the main quadrangle with its rectangle of grass, and terracotta pots of red geraniums. On the right, Bob the head porter watched them through a sliding panel of glass from his seat inside the porters' lodge. Martin introduced Bernie.

'Hi Bob! This is Dr Bernie Fazakerley. She used to be Applied Maths fellow at St Luke's.'

Bob nodded towards Bernie by way of a greeting and waited for Martin to go on. Long years of experience with both undergraduates and staff led him to believe from the don's demeanour that some sort of request was being formulated.

'This is a bit left field, I'm afraid,' Martin continued, 'but we're hoping you may be able to help us track down a missing parcel.'

'Go on,' Bob murmured, smiling back enquiringly. 'Tell me about it and I'll see what I can do.'

'I'm afraid it goes back rather a long time,' Martin apologised. 'You see – Bernie and I wrote a joint paper last year with Professor Wellesley. Paula was the corresponding author, so the authors' copies were sent to her. Now Bernie's been asked for a copy by a postgraduate student, and she's realised that she's never had any. So she asked Paula about it, and Paula can't remember ever having received them. We were wondering if you have any record of parcels that are delivered to college?'

'That depends,' Bob answered. 'If a package is small enough to fit in the pigeon-holes, we'd just put it straight in. Larger parcels, and ones that have to be signed for, we log in the book and ring through to let the person know it's come. Then we get them to sign the book when they collect it. Would your parcel have been one of those?'

'I'm not sure,' Martin appeared to think. 'I don't imagine the publisher would require a signature, and the package shouldn't have been all that big – although, you never know. It rather depends how they wrapped them, doesn't it? Do you think we could have a look at the book, just to check? It'd be round about the middle of May, I think.'

'OK. Just a minute.' Bob disappeared inside the lodge. A few moments later, he returned with a large ledger, which he placed on the counter in front of them. He opened it and thumbed through the pages until he found the entries for the previous May. He ran his fingers down the page, murmuring names to himself as he scanned the entries. Then he stopped and turned the book round to show Martin.

'Would this be the one?' he asked, holding his index finger above the words "Prof. P Wellesley" in the left-hand column of the table. 'It says a parcel arrived on the morning of Saturday the twelfth of May and it was collected by Prof Wellesley at eleven thirty-four. Here's her signature – look!'

Martin and Bernie both peered closely at the entry in the book.

'That must be it!' Bernie declared. 'So Paula did get them after all!'

'It certainly looks like it,' Martin agreed. He flashed a wry smile at Bob. 'Thanks for that. I expect she put them down in her room and then they got covered with other things – you know what fellows' desks are like! We'll go along now and help her hunt for them.'

'You are sure Paula collected the parcel herself?' Bernie asked, as Martin turned to go. 'She didn't ask her scout[17] to bring it up for her or anything?'

'No. She definitely picked it up herself,' Bob said confidently. 'In fact,' he added, to Bernie's great delight, 'I

---

[17] The domestic staff in Oxford colleges are known as scouts.

think I remember the occasion. I didn't get any reply when I rang her rooms, so I settled down to send her an email. And then, just as I was about to click "send", in she comes through the wicket gate, so I didn't need to after all.'

'Thank you!' Bernie exclaimed, surprising Bob greatly by her enthusiastic response. 'You must have a wonderful memory to be able to remember all that.'

She followed Martin out, smiling broadly.

'You're a very good liar,' she said to him, when she caught him up, halfway across the quadrangle. 'I almost found myself believing in that paper of yours!'

'Ours,' Martin corrected her with a grin. 'You were a co-author too, remember!'

'And we did get lucky, as you put it,' Bernie went on. 'If our Paula was working innocently in her room all morning, how come she was coming *in* through the gate at eleven thirty?'

'I'm sure there are plenty of explanations,' Martin argued. 'She may just have stepped out for a moment, and Bob didn't see her because he was busy on the phone trying to ring her.'

'Stepped out for what?' Bernie asked. 'And what was she doing down there at all? She didn't know she had a parcel to collect, because he hadn't got through to her yet.'

'I don't know,' Martin shrugged. 'And I know you're going to ask her in a minute or two, so let's wait, shall we?'

He led the way to a doorway, which opened on to a narrow winding staircase of worn wooden steps. Bernie grasped hold of the rickety handrail and followed him up. Reaching the top, they found themselves facing an ancient-looking door, with the words, "Professor Paula Wellesley" in gold lettering on a wooden plaque attached to it. There was a bell-push on the door frame and a paper note, pinned below it, which read: "please ring for attention." Martin pressed it firmly and they could hear a buzzer sounding faintly behind the heavy door.

They continued to listen for signs of Paula's presence.

There came the sound of a door closing and then muffled footsteps – and then the door opened and Paula Wellesley looked out.

'You again!' she exclaimed, with look of amusement on her face. 'No police backup this time?' she added, peering behind them as if expecting Peter and Jonah to appear out of the shadows. 'I take it you haven't come to arrest me then? You'd better come in.'

Bernie's first impression, as she stepped through the doorway, was that this looked more like the living room of an ordinary house than the study of an Oxford don. The sofa and easy chairs looked much more modern and in better condition than most that she had experienced during her long time at the university – first as an undergraduate, then while studying for her doctorate, and finally when she became a fellow herself. Both chairs and sofa were strewn with cushions embroidered with cross-stitch designs featuring Oxford buildings. There was no desk and no whiteboard. The sofa faced a large television screen with a DVD player on a shelf beneath it. The coffee table in front of the sofa was empty apart from a pile of coasters.

'Sit down. Would you like some coffee – or tea?' Paula added as an afterthought.

'No thanks,' Martin said hastily. 'We won't keep you long. Bernie here just wanted to ask you something about the day your brother died.'

'Oh?' Paula turned to look at Bernie with an expression that conveyed innocent wonder, but also defiance.

'According to your porter, you didn't stay in your rooms quite *all* morning, as you told the police at the time,' Bernie began, judging that a direct approach was likely to be the most productive when dealing with this intelligent and straight-talking woman. 'He told us just now that, when you collected your parcel that day, you came into the lodge from outside the college. How do you account for that?'

'I forgot,' Paula answered with a smile. 'It's a long time ago now. I was having trouble deciding how to put the paper I was working on together, so I went for a walk while I thought it out.'

'It wasn't so long ago when the police interviewed you,' Bernie pointed out. 'A day – two at the most. I'd have thought you'd have remembered then.'

'They weren't that interested. I said I was in Oxford working on a paper and they left it at that. Anyway, what does it matter? Bob's confirmed that I was here in Lichfield at eleven thirty; so I couldn't have been over in Evesham murdering Chris at ten, could I?'

'It's only an hour's drive,' Bernie pointed out. 'That could be where you'd been when Bob saw you coming in.'

'Except I don't have a car,' Paula answered smoothly. 'I don't need one, living here in the middle of Oxford. I can get everywhere I need to go on my bike.'

'Cars can be hired – or you could have used a taxi,' Bernie argued.

'That'd be a rather foolish way of going about planning a murder.' Paula continued to smile complacently. 'Leaving a nice easy trail for the police to find with the car hire firm or the taxi company!'

'But I don't think it *was* planned,' Bernie persisted. 'Whoever killed your brother, I think it was more or less accidental. How about this? You decide that it's time you tried to make peace with your estranged brother. You go over there, intending to offer him an olive branch, but he isn't having any of it. He taunts you with the way your father favoured him and cut you out of his will. He makes fun of your career and tells you that no man is ever going to look at a woman like you who thinks she's cleverer than they are! Perhaps he even casts aspersions on your relationship with good old Uncle Angus – implying that there was something sinister or unnatural about it. You argue. Tempers flare. You say something that makes him so angry that he picks up a hammer off the bench and threatens you with it. You retaliate by grabbing a screwdriver and holding it between you. He drops the hammer and lunges for your throat, falling on to the screwdriver, which you are still holding up, trying to fend him off. He falls to the floor and you think he's dead. Realising that it will not look good if you're found there with him, you make off back to Oxford, leaving Vanessa to find him an hour or so later.'

'Well, that's a very interesting story,' Paula said, still smiling. 'But it didn't happen. I really *was* in Oxford all day and I didn't ever have any thoughts of trying to make things up between me and Chris. I'm not that forgiving – or that stupid!'

'Oh well!' Bernie shrugged, smiling back. She was secretly relieved that Paula had not confessed, although had she done so it would have been a feather in her cap and evidence that she was as good a detective as Peter and Jonah. 'It was a good try. We will have to check that you didn't have access to a car that day, but …'

She got up to go, but Paula motioned to her to wait.

'Hang on! I've got something for you. It's in the other room.'

She disappeared through a door at the side of the room, returning within minutes with something in her hand. She held it out towards Bernie, who immediately recognised it as a Yale-type key.

'It's the key to the front door of twenty-six Wilbraham Avenue,' Paula told her. 'Or it was, back in ninety-two. As I said before, they've probably changed the locks by now.'

'But they may not,' Bernie answered, taking the key. 'Thanks. Where was it?'

'In an old bag of mine that I'd left in my room when I moved out. After Chris told me I had to clear everything out, I put a load of stuff into storage and that was in with it. I got it all out again when I came back to Oxford, but most of it is still lying around in boxes waiting for me to get round to going through it.'

'Well, thanks,' Bernie repeated. 'And thanks for your time too. We'd better go and leave you in peace.'

She went out, but Martin hesitated in the doorway. Paula looked enquiringly towards him.

'You don't happen to fancy an afternoon in a narrow boat, do you?' he asked at last.

'I might,' she smiled back. 'Tell me more.'

'I've got one on the canal. It's moored down behind Worcester. I take it out most Saturdays. My regular crew mate has deserted me for ten weeks, so I wondered if you'd like to come to keep me company.'

'He means my daughter, Lucy,' Bernie explained. 'She's just gone off for her first term at university and it's left Martin with nobody to help him with opening the locks and pushing the boat off the mud banks when it gets grounded.'

'It sounds like fun. What time?'

'One thirty at the porters' lodge? We can cycle down together.'

'That's fine. Thanks. I'll look forward to it.'

***

The following day, Jonah had an appointment at the hospital for one of the periodic reviews of his health, which were necessary in order to detect the first signs of any of the numerous complications to which people with spinal cord injuries are prone. Bernie was to accompany him, so it fell to Peter to drive over to Evesham to check whether the key that Paula had given Bernie still opened the Wellesley front door.

As he walked up the short path from the road, he scrutinised the front of the house. The window frames had been replaced with modern white plastic, but the door looked as if it could well be the original one installed when the house was built. It was made of fine-grained wood, stained dark and with a coat of varnish. There was a Yale lock at shoulder height and a keyhole lower down.

Peter tried the key. It slid easily into the lock. When he turned it, he could feel the bolt sliding back, but the door would not open. Presumably the mortice lock below had also been turned, to make the house secure while it was empty; but Christopher Wellesley had been at home when his killer entered the house, so the deadlock would not have been applied, and anyone with a key to the Yale would be able to gain entry.

'Excuse me!' A man's voice caused him to look round. 'Can I ask what you're doing there? Nobody's supposed to go in, you know – it's a crime scene.'

'Yes, I know,' Peter answered mildly, turning to see a youngish man dressed in jeans and a rather grimy sweatshirt looking over the fence from number twenty-four. He walked over to the fence and put out his hand. 'I'm Peter Johns. I'm a detective working with the defence team, trying to prove that Mrs Wellesley didn't kill her husband. You must be Jeremy Willard, I assume.'

'That's right,' the man admitted, shaking hands perfunctorily. 'Isn't it a bit late for that – seeing as the trial's already started?'

'I hope not, but in any case, there's always the possibility of an appeal.'

'I can't say I blame her,' Willard went on. 'He must've been hell to live with.'

'I saw from the police report that you were at home when it must've happened,' Peter said cautiously. 'It's a pity you didn't see or hear anything.'

'I'm not sure I'd have done anything to help him if I had,' Willard admitted grimly. 'He deserved it. Did they tell you what he did to my cat?'

'I heard he turned the hose on ... him,' Peter replied, hesitating slightly over the choice of pronoun to describe Willard's precious companion. He knew that some pet-owners were sensitive about their animals being described as "it".

'Too right he did!' Willard confirmed explosively. 'And

not just a gentle spray to warn her off; he went at her full blast! She was back over the wall like a bat out of hell, scared out of her wits and soaked to the skin. If he hadn't gone back inside and locked the door, I'd have been over that fence to strangle him with my bare hands!'

'How did he get on with the other neighbours?' Peter asked when Willard's tirade died down. 'Did any of them have complaints about him?'

'He put a note through Gladys Frimpton's door – that's the house on the other side of the Wellesleys – telling her to stop her dog barking,' Willard answered grumpily. 'Apart from that, I wouldn't know. He kept himself to himself – no community spirit. Anyway,' he added turning away, 'I can't stand here gossiping all day. I've got to get the car fixed or I'll have to take another day off work.'

Peter put the key back in his pocket and returned to the car. He pondered on the situation as he drove back home through the rolling Cotswold Hills. Jeremy Willard did seem disproportionately upset about Wellesley's treatment of his cat. Could he have put into practice his threat to climb over the wall and accost him? But if he had done so, surely he would have tried to conceal his anger after the event in order to avoid suspicion?

If Paula Wellesley had wanted to enter the house and confront her brother in his workshop, she had the means to do so. Her lack of a vehicle to make the journey was not such a great impediment. She could easily have hired or borrowed a car for the purpose. There was also a rail service between Oxford and Evesham. He must check the train times to see if she could have got back by that method in time to be entering Lichfield College at eleven thirty.

On the other hand – why had she given Bernie the key, if she had used it to enter the house and kill Christopher? Surely, it would make more sense for her to maintain that she did not have one? Or was she counting on them thinking that, and the key was a bluff intended to put them off the scent?

Who else might have a key? Now that they knew that the door and lock had not been changed since before Paula left home, there were other possibilities – Leanne, for instance. She must have had a key when she was living in the house with Christopher. Had she kept it when they split up? But she could not be the murderer, because she was securely locked away at the time!

Might Christopher have kept a spare set of keys at his office? If so, another member of the staff there could have got hold of them. Uncle Angus might well have had a key – who had been responsible for clearing his flat after he died?

Peter sighed. All this was mere speculation. The chances were that Christopher had opened the door to his killer himself and invited them in to see whatever it was that he was working on in that outbuilding at the back of the house, never dreaming of the dire consequences that were to follow.

11. ON TRIAL: DAY 1

A jury consists of twelve persons chosen to decide who has the better lawyer.
Attributed to Robert Frost (1874-1963)

Peter, Bernie and Jonah were outside Worcester Crown Court, waiting for Yasmeen to come and escort them to the courtroom where Vanessa's trial was to be held. The magnificent neo-classical building was of historical significance, which provided an excuse for the note next to the familiar blue disability symbol on the court website: "This is a listed building and therefore access may be restricted. Please contact us to discuss your needs."

With quiet persistence, Jonah had negotiated that they would all three be permitted to sit with the defence lawyers, which would be more convenient for him in his wheelchair than the public gallery.

A red fiesta pulled up on the opposite side of the road, and Deborah and Patrick got out of it, accompanied by Father Gerard. They waited until it drove off again, and then came across to wait with the others.

'We won't go in until Louise gets back,' Deborah told them. 'She's just finding somewhere to park the car.'

'I hope she gets here soon,' Patrick said, looking nervously at his watch. 'They may not let us in if we're late.'

'I wouldn't worry about that,' Peter assured him. 'It's still half an hour before the trial's due to begin, and anyway, there are lots of preliminaries to be gone through, which take far longer than you'd imagine.'

'And the defence solicitor is only just arriving herself!' Bernie added, seeing Yasmeen approaching, dressed more sombrely than when they had met her in her office, in a black trouser suit and a grey hijab.

'I'm sorry I'm late,' she apologised. 'The traffic was horrendous.'

She turned to speak to the O'Sheas.

'Once you're through security, make your way to Court 2,' she told them. 'There are signs up, but if you get lost, just ask someone and they'll direct you to the public gallery.'

'How's Vanessa?' Deborah asked anxiously. Their daughter had been kept in a cell overnight, in order to ensure that her journey to court could be done discretely without attracting unwelcome press attention.

Yasmeen hesitated.

'Apprehensive,' she said at last. 'As you would expect. And anxious about Leah. But I think she's also quite glad that the waiting's going to be over soon. Anyway,' she added, turning to Jonah and his friends, 'we'd better get on. Are you all coming?'

'No,' Peter answered. 'Bernie and Jonah are going to watch the show, while I carry on trying to find who really killed Christopher. I've arranged to meet the parents of that old girlfriend of his that I told you about, and I'm going to try to find the postman who delivered to their road that morning while Vanessa was out, in case he saw anything.'

'OK,' Yasmeen said without enthusiasm. 'Just try to remember what we told you about how we only want to hear about evidence that points towards Vanessa's innocence. If this girl was in a secure unit when it happened, there doesn't seem much point talking to her family.'

She looked down at Jonah and then at Bernie.

'Right! Are we ready?'

***

Bernie looked round with interest as she sat waiting for the trial to begin. This was the first time that she had been inside a courtroom. She and Jonah were sitting with Yasmeen, just behind Christabel and Justin, who were now attired in the familiar black gowns and small horsehair wigs that she had seen in TV courtroom dramas. Opposite them, behind a wide bench, sat the clerk to the court. Next to him was a stenographer, whose job would be recording everything that took place. High above them, behind another wide bench, there sat a middle-aged woman with black glasses and curly grey hair just visible beneath a much larger judge's wig.

The public gallery was behind her. She turned to see Patrick and Deborah O'Shea coming in and taking their seats, accompanied by Louise and a man whom she assumed must be her partner. There was also a small group of journalists with notebooks and pencils, and about a dozen other members of the public whom she could not identify. They were probably just local people with time on their hands who thought that a murder trial would make interesting entertainment, she supposed.

Peter had been right in predicting that the preliminary proceedings would take some time. It was nearly lunchtime before the jury had been sworn in, the charge read and Vanessa's *not guilty* plea confirmed.

First, the jury members were called in one at a time. Once they were all assembled, the Judge turned to speak to Vanessa, who looked very small and unsure of herself, sitting in the dock. She nodded and then shook her head, as she was asked if she had any objection to the jurors who had been selected. Christabel stood up and confirmed, on her behalf, that the defence was satisfied that there was no reason to suspect that any member of the jury was likely to be biased against the defendant. Vanessa flashed her a grateful look and swallowed hard.

The judge then directed the jurors to take their seats in the jury box. They meekly followed her instructions, most of them clearly almost as over-awed by the proceedings as Vanessa herself. Then the clerk approached each juror in turn offering them a small New Testament to hold while they swore that they would "faithfully try the defendant and give a true verdict according to the evidence". Jonah noted that three members chose to affirm and one requested, and was given, a copy of the Qur'an in place of the testament.

The judge addressed the jury at some length, emphasising the importance of taking careful note of all the evidence presented, and to base their conclusions on that evidence alone. She would advise them on the law, and if they were unsure on any point, they should ask her for clarification. They would hear evidence from a number of witnesses, some of which might be detailed and technical. They must, therefore, pay attention and study both the words of the witnesses and any exhibits and documents presented to them.

She then proceeded to warn them that nothing that was said inside the jury room was allowed to be disclosed and that the penalties for such contempt of court were severe. Mobile phones and other devices should already have been handed in, and absolutely no communication was allowed between members of the jury and anyone outside the court.

At the end of her address, the judge looked up at the clock on the wall. She gave the jury a brief explanation of the nature of the charge being brought and spoke to Vanessa again, confirming that she did not wish to change her *not guilty* plea. Then she announced that there was not sufficient time that morning to begin hearing the prosecution evidence and adjourned the court until after lunch.

***

Peter, meanwhile, was sitting in a coffee shop with John and Lesley Binns, Leanne's parents.

'It's no good asking me to feel sorry for that devil,' John declared forcefully. 'I was nine-tenths of the way to doing it myself the day we went to see her after the abortion. If he'd walked in at that moment, I'm afraid I might not have been able to restrain myself from strangling him with my bare hands.'

He was a large, muscular man with a red face and very little hair. Looking at him, clenching his fists as he remembered the man who had taken his lively bright sixteen-year-old daughter away from home and returned her seven years later, in a state of mental collapse, Peter did not doubt that he would have been capable of carrying out such a threat. Could he have somehow got into the house and thrust the screwdriver into Christopher's chest?

'I hope the judge will be understanding,' Lesley chimed in. 'That poor woman! She must have been desperate – if he put her through anything like what he did to Leanne.'

'Ah yes,' said Peter, looking at her short black hair and wondering if she could have been the woman that Jacqueline Lindhurst had seen on the morning of Christopher Wellesley's death. 'Now that's something I'd like your help with. You see, the judge will be much more likely to believe Vanessa's account of her marriage, if there's independent evidence of her husband's behaviour to back her up. I know it must be painful for you, but do you think you could tell me a bit more about what happened to Leanne when she was living with him? What's this about an abortion, for instance?'

'It was while they were living together in Southampton,' John told him. 'I suppose you know that they ran away together?'

'Well, it wasn't quite running away,' Lesley put in. 'At least, not for him. He was at university there and his rich daddy had bought him a little house to live in, which I suppose encouraged him to think he was a man of the world and could do just as he pleased.'

'Anyway,' John resumed, 'Leanne was quite blown

away by this university student taking an interest in her – with her being only sixteen and still at school. He persuaded her to go to live with him there. Of course, we went straight off down there to try to get her back, but she said she was happy there and wanted to stay.'

'She shut herself up in the bathroom and shouted at us to go away,' Lesley recounted. 'And that awful young Christopher told us in a high-and-mighty voice that we were trespassing on his property and if we didn't leave he would call the police.'

'We came away in the end,' her husband continued, 'because she was getting hysterical. We went to speak to the boy's parents, thinking that they would agree with us that she ought to come back to live with us at least until she was eighteen.'

'We tried reasoning with his father,' Lesley told Peter, looking at him earnestly, as if she felt the need to justify their actions. 'But in his sight, Christopher could do no wrong.'

'He acted like he thought they were doing Leanne a favour *allowing* her to live with him,' John added indignantly. 'We thought of trying to get some sort of court order for her to come home, seeing as she was still a minor, but the father told us that sixteen was old enough to choose where you wanted to live. He was a lawyer so we believed him – I don't know if it's really true or not.'

'Technically he's correct,' Peter told them. 'You'd only be able to get a court to force her to come home if she was deemed to be in danger. A sixteen-year-old living with a nineteen-year-old might be vulnerable, but the chances are, if the girl herself wanted to stay, the court would think that the age difference wasn't big enough in itself to warrant taking action, unless the man had a history of violence against women or something like that.'

'Whatever the law really says, he managed to browbeat us into giving in,' Lesley said. 'And we were afraid that it would only make Leanne even more determined not to come home if we made too much fuss, as well. So we let them alone and told ourselves that she'd come back when she was ready.'

'But you were going to tell me about an abortion?' Peter prompted.

'Yes,' John answered grimly. 'As I said, that happened while she was living with him down in Southampton. She wanted to keep the baby, but Christopher put pressure on her to get rid of it.'

'We didn't know what to do for the best,' Lesley interjected. 'We couldn't help agreeing that Leanne wasn't ready to become a mother, but ...'

'And a baby might have made her even more determined to stay with him,' John added.

'But she did really want it,' Lesley continued. 'I could see it was making her really upset – the thought of ...'

'His father arranged it all at a clinic down there,' John went on. 'We only got to know about it the day it happened. We went down right away and there she was, very tearful and upset. And there *he* was with flowers and chocolates and all very concerned and telling her not to worry – this was just the wrong time for a baby, there would be plenty of time later, after he was qualified.'

'He could be very charming when he chose,' Lesley agreed. 'At the time we were rather taken in. It wasn't until after they moved back up here that we discovered how violent he could be.'

'If we'd known about that sooner, we might have persevered with getting the court order,' John growled. 'But he was always very polite when we went down to visit them, and Leanne did seem happy – up until the business with the baby.'

'I suppose, to be fair, it was probably only later that he started knocking her about,' Lesley admitted. 'I think he didn't like her coming round to see us. While they were living down there, he had her to himself. She didn't have any friends down there. She didn't know anyone except him. Back here in Evesham, she started to have a social life of her own, and he didn't like it.'

'It was the same with his wife,' Peter told them. 'The weekly shopping trip seems to be the only time he allowed her out without him. If we can't prove that she wasn't responsible for his death, we may at least be able to convince the judge to be lenient to her, if we've got evidence of the way he behaved towards her. Would either of you be willing to come to court to tell them about your daughter's experience? It would show them the sort of man he was.'

'Like a character witness, you mean?' asked John suspiciously.

'Sort of. Only this would be evidence of his *bad* character, which isn't what you usually mean by that,' Peter smiled.

'I don't think so – sorry,' Lesley said quickly. 'It might upset Leanne if she got to know about it.'

'That's right,' her husband agreed. 'We've been trying to help her put all that behind her. No point raking it all up again.'

'It'd be like airing her dirty linen in public,' Lesley added. 'I do hope you understand.' She looked Peter full in the face. 'We'd like to help that poor woman, but we have to put Leanne first.'

'Yes, of course. I do understand,' Peter assured her. 'How is your daughter? I heard she'd been ill.'

'She's not at all well, still,' Lesley answered. 'She's out of hospital, which is a start, but she's definitely got a long way to go before she'll be right again. Russell – that's her boyfriend – is very patient with her, and very kind. I don't know what sort of state she'd be in if it weren't for him.'

'He's everything that louse Christopher wasn't,' John agreed. 'He encourages her to do things and tries to boost her confidence – instead of always putting her down and telling her she's useless!'

'He's like the son we never had,' Lesley continued,

'while Christopher always wanted to keep Leanne away from us.'

'When did you hear about Christopher's death?' Peter asked, trying to manoeuvre the conversation round to a position where he could ask them about their movements that day.

'It must've been the same day it happened,' John said promptly. 'It was on the local news that evening.'

'They only said "a local solicitor" and "police are treating his death as suspicious",' Lesley added, 'but they showed a picture of the house, and we recognised it from that.'

'And then the next day, they gave his name and said his wife was being questioned under caution,' John continued.

'We were glad Leanne was still in the hospital,' Lesley added. 'So she didn't hear about it until later, and we were able to prepare her for it. We were afraid it might … I mean, she might have … Well, it might have brought it all back for her, if you see what I mean. But, touch wood, so far she seems OK.'

'It must have been quite a shock for you, hearing about someone you know on the television news like that,' Peter suggested. 'I suppose it will be like they always say about the assassination of President Kennedy – you'll always remember what you were doing that day.'

'Well I don't know about that!' John laughed. 'I do remember that I was out fishing all day, but that's nothing unusual for a Saturday, so I reckon I'd be able to tell you where I was without anything like that to jog my memory.'

'And I went shopping, like I always do,' Lesley added. 'I took the car to Tesco on Worcester Road and called in at the chemist on the way back for John's repeat prescription, and then, just as I was walking in the door, Russell rang me from the hospital with an update on how Leanne was doing and letting me know he was coming over. It was getting on by then – eleven o'clock or so – so I invited him to stay for lunch.'

'You and Vanessa must have been at Tesco at the same time,' Peter remarked, making conversation and carefully keeping out of his voice any sign that he had a particular interest in their movements that day. 'She went there that morning too – and then when she got home, she found Christopher on the floor with a screwdriver in him.'

'Or so she says,' John grunted.

***

When the trial resumed that afternoon, prosecuting counsel stood up and addressed the jury. He outlined the case against Vanessa, emphasising the lack of any sign of a break-in or any other evidence that anyone other than she and toddler Leah had been in the house with Christopher that day. He said that he intended to prove that, on the 12th of May 2018, Vanessa Wellesley had stabbed her husband with a screwdriver from off his workbench, and then gone off shopping with their young daughter, leaving him to die on the floor of their house.

He would further prove, he told the jury, that when, on returning home, she had discovered that he was still alive, she had removed the weapon from his chest, causing him to bleed to death; and that she had then waited for some time before calling for medical help, with the aim of ensuring that he would never regain consciousness and so would be unable to name her as his attacker.

He went on to inform the court that the Wellesleys' marriage had been under strain for some time and that Vanessa was known to have blamed him for the recent stillbirth of their second child. It was, therefore, unsurprising that anger and resentment had caused her to do away with her husband. Her refusal to admit to her crime and her lack of remorse, demonstrated that this was a deliberate act, and therefore an act of murder.

Christabel then got up and gave a brief statement, acknowledging the basic facts of Christopher's death and suggesting that there was every possibility that someone else could have come into the house and killed Christopher while Vanessa was out. She told the court that Vanessa denied having stabbed her husband, and that she did all she could to summon medical help for him after she returned home and discovered the extent of his injuries. She admits to having pulled the screwdriver from the wound, but this was done in a moment of panic and in the misguided belief that it would relieve his pain.

Bernie turned in her seat to look up at Vanessa, sitting in the dock. She looked very young and frightened – and very alone. She watched wide-eyed as the prosecution barrister called his first witness, the police constable who had been summoned by the paramedics attending in response to Vanessa's 999 call.

He described the scene when he arrived at the house: Vanessa sitting in the kitchen staring into space while the paramedics worked on stabilising Christopher and preparing him for the journey to hospital. He went on to confirm that, after seeing the bloodied screwdriver and hearing the paramedics' description of the wound inflicted on Christopher, he had radioed for backup to assist him in securing what he had become convinced was a crime scene.

The jury was then invited to study photographs of the murder scene displayed on a screen at the front of the court. First came the photograph taken by the paramedics on arrival, showing Christopher Wellesley unconscious on the floor with the screwdriver a few feet away. Then there was a sequence of pictures including a close-up of the screwdriver, views of the interior and exterior of the house, and a plan showing the relative positions of the front door, kitchen, utility room and workshop.

When asked whether Mrs Wellesley appeared distressed by her husband's injuries, PC Tyler Evans looked apologetically towards the dock, before answering, 'not distressed as such. She was a bit shell-shocked, I reckon. We asked her if she wanted to go in the ambulance with her husband and she said, no, she needed to stay with her little girl.'

When Christabel rose to cross-examine this witness, she had only one question to put to him: 'Can you remember what Mrs Wellesley said when the call came through that her husband had died?'

'Yes,' he replied, 'she said, "but I've just bought half a pound of that blue cheese he likes." And then she turned to me and DC Burgess and said, "Would you like it? It'll only go to waste, because I never eat it." Like I said, I think she was a bit shell-shocked.'

***

Peter, meanwhile, was at the Royal Mail delivery office, talking to postal worker Alan Green, who had delivered to Wilbraham Avenue on the day of Christopher's death. Green had read about the case in the paper and was excited at the prospect that he might be able to throw light on what had happened. He answered Peter's questions readily.

'It wasn't my usual round,' he explained. 'I was covering for Simon, who was off sick. I got the shock of my life when I turned on the telly and saw all police tape and stuff round one of the houses I'd delivered to only a few weeks before!'

'So, you actually delivered to number twenty-six?' Peter asked with interest. 'To the house where the man was killed?'

'Oh yes! I remember it distinctly. I knew it at once when I saw it on the box. You couldn't mistake it 'cos of that massive bush in the front garden. I got there just as this woman was letting herself in at the front door. So I handed the letters to her.'

'You actually met someone going in?' Peter asked in surprise. 'On the day that Mr Wellesley was killed?'

'Yes. Like I said, I gave her the letters, and she thanked me, and then I went on. I didn't hang about because, with it being an unfamiliar round and everything, I was afraid of getting behind.'

'And what time was it?' Peter asked. 'When you delivered the letters to number twenty-six, I mean.'

'Dunno,' Green shook his head apologetically. Then he brightened up. 'But I could find out for you – or find out near enough anyhow. I had a couple of items in that road that needed signing for. One was before I called at number twenty-six and the other was after. I can find the times when I delivered those, and number twenty-six must've been in between, mustn't it?'

'Yes. Thank you. Can you do that for me?' Peter asked excitedly.

It turned out that Green had visited number ten Wilbraham Avenue at nine thirty-eight that morning. He had then proceeded along the even-numbered side of the road to the last house, which was number thirty-two. After that, he crossed over and delivered to the odd-numbers, starting with number thirty-one. At ten twenty-three, he delivered a parcel to Mrs Lowndes at number twenty-seven. That put the time of his visit to number twenty-six at approximately ten o'clock.

'Thank you,' Peter repeated, noting in his mind that they now had accurate times both for the arrival of some mystery woman at the house and for the departure of the woman in the green coat. 'That's very useful indeed. Did you tell any of this to the police at the time?'

'No. They never asked me about it and I didn't realise it was the same day I delivered there, so I didn't think to come forward and tell them about it. It was only just now, when you came asking about who was doing that round that day, and we checked back at the roster that I realised. If I'd had any idea I could have important evidence about the wife's movements the day the poor bloke was killed … well! I'd have been on to them like a shot. As it was, I just says to the wife, "look at that! I remember delivering there only a couple of weeks ago." And she says, "How can you be so sure?", and I says, "I recognised the house, 'cos of that whopping great bush in the front, stopping you seeing the number next to the door." Fancy me actually talking to someone who ends up being charged with murder!'

'So it was Mrs Wellesley that you saw going in at ten o'clock?' Peter asked sharply as soon as the postman's eloquence subsided. 'Are you sure of that?'

'Well, like I said she had a key, so it stands to reason, doesn't it?'

'She might not be the only person with a key,' Peter told him 'and Mrs Wellesley was out shopping at that time.'

'Really?' Green's eyes lit up with excitement. 'So do you think I could've seen the murderer going in to do him in? Could my evidence unmask a killer?'

'Well don't go round telling anyone about that,' Peter warned. 'It's always possible that Mrs Wellesley got back earlier than we thought. What did she look like, this woman that you gave the letters to?'

'Dark hair, I think,' Green said slowly. 'Not specially tall, but not that short either. I'm afraid I didn't really notice.'

'Do you remember what she was wearing?'

'No – sorry. Nothing very way-out or I'd have remembered.'

'Never mind. Now tell me – do you remember seeing a car outside the house at all? Maybe in the road or it could have been on the drive or under the carport at the side of the house.'

'No.' Green shook his head. 'I don't think there can have been one on the drive, because I'd have had to walk past it to get to the house, but there could've been one round the side, and there were quite a few cars parked out in the road. I can't remember if any of them were outside number twenty-six.'

'Not to worry,' Peter assured him. 'It's probably not important. Now, could you have a look at this and tell me if it could have been the woman you saw?'

He took out a photograph of Vanessa from his pocket and held it out. Green studied it carefully. Then he looked up and shook his head.

'I suppose it could've been, but I honestly don't think so,' he said regretfully. 'To be honest, I'd have put her down as a bit older, but I'm not that good at telling women's ages. Maybe she just didn't have her makeup on or something.'

'OK.' Peter put the picture away again. 'Now, I want you to undertake not to talk about this to anyone – unless the police interview you about it, of course.'

'Yes. Of course,' Green agreed eagerly. 'Will I be called as a witness?'

'I don't know. That will be for the lawyers to decide, after I tell them what you've just told me and after we've had a chance to think through what it means for the case against Vanessa Wellesley.' Peter got up and handed Green a card with his telephone number on it. 'I'd better get back to them now. I'll be in touch to let you know if you're going to be needed in court. Meanwhile, if you think of anything else we ought to know, give me a ring.'

***

'Surely this new evidence settles it?' declared Bernie, when Peter told the postman's story to the defence team after the court had adjourned for the day. 'I mean, the prosecution can't continue to maintain that Vanessa must have killed him, now that we know that someone else got into the house after she left for the shops.'

'I'm not so sure,' Jonah said, turning to Christabel. 'If you were prosecuting, how would you deal with this?'

'I'd draw attention to the fact that, until Peter sowed doubt in his mind, Green believed that it was Vanessa herself whom he met,' Christabel answered.

'But she'd already gone out,' Bernie argued, 'and it was too early for her to have got back from the shops.'

'Bernie's right about that,' Peter added. 'We know she wasn't back until after eleven thirteen, because that's the time-stamp on her supermarket till receipt.'

'Yes, but what time was it she said she left that morning?' Christabel countered. 'Half past nine, wasn't it? But how about if it was later than that? When you've got young children to deal with, often the time you *start* going out is a long way before you actually make it into the car and down the drive. What if Green misinterpreted what he saw, and she was actually on her way out when he saw her?'

'I see what you mean,' Peter nodded. 'She could have put Leah in the car and then gone back to the house for something, and that was when Alan Green saw her, apparently letting herself in with a key, when in reality she hadn't left yet.'

'Yes, I suppose the door could've blown shut,' Yasmeen agreed, 'so that she needed her key to get back in to get her handbag or her coat or something – or to say good bye to her husband.'

'And we don't know for certain what time it was that Green got there,' Christabel added. 'If there were no letters for the intervening houses, he could have got from number ten to number twenty-six in only a couple of minutes.'

'Surely you could at least ask the judge to adjourn the trial while there's further investigation, couldn't you?' Bernie asked. 'I mean – this is new evidence that *could* exonerate Vanessa. Shouldn't the trial be stopped while the police try to find out who this woman was that Green met on the doorstep?'

'I can try,' Christabel agreed doubtfully, 'but Her Honour Judge Freeman QC is notorious for being reluctant to interrupt a trial once it's started.'

'In that case, we'll just have to get a move on and find the evidence before the trial ends!' Jonah declared. 'So now, what's our next move?'

12. ON TRIAL: DAY 2

Blessed is anyone who endures temptation. Such a one has stood the test and will receive the crown of life that the Lord has promised to those who love him.

James 1:12, NRSV Anglicised Edition

The next day, Jonah and Bernie were once again seated on the floor of the courtroom watching the trial, while Peter continued with the investigation. He had just decided that he ought to find out whether the forensics team had looked for fingermarks on the outside of the utility room door – marks which could possibly provide evidence of Jeremy Willard having entered the premises – when his mobile phone rang. It was Russell Cochrane, Leanne's boyfriend.

'Lesley and John told me you were looking for people to give evidence against Christopher Wellesley,' he said belligerently. 'I wanted to tell you I'd be glad to tell the world what sort of scumbag he was – especially if it helps that wife of his who topped him.'

'OK,' Peter answered cautiously, wondering whether this particular witness might turn out to be more trouble than he was worth. 'Perhaps we could meet?'

'Where? You can't come here – I don't want Leanne to know anything about it. It might set her off again.'

Peter thought for a few moments, and then gave the address of Yasmeen's offices.

'Right you are,' Russell agreed. 'Will half ten be alright for you?'

***

The morning of Day Two of Vanessa's trial was occupied by evidence from the police and forensics team, detailing their examination of the crime scene. Prosecuting counsel drew out from them clear statements that there were absolutely no signs of any attempt at a break-in and no evidence that anyone had been in the house that morning apart from Mr and Mrs Wellesley and their infant daughter.

When it was her turn to question the police officer in charge of searching the house, Christabel asked whether they had found a green waterproof coat.

'No,' replied the detective constable nervously. 'But then, we didn't look for one.'

'Not even after you were informed that such a coat had gone missing from the hall on the day that poor Mr Wellesley met his death?' demanded Christabel in forbidding tones.

'I – I don't remember anyone saying … I mean, I wasn't made aware of that,' DC Amanda Burgess stammered, looking nervously round the court.

'Mrs Wellesley's solicitor informed your superior on … let me just check my notes – we want to be sure that this is accurate …,' Christabel said smoothly, making a display of consulting a sheaf of papers on the desk in front of her. '… Yes, here we are! On Friday the twenty-first of September, which should have given you ample opportunity for a return visit to the property to look for the missing item.'

'Perhaps you could enlighten us as to why this particular garment is of significance to the case,' suggested the judge, looking down from the bench and gazing sternly at Christabel.'

'I will be happy to do so, Your Honour. As I shall demonstrate, we have a witness who saw a woman wearing such a coat leaving the vicinity of twenty-six Wilbraham Avenue on the morning in question. And I will provide compelling evidence that this unidentified woman took the coat from the house, after stabbing Mr Wellesley with the screwdriver, which we have seen so graphically displayed on the screen in front of us.'

A small gasp went round the room as both the jury and the viewers in the public gallery realised for the first time exactly what the defence case was to be. Several of the reporters began scribbling frantically in their notebooks, eager to make the most of this unexpected development. Until now, they had assumed that the outcome of the trial was a foregone conclusion and that the defence counsel would be concentrating on providing mitigating evidence in the hope of obtaining a light sentence for her client.

'Advantage Bagshott-White,' murmured Bernie in Jonah's ear.

DC Burgess stepped down and was replaced in the witness box by the forensic scientist who had examined the murder weapon.

He confirmed that the only fingerprints found on it were those of Mrs Wellesley. Under cross-examination, he admitted that it was a little surprising that Christopher Wellesley's prints were not also present, since the screwdriver had belonged to him and he had presumably used it. However, during re-examination by the prosecuting barrister, he went on to say that it was quite possible that any such prints had been obliterated by Mrs Wellesley's taking hold of the tool with bloodied hands.

'Deuce,' Bernie commented in an undertone.

***

When Peter arrived at the solicitor's office, he found Russell Cochrane waiting for him. Yasmeen's secretary led them both into a private room at the back of the main office.

'Thank you for coming forward,' Peter began, not totally sincerely. 'It's very good of you to offer to testify, but we need to be clear exactly what you are able to tell us. You didn't actually know Christopher Wellesley yourself personally, I take it?'

'No, not personally,' Russell admitted. 'But I didn't need to have met him to know what sort of scumbag he was. I saw what he'd done to Leanne and that was enough for me to know he deserved whatever he got and more.'

'And what exactly did he do to Leanne?' asked Peter.

'I thought you knew? I thought Lesley and John had told you.'

'They did,' Peter answered patiently, 'but they aren't prepared to testify, so I need to hear it from you.'

'He conned her into thinking they were in love and got her to leave home and go with him to Southampton. He got her pregnant and then forced her to get rid of the baby. He arranged for it to be done in a clinic where they messed up so bad that now she can't ever go to full term. He messed up her mind so that she thinks it's all her fault. He … what more do you want?' Russell broke off, looking defiantly into Peter's eyes.

'I'm sorry- ,' he began, but Russell had got his breath back and continued regardless.

'We've been together eleven years now. We wanted to start a family. Six miscarriages Leanne's had now! The last one was only at the beginning of May. The doctors say that there was damage to the cervix when she had the abortion, which is why she keeps losing her babies. Leanne thinks it's all her fault for agreeing to have it done – but he never gave her any choice! It made me sick when I heard on the news that he had a kid of his own now. He didn't deserve it, after what he did to poor Leanne.'

'I'm very sorry,' Peter murmured, unable to think of anything more to say.

'So now you see why I don't want this trial to make him seem like an innocent victim,' Russell concluded. 'I want the world to know what he was like.'

'I see. Thank you,' Peter said rather formally, getting to his feet. 'Well, thank you again for coming. I'll explain all this to the defence lawyers and they'll be in touch if they want you to testify. Oh! Just one more thing: if you do go in the witness box, the prosecution are bound to ask, so I'd better clear it up now. Where were you between nine and twelve on the morning of Saturday 12th May?'

'That's easy,' Russell replied promptly. 'I was visiting Leanne in the secure unit. I was with her from before nine until ten fifteen, ten thirty maybe. After that I had a coffee in the coffee bar they have there for visitors and I rang Lesley from there to give her an update on how Leanne was.'

'Good. That sounds fine. I just needed to check. We don't want to end up landing *you* in the dock in place of Mrs Wellesley, do we?'

***

'Russell Cochrane is a very angry young man,' Peter told the others later, when they met up over lunch.

The members of the jury were spending the afternoon being taken to Wilbraham Avenue to view the scene of the crime, so the defence team had several hours in which to make plans for the days ahead. 'I'm not sure that calling him to give evidence is a good idea. He may just come over as vindictive.'

'I agree,' said Yasmeen firmly. 'He sounds like a bit of a loose cannon.'

'Perhaps,' Christabel mused, weighing up the arguments for and against in her mind. 'On the other hand, I think I could work with it. The jury looked bored to tears with all that technical stuff about fingerprints and footprints and blood spatter analysis, this morning. A bit of drama always goes down well and it sounds as if he'll certainly dispel any sympathy they may still have for Christopher Wellesley.'

'But I thought we were trying to prove that Vanessa didn't kill him,' Peter objected. 'It's all very well showing what a bastard he was, in order to make the jury sympathise with her, but it also gives her a very good motive for wanting to do away with him.'

'I think the most interesting part of his evidence is what he said about the phone call to Lesley Binns,' put in Bernie. 'He confirms her alibi for eleven o'clock, which means that she can't possibly be the woman who was hanging about outside peering in through the windows not long after that.'

'It seems clear to me that, whoever that was, wasn't the killer,' Jonah interjected. 'Surely *that* must've been the woman the postman spoke to, who actually went inside and then apparently came back out wearing the green mac.'

'OK, let's do this systematically,' said Peter, pushing his plate away and taking out a pad of paper from the storage space at the back of Jonah's chair. He put it on the table and started writing a list of names. 'These are the people that I reckon could have been the woman the postman saw. He didn't recognise Vanessa's picture when I showed it to him, but we can't entirely rule that out.'

'She can't have been the woman in the green coat, though,' Bernie pointed out. 'She wouldn't have gone off in someone else's car and left Leah behind. So, if we think those two are the same woman, that rules out the possibility that the postman actually met Vanessa on the way out.'

'Anyway, Vanessa says it wasn't her,' put in Yasmeen. 'She's sure she would have remembered if she'd taken in the letters on her way out of the house.'

'Then there's Lesley,' Peter continued, noting down these comments against Vanessa's name on his list. 'She says she was out shopping, but we don't have any independent evidence for that. We have Russell's confirmation that she was back home by eleven or thereabouts. Would she have had time to kill Christopher before that?'

'We'd better check that out,' Jonah said. 'As far as I can remember, the two houses aren't very far apart, but it's difficult to know without testing the route directly. And we ought to ask the pharmacist if she really did call for a prescription that morning. They probably keep records of repeat prescriptions.'

'How will you know which pharmacist it was?' asked Yasmeen.

'We won't,' Jonah answered cheerfully. 'We'll just have to keep asking until we find the right one.'

'Then there's Louise,' Peter went on, adding another name to his list. 'She also claims to have been shopping – this time in Swindon. And there's Paula, who claims to have been in Oxford.'

'I'll have another word with her, if you like,' Bernie volunteered.

'And finally, Deborah,' Peter concluded. 'Her only alibi is her husband, which might normally call it into question. However, in this case, I think they must be telling the truth, because they surely wouldn't allow their daughter to be convicted of a crime that they had committed themselves!'

'I want to speak to this postman,' Christabel announced, when Peter had finished making his list. 'And I want him to have a look at pictures of Vanessa, Deborah and Louise.'

'I've already shown him Vanessa's photo,' Peter told her, 'and he said he didn't think it was her.'

'That's right,' Christabel agreed. 'And I'd like him to have another look and to be a bit more definite than that. It doesn't matter if he can't identify the woman he saw – in fact, it's better if he can't – so long as he can say categorically that it wasn't Vanessa (and preferably that it wasn't her mother or sister either). The purpose of his evidence is to convince the jury that *someone else* – someone who hasn't been investigated by the police – was in the house that morning. We don't want to know who it was, in case they turn out to have a perfectly innocent explanation of what they were doing there.'

***

'OK,' Jonah said from the back of the car, which was parked outside number thirty Wilbraham Avenue, in approximately the place that Hazel Lowndes had described the red hatchback as having been when the woman in the green coat got into it. 'Let's imagine that we're Lesley Binns. We've just stabbed Christopher Wellesley and now we're making our getaway. It's ten twenty-three.' He looked down at his computer screen to check the actual time. 'So now let's see how long it takes to get back to her house from here.'

Soon they were out on the main road. They drove past the railway station and on through the centre of the town, slowing down as they reached the shops where parked cars, buses and pedestrians impeded their progress. Despite those hazards, they reached the bridge over the river within minutes. They turned right and followed the road alongside the river, which was shielded from view by the queue of traffic coming into Evesham from the West.

Three more minutes and they were outside the Binns family home. Peter drove past and pulled up round the corner where there was no chance of the car being recognised by anyone looking out from the house. He turned round in his seat to speak to Jonah.

'Well? How did we do?'

'Just on twelve minutes,' Jonah replied. 'Which gives us as much as, say, twenty minutes for the trip to the pharmacy.'

'And I think I spotted a pharmacy on the way here,' Peter added, 'next to that little corner shop where we turned right just now.'

He turned the car round and drove back the way they had come. Sure enough, there was a small chemist's shop, sandwiched between a general stores and a hairdresser's, on the corner of the next road. Peter parked the car and they got out to investigate.

Luck was on their side and this proved to be the correct place. The pharmacist knew both Mr and Mrs

Binns well. It was also lucky that she recognised Jonah at once from having seen press reports of his exploits as the only police officer in the country who continued to investigate cases, despite needing to use a wheelchair. She readily looked up her records and informed him that Mrs Binns had, indeed, come in for a repeat prescription on the morning of the twelfth of May. The time-stamp on the label was ten fifty-three.

'Giving her seven minutes to get back home for Russell's telephone call,' observed Jonah to Peter, once they were back in the car.

'And also giving her a few spare minutes during her journey to the pharmacy from Wilbraham Avenue,' added Peter, 'unless the traffic was even worse than it was today.'

***

Bernie, meanwhile, was walking along the path behind Merton College, known as "Dead Man's Walk" in the company of Paula and Martin.

'I came along here,' Paula was saying, 'and then I went for a look round the Botanic Garden.'

They followed the path, with its beds of lavender on one side and the grassy expanse of Merton Field (just beginning to recover from the unusually dry summer) on the other, and made their way to the entrance of the Botanic Garden.

'I can give you a copy of the paper I was thinking out, if you like,' Paula added, 'though I realise I can't *prove* I was writing it that morning.'

'The thing is,' Bernie told her, 'we're really struggling to work out who those two women could have been who called at your brother's house that morning. And from the descriptions that we've got, either of them could easily have been you. They can't both be the murderer, so we're hoping that the other one will eventually admit to having been there, because they might have valuable information to give us about what they saw.'

'Such as?' asked Martin suspiciously.

'Well, if the murderer was the first one to come, the other woman could have seen Christopher after he'd been stabbed,' Bernie answered. 'Or, if it was the other way round, she could confirm that Christopher was still unharmed when Vanessa left for the shops. The prosecution is alleging that she stabbed him before she went out and then finished him off by pulling out the screwdriver from the wound when she got back.'

'I see,' Paula said thoughtfully. 'Well, I'm sorry. I still didn't go over there that day – or any other day, for that matter. I washed my hands of my family a quarter of a century ago and I haven't looked back since.'

***

Back in Yasmeen's office later that afternoon, Alan Green was enjoying being the centre of attention. He looked at the photographs of Vanessa, Louise and Deborah, which Yasmeen showed to him, and shook his head.

'No,' he said firmly. 'I'm sure it wasn't any of them. Her eyes were different somehow. I can't describe it, but I'm sure I'd know if it was her.'

'Good,' said Christabel approvingly. 'That's very good. And you'd be willing to stand up in the witness box and repeat that under oath?'

'Yes – yes I would.'

'Good,' Christabel repeated. 'And you're quite sure of the date? There's no chance that, if the prosecuting counsel suggests that you could be remembering a different day, you might not be completely certain about it?'

'Oh no! Definitely not,' Green assured her. 'After all, we've got the tracking on those parcels, haven't we? There couldn't be two days when I had to get signatures from houses on either side of number twenty-six *and* bumped into someone going in there, all on the same day, could there? And especially not when I only did that round for three days, while Simon was off.'

'Excellent,' purred Christabel. 'That's what we want – a witness who can stand his ground under cross-examination and who knows how to back up his words with independent evidence. Thank you very much, Mr Green. We'll be in touch to let you know when you need to attend court. You'd better warn your employer that you'll have to take time off, probably the day after tomorrow, but it'll depend on how soon the prosecution finishes their case. They seem to be making a bit of a meal of it at the moment – which is all to the good because it gives us more time.'

Yasmeen opened the door and Green got up to go.

'I've got a picture of Paula off her university web page,' Bernie volunteered, looking across at Christabel. 'Shall I show it to Alan before he goes?'

'No, no,' Christabel answered quickly. 'We've got all we need.' She turned to look at Green, who was hesitating in the doorway. 'Thank you again, Mr Green. As I said, we'll be in touch.'

After the door had closed behind him, Bernie turned to Christabel.

'Why didn't you want him to see Paula's picture?' she demanded. 'We might have been able to rule her out too.'

'And then there would have been one fewer potential suspect to set up against Vanessa,' Christabel replied smoothly. 'Or else, he might have confirmed that she was the woman that he saw, which would have been fine until she produced a cast-iron alibi and discredited his evidence altogether. Don't you understand? The beauty of this witness's evidence is that it proves that someone else entered the house while Vanessa was out, but it *doesn't* point the finger at anyone in particular. The jury will have to accept that there is reasonable doubt that Vanessa killed her husband, but we don't have to deal with all the risks associated with making an accusation against a specific person.'

13. ON TRIAL: DAY 3

You will be in the right, O Lord, when I lay charges against you; but let me put my case to you. Why does the way of the guilty prosper? Why do all who are treacherous thrive?

Jeremiah 12:1, NRSV Anglicised Edition

They were preparing to set out, Bernie and Jonah for Worcester and Peter for Evesham, when Jonah's mobile phone rang. It was Jacqueline Lindhurst, very excited and speaking very fast and rather incoherently.

'I've seen her!' she told him. 'I was just pouring the milk on my bran flakes and there she was! It went all over the table and started dripping on the floor, but I'm sure it was her! The way her hair was tied up and the way she walked – a bit high-and-mighty, like she owned the place. I simply know it was her.'

'Hold on,' Jonah said. 'Can we go back a bit? Who is it you saw?'

'The woman who was trying to get into number twenty-six, of course!' Jacqueline replied impatiently.

'And where was it you saw her?' Jonah asked forbearingly.

'On the breakfast news. They showed the family arriving at court to watch the trial. There was this older couple – the parents, I suppose – and a younger woman, who looked a bit like Vanessa, only not so submissive and hangdog. I'm sure it was the same woman I saw trying to get into their house the day Christopher was killed.'

'Louise!' gasped Bernie and Peter together.

'Thank you, Mrs Lindhurst,' Jonah said after a long pause. 'That's very important information. I'll pass on what you've told me to the defence team and I'm sure they'll be in touch shortly.'

He ended the call and looked round at the others. They sat together in silence for several minutes.

'So, Louise has been lying to us,' Peter said at last.

'Do you think she did it?' asked Bernie. 'I wouldn't have thought she'd have allowed Vanessa to take the blame like this, if she had.'

'I suppose that rather depends on whether she's as fond of her sister as she makes out,' Jonah suggested. 'Maybe it's all put on and she's actually pleased to see Vanessa in the dock.'

'I suppose she did say explicitly that she thought Vanessa had done it,' Bernie admitted.

'But why would Louise kill Christopher, except to protect Vanessa?' Peter argued. 'As soon as you start suggesting that she didn't care about her sister, you also remove any motive she might have had for killing her brother-in-law. I don't think Louise killed him, but she does need to explain what she was doing there that morning and why she didn't tell us about it.'

'What do we do now?' asked Bernie.

'Well you and I need to get off to Worcester right away or we'll be late,' Jonah said briskly. 'I assume Louise will be in the public gallery again, so we can confront her when the court adjourns for lunch. What about you Peter?'

'I've got to go over to Evesham this morning. I've got an appointment with the temp agency that supplied Kelly Phillips, and then after that I was planning to walk the route from Wilbraham Avenue to the Binns' house, in the hope of finding evidence that it was Lesley Binns, who drove away in a red hatchback that morning. I thought she might have been picked up on CC-TV cameras or something; but I think I'll give that a miss. It was always a long shot. I'll go to the agency and then come over to

Worcester. I'll meet you outside the court when it adjourns for lunch, so we can all talk to Louise.'

The traffic was bad that morning, with the result that the prosecuting counsel was already on his feet preparing to call his first witness when Jonah and Bernie entered the courtroom and hurried to their places. Bernie turned to look up at the public gallery and soon spotted Louise, sitting on the front row next to her mother. Deborah appeared anxious, constantly switching her gaze between her daughter, below her in the dock, and her husband, sitting beside her. Louise, by contrast, was more composed, staring down at the prosecuting barrister with an expression of grim determination, as if willing him to abandon the case.

The morning passed slowly, with detailed evidence being given by the paramedics who had attended Christopher at his home, the medical staff at the hospital, and finally the pathologist who had conducted the post-mortem examination. Bernie watched the jury as they tried to take in facts and figures which meant little to them. By the time Christabel stood up to cross-examine the pathologist, they were starting to fidget and to look longingly towards the clock on the wall.

'Just to be quite clear on that point,' Christabel said finally, 'you are saying that it is not possible to tell, from the condition of the corpse, how much time had passed between the wound being inflicted and his final demise?'

'That is correct,' the pathologist agreed.

'So you are not able to tell what time it was when Mr Wellesley was stabbed with the screwdriver?'

'That is correct,' the pathologist repeated.

'Thank you. No more questions.' Christabel sat down.

The judge adjourned the court, to the evident relief of the jury, who immediately filed out to their room, eager for the sandwiches that awaited them there. Bernie, Peter and Jonah also hastened out of the court and intercepted Louise and her parents as they came out of the public gallery.

'Do you mind if we join you?' Jonah greeted them.

'No, of course not,' Deborah O'Shea responded. 'We were planning to go to the museum for lunch. There's a nice little café in there, and it's just next door.'

'Sounds good to me,' Jonah concurred cheerfully. 'You lead the way and we'll follow.'

***

Peter was waiting for them when they stepped out into the watery October sunshine. They walked together the short distance to the Museum and Art Gallery. Jonah's wheelchair could not manage the steep steps at the front entrance, but they eventually found an alternative way in down a side road and a lift to take him to the first floor where the balcony café was situated.

Once they were all settled comfortably round a small table, with plates of food in front of them, Jonah looked across at Louise and caught her eye.

'Tell me, Louise, why did you deny going to Evesham to see your sister the day her husband died?'

'Because I didn't go there,' Louise answered promptly. 'Why d'you think?'

'But there's a witness who positively identifies you as the woman that she saw trying to get into the house round about eleven that morning. How do you account for that?'

'She's lying,' Louise spat back immediately. Then, in more measured tones, 'or else she's made a mistake. I told you – I was fifty miles away, shopping.'

'Would it help you to know that we don't believe that the woman who was knocking on the door and peering in at the windows at eleven o'clock was the person who killed Christopher?' Peter asked gently. 'We think that Christopher had already been stabbed before that.'

'By a different woman, who let herself in with a key about an hour earlier,' added Jonah. 'So now, will you please tell us what you were doing there? You may have seen something that could help exonerate your sister.'

'Louise?' Deborah said anxiously, looking across at her daughter with eyes wide and frightened.

'Go on Lou,' Patrick urged. 'If you were there. You ought to answer the inspector's questions.'

Louise looked round at all the expectant faces, their eyes fixed on her, waiting for her reply. Then she took a deep breath and began her story.

'Yes, OK, I was there,' she admitted. 'Vanny sounded so low on the phone the night before that I was really worried about her. I decided to go over and try to reason with Chris. I tried to believe that he did actually care for her deep down, and I was hoping that if I could explain to him what he was doing to her, maybe, just maybe I could get him to stop. I knew she did a big shop every Saturday morning, so I thought, if I went over then, I'd be able to get him alone. I knew if she was there, I wouldn't be able to say any of the things he needed to have said to him. So, after I'd done my own shopping, I went over there.'

'What time would that have been?' Jonah asked.

'I didn't get away until gone ten, so it must've been after eleven – quarter past, maybe. The car was gone, so I knew Vanny was still out. I rang the bell and hammered on the door, but he didn't answer.'

'So then you started looking in at the windows,' Jonah continued for her.

'That's right. I looked in at the lounge window, but he wasn't there. The blinds were closed on the front window of the dining room, so I went round to have a look through the side window. He wasn't there either. I tried the gate, but it was locked, and I called through it, in case he was in the back garden. Then I came back and tried the front door again, but he still didn't answer, so I gave up and came home.'

'That's better,' declared Jonah with an air of satisfaction. 'That's much better. Now think back and tell us if you noticed anything – anything at all – that was unusual or out of place when you were there that morning.'

Louise paused for a few seconds; then she shook her head.

'No, I can't think of anything. It all just seemed the same as always – but then, I don't go over there that often, because I'm not welcome.'

'Why didn't you tell us about this before?' Patrick asked in a puzzled voice.

'I was afraid the police would think that I might have done it,' Louise admitted. 'And …,' she hesitated before continuing, 'I was afraid that Vanny might think so too – if she really didn't do it herself.' She turned to Jonah. 'Do you really think it was this other woman – the one who was there earlier?'

'Yes,' Peter answered, before Jonah could speak. 'Yes we do – and what you've just told us fits in with that. It's not surprising that Christopher didn't answer the door when you rang, if he was already lying helpless on the floor of the workshop.'

'Not that that, in itself, proves that your sister is innocent,' Jonah added hastily, 'because the prosecution is alleging that she stabbed him and then proceeded to go calmly off to do her shopping. Still, it does make it highly unlikely that she stabbed him after she got home, which rules out that fall-back position, which they could adopt if we manage to show that he was alive when she left.'

'We'll have to tell the defence team what you told us just now,' Peter warned Louise, 'and there's a chance that they'll want to call you as a witness. I doubt it, but it will be as well for you to be prepared.'

'Will anything happen to me?' Louise asked in a frightened voice. 'Because I lied to the police, I mean.'

'I don't know,' Peter tried to sound reassuring. 'If I was in charge, I don't think I'd bother to pursue it, but technically you could be accused of attempting to pervert the course of justice.'

'And wasting police time,' Bernie added, 'but I wouldn't worry about it. It's not as if it's actually made any difference to anything.'

'And if we can find out who the other woman was – the one who let herself in and then made off in Vanessa's mac – there won't be any reason why you even need to tell anyone else about it,' Jonah added. 'So now, the main thing for us to decide it how we find out who that was!'

There was no time to tell the lawyers about Louise's new account of her movements before the court reconvened for the afternoon session. They all sat impatiently watching more evidence from the police, describing the extent of their enquiries into all possible alternative explanations of how Christopher Wellesley met his death. DI Wilding – who had been the Senior Investigating Officer – appearing to be somewhat on the defensive, insisted on relating, in great detail, all the interviews that they had conducted and statements that they had obtained from neighbours, friends and colleagues of the deceased.

Christabel declined to cross-examine this witness, contenting herself with a few words of thanks to the police officer for his clear presentation of the evidence and for the thoroughness of the police investigation.

To everyone's surprise, the next prosecution witness was Linda Hayes the receptionist at *Wellesley, Bracknell & Wellesley*. She confirmed that Vanessa rarely, if ever, attended social functions where the spouses and partners of other members of the firm were present, and conceded, perhaps a little reluctantly, that this indicated that the Wellesleys' marriage was under strain. She also admitted that Christopher was notorious among his employees for making inappropriate advances on female members of staff, and that she had taken steps to avoid him being left alone with them. When asked whether she thought that this behaviour must have made Mrs Wellesley angry with her husband, she hesitated for a moment and then replied,

'I really couldn't say.'

The O'Sheas and their supporters, who had drawn in breath sharply at this question, breathed a sigh of relief at Linda's answer. However, this relief was short-lived, since she then went on to say, '*I* would have been very angry, but Mrs Wellesley may not have minded.'

Christabel was on her feet at once, appealing to the judge to disallow this question, which was one of opinion rather than of fact. The judge acknowledged her objection, and instructed the jury that, while they could take into account the evidence that Mrs Hayes had given regarding Christopher's reputation within the solicitor's firm, they should draw their own conclusions as to the probable effect that this might have had on the defendant.

The final prosecution witness came as a complete surprise to Bernie and her friends. It was the consultant who had delivered Vanessa's stillborn baby.

'Why isn't he appearing for the defence?' Bernie whispered to Yasmeen, who was sitting in front of her.

'Vanessa wouldn't let us call him,' the solicitor whispered back. 'This is a bit of luck for us – I hope!'

Mr Maurice Lampard was a small, fussy man with grey hair, a high forehead and reading glasses, which he took on and off his face as he alternated between consulting his notes and facing his questioners.

Under questioning from the prosecuting counsel, he told the court that Mrs Wellesley had been admitted to the maternity unit where he worked, after going into labour at thirty-five weeks gestation following a fall – or so she claimed. In his opinion, it was far more likely that the bruising to Mrs Wellesley's abdomen had been caused by her having been kicked or punched. He had been sufficiently sure in this assessment that he had gone so far as to report the situation to Social Services, in case it might be a case of domestic abuse, bearing in mind that the couple had another young child at home.

Did he believe that it was this abuse – if it were a case

of abuse – that had caused the child to be born dead?

It was impossible to be certain, but there had been no prior indications to suggest that the foetus was not perfectly healthy up to that point or that Mrs Wellesley was in danger of miscarrying.

Did he have any experience of such maternal injuries causing stillbirth?

Yes, he had seen at least two similar occurrences previously.

Had he told Mrs Wellesley that he thought that her "accident" had been the cause of her baby's death?

No. He did not consider that it would be helpful to her to be made aware of that. She already appeared quite depressed by her experience, and he did not want to increase her distress by suggesting that she had in any way contributed to the tragedy – even if only by taking insufficient care when descending the stairs.

The prosecuting barrister thanked the witness and sat down. Christabel signalled to the judge that she did not have any questions. The judge gave the witness permission to stand down and then adjourned the trial until the following day.

***

'I'd already been thinking that we ought to drop Mrs Lindhurst as a witness,' Christabel said, when she heard about Louise's admission that she had been the dark-haired woman who had been seen peering in at the windows of twenty-six Wilbraham Avenue. 'Now I'm sure of it. There's no point at all in letting the jury know that the defendant's sister was there that day. What conclusions will they draw from that? Very likely that the two of them were in it together, or at very least that Vanessa called Louise to come over and help her in some way after she stabbed Christopher. No, we need to keep Jacqueline Lindhurst out of the witness box and make the most of Alan Green's evidence that another woman actually went inside the house while Vanessa was out.'

'I agree,' nodded Yasmeen.

'Isn't his testimony enough to warrant stopping the trial?' asked Bernie. 'Surely it would be in the interest of justice to adjourn it for a few weeks, to give the police time to try to find this woman, whoever she is?'

'Perhaps,' Christabel admitted, 'but I have to think of my client. It may not be in her best interests to stop the trial now. Quite apart from the stress of having to wait, perhaps for several months, while the police hunt for someone who may never be found, her best chance of acquittal may well be to shock the jury into believing her story by springing Green's evidence on them unexpectedly. Think about it. You've listened to the prosecution case that Vanessa stabbed her husband and then went off to the shops with her little girl. You've heard how there was no sign of a break-in and no clue that anyone else was in the house that day. You've drunk it all in and believed it all. Then, all of a sudden, here's this man saying that he saw another woman going into the house at just the right time to be the real killer.'

'And just before the time that the next-door-neighbour heard shouting coming from that direction,' Jonah added, remembering Jeremy Willard's statement.

'Exactly,' Christabel agreed. 'You'd start to wonder, wouldn't you? And then, when another neighbour says that she saw a woman getting into a car and driving away a short while later – a woman wearing a long coat with the hood up, even though it was a warm day – you'd think that the prosecution had been deliberately concealing facts from you in order to convince you that Vanessa was guilty, when in fact it was this mystery woman all along.'

'So, we're not calling Mrs Lindhurst after all, and we *are* calling Mr Green and Mrs Lowndes?' Justin asked, looking up from scribbling notes in a small spiral-bound book. 'What about Mr Willard?'

'He's a bit of a loose cannon,' Peter warned them.

'He'll probably insist on going on about his cat and how badly Christopher treated her.'

'That may not be any bad thing,' Christabel mused. 'Hearing about that certainly won't endear Christopher Wellesley to the jury. Yes. I think we'll call Green first, to sow the seeds of an alternative murderer in the jury's minds. Then we'll have Willard to tell them that there was something going on in the house or garden *after* we know that Vanessa had already left for the shops. And finally, we'll get Mrs Lowndes telling them about the sinister woman in the green coat, slinking away from the crime scene. After that, there shouldn't be any question that they'll conclude that there's reasonable doubt and bring in a *not guilty* verdict.'

'And Russell Cochrane?' Justin asked, quietly determined to get the list of defence witnesses clear. He found it very confusing to have these changing after the trial was underway. 'Are we still going to call him?'

'Oh yes, I think so,' Christabel told him. 'You've got to remember that juries rarely succeed in behaving rationally – regardless of their having sworn to try the defendant in accordance with the evidence. If we can begin by turning them against Christopher, allowing them to think that we are making a case for self-defence and instilling in them sympathy for Vanessa, and then spring on them the fact that there is an alternative explanation, another potential murderer, then they will leap on the suggestion because it's what they want to believe!'

***

'I'm sure Christabel is a very good barrister,' Peter said, as they drove home that evening, 'but I can't say I like the way she treats the trial as some sort of game. And I wish I could believe that she actually cares about finding out what really happened.'

'I almost think she'd rather it *was* Vanessa who killed Christopher,' Bernie agreed. 'It's as if she wanted to make a point about women defending themselves against violent and controlling men.'

'Well, with a name like hers, you'd expect her to be a rampant feminist,' Jonah chuckled. 'I imagine she must've imbibed hatred of the patriarchy with her mother's milk!'

'Personally, I always preferred Sylvia Pankhurst[18] to Christabel or even Emmeline,' Bernie declared. 'She remained a socialist and stuck up for the working class – and she didn't jump on the nationalist bandwagon when the first world war started.'

'I suppose, if Christabel can get Vanessa acquitted, the police will have to re-open the case and look for the woman that the postman saw,' Jonah commented. 'So I suppose she would argue that that's the best way to go about finding out what really happened.'

'I suppose so.' Peter still sounded dissatisfied.

'And meanwhile,' Jonah continued, 'there's nothing to stop us trying to find out for ourselves.

'I suppose we ought to try to think who might have had a key to the house,' Bernie suggested. 'We know that Paula did, but I really don't think she killed Christopher. Who else is there?'

'Vanessa could have given one to her parents or to Louise,' Jonah conjectured. 'It would be a natural thing to do. We know Louise couldn't get in when she came along later, so how about Deborah as the mystery woman?'

'Green didn't recognise her,' Peter pointed out. 'And I'm sure she would have admitted it if she'd killed Christopher, rather than allowing Vanessa to take the blame.'

'Well there's always Leanne, isn't there,' Bernie reminded them. 'I know she couldn't have done it, but if

---

[18] Emmeline Pankhurst and her daughters Christabel and Sylvia were founding members of the Women's Social and Political Union, a society dedicated to obtaining women's suffrage in the early years of the twentieth century.

she had a key then her partner or parents could have got hold of it. It seems to me that Lesley Binns is the perfect match for both the woman with the key and the woman in the green coat.'

'But why now?' asked Peter sceptically. 'I could have understood if she'd gone round and had it out with him back then when they were living together – or just after they'd split up – but why rake it all up again now?'

'So, who else might Christopher have given a key to?' Jonah mused. 'Why would a woman be letting herself into the house like that?' He fell silent, deep in thought. Bernie turned the car in at the drive of their house and pulled up a few feet from the front door.

'I know!' Jonah greeted her, as she opened the back of the car to let him out. 'How about this? What if Christopher had a mistress? What if the mystery woman was coming to see him because they knew his wife would be out for the morning and they'd have the house to themselves?'

14. ON TRIAL: DAY 4

You are those who have stood by me in my trials
Luke 22:28, NRSV Anglicised Edition

The fourth day of Vanessa's trial opened with a speech from the prosecution barrister, summing up the case against her and presenting some items of written evidence. He stood up ponderously and turned to address the jury, speaking slowly and solemnly.

'Ladies and gentlemen of the jury, you have now heard the evidence of a number of witnesses, evidence which indicates in the strongest possible way that Mrs Vanessa Wellesley was responsible for her husband's death. Let me remind you first of the sequence of events surrounding his death, which are not disputed by the defence. On Saturday the twelfth of May, Christopher Wellesley was alone in the workshop at the back of his house, intent on making a piece of furniture for his daughter's bedroom. His wife – the defendant – and their young child were the only other people in the house.

'At nine thirty, or thereabouts, the defendant left the house with the child. By the time they returned, sometime after eleven o'clock, Christopher had been brutally stabbed with one of his own screwdrivers from off the bench in his workroom. The defendant's reaction, on discovering her husband unconscious on the floor with a nine-inch screwdriver protruding from his body, was to pull the weapon out of the wound. This action caused him to bleed to death.'

The barrister paused and looked round the court, allowing time for this statement to sink in.

'What did Mrs Wellesley do then?' he resumed in a booming voice, which echoed around the chamber. 'What would any person of goodwill do upon finding another human being seriously injured, lying helpless on the floor with blood gushing from an open wound? Surely the natural reaction would be to telephone the emergency services immediately, while also administering whatever first aid one was able to provide? Is that not what any one of you would have done?'

He looked slowly along the line of jurors, as if daring them to disagree, before continuing his speech.

'I ask again, what did the defendant do, when she realised that her husband was mortally wounded? The answer appears to be nothing! Or at least nothing for a full twenty minutes! In her statement to the police, which you have before you, she puts her arrival home at half past eleven. This accords with the time stamp on the till receipt that they found in her purse, which shows that she had completed her shopping and was on her way home by eleven thirteen. And yet, she does not call for an ambulance until eleven fifty-one. Why this delay? How could *any* delay be justified, when a man lay bleeding to death for want of medical attention?'

He fixed the jury with his eye and then slowly turned to look towards Vanessa, sitting pale-faced in the dock with her hands clasped tightly together in her lap. The jury, following his gaze, stared at this woman who had behaved so callously and unnaturally.

'The defence will try to convince you that the deadly blow was struck by some intruder, who entered the house while Mrs Wellesley was out,' the prosecuting barrister resumed. 'However, as you have heard, the police, despite diligent searching, have been unable to find any trace of such a person. There was no sign of a break-in, and no footprints or fingerprints, except those of Mr and Mrs

Wellesley. Extensive house-to-house enquiries failed to produce a single witness who saw anyone entering the house that morning. Is it credible that a murderer should enter a house, brutally kill the householder and then walk nonchalantly away, all without leaving any trace of their presence, and without being observed by any of the neighbours? If she did not kill her husband, why are Mrs Wellesley's prints the only ones on the murder weapon?'

He paused again and took a sip of water, allowing time for the jury to consider these questions.

'But let us suppose for a moment that such an interloper did exist. Who could that be? And what motive could they have for wanting Mr Wellesley dead? Could the incident perhaps be a burglary that went wrong? Could it be that Christopher Wellesley surprised a thief, who stabbed him in order to incapacitate him for long enough to make a getaway? But there was no sign of a forced entry, and nothing was stolen.

'We are compelled to the conclusion that whoever stabbed Mr Wellesley must have been in the house with his consent. It must have been someone known to him, and trusted by him. Who among his acquaintances could have borne him such ill will as to deliberately drive a lethal weapon into his chest and then leave him for dead?'

He waited, as if expecting the jury to produce some suggestions in answer to this. Bernie leaned across and whispered in Peter's ear, 'He hasn't thought of the possibility of someone else having a key.'

'Or else, he doesn't want the jury to think about that possibility,' Peter whispered back.

'What had Christopher Wellesley done to engender such hatred? We are not talking here of some disagreement among colleagues in the office or some dispute with a client over fees charged for his services. No! The defence would have us believe that someone – so far unknown, whom the police have searched for in vain – bore such malice against the victim as to travel to his house in order to stab him to death with a sharp instrument in his own home! I ask you, members of the jury, is this credible?'

Looking along the line of jurors, Bernie thought that she could detect a mixture of reactions to this diatribe against the supposed defence case. Probably the majority were looking on approvingly, but a sizeable proportion of them appeared bored with the length and wordiness of the speech, and one member – a middle-aged woman in a business suit – exhibited undisguised hostility towards the prosecuting counsel. A feminist, perhaps, who had listened to Linda's testimony about Christopher's behaviour towards female members of staff and believed that he deserved the fate that had befallen him? Or was she simply anxious to complete her jury service and get back to her job, and considered this long-winded repetition of what they had heard from the various witnesses a waste of her valuable time?

'However,' counsel for the prosecution continued, 'let us not be hasty in our judgement. Let us suppose that Christopher Wellesley, a well-regarded local solicitor with an unblemished reputation, did possess such an enemy. That someone did entertain such hostile feelings towards him as to wish to see him dead. Why would he open his door to that person? Why, having opened the door, would he invite them into his home? And, more significantly, why would he allow them into his house when he was alone, and hence vulnerable were they to make an attack upon his person?'

'Because it wouldn't have occurred to him that anyone would dare to,' Bernie muttered. 'And because he wouldn't have realised that he'd done anything to upset them.'

'But, let us not dismiss this scenario out of hand,' the barrister went on, after short pause. 'Unlikely as it must seem, it is not completely impossible that there could have been such a person: known to the victim, trusted by him sufficiently to be invited into his home when he or she called unexpectedly at his house, and yet, intent on doing him serious injury or even wishing him dead.'

He paused again, allowing his hearers to dwell briefly on his magnanimity in considering every possible explanation that might be used to exonerate the defendant.

'I ask you, ladies and gentlemen of the jury, to consider this: when a visitor calls on your home and you invite them in, where do you receive them? Do you lead them through your kitchen and utility room into a small, cluttered, dirty workroom at the back of the house? Do you entertain them among the debris of your DIY projects? Do you expect them to stand while you conduct whatever business it is that they have come about? No! Of course you would not. I am confident that none of you would be so discourteous.'

He smiled round benevolently at the jury, before continuing, 'No. You would do what any other rational person would do. You would show them into the lounge, where you can both sit in comfort. And yet, it is not there that the victim was found lying mortally wounded. And it was not from there that the murderer seized the weapon with which the deadly blow was struck!'

He paused dramatically once more, looking along the lines of jurors, who stared back waiting for him to go on.

'And so,' he resumed, 'having considered every possible alternative, we are inevitably led to conclude that the likelihood of any outside agency being responsible for Christopher Wellesley's death is so small as to be negligible. Firstly, there is no evidence that anyone else ever entered the house that day. Secondly, if anyone did enter, it must have been by the invitation of Mr Wellesley himself. Why would he invite his own murderer into his home? And, assuming that he was sufficiently unsuspecting as to do so, why would he entertain them in the most inauspicious room in the house?'

He left the question hanging in the air while he took another draught of water from the glass on the desk in front of him. Bernie noticed several members of the jury glancing up at the clock on the wall, as if hoping that the lunchtime adjournment would come soon. It was not yet eleven. How much more of this oratory were they to be subjected to?

'As we have seen,' learned counsel for the prosecution resumed, 'the only person whom we can be confident had the opportunity to commit this crime is the defendant. She alone had access to the house where he was so brutally assaulted. She alone had reason to go into his workroom – the inner sanctum where he was accustomed to retreat during his hours of leisure – the one place where he could be confident of escaping the rigours and burdens of his weekday toil.'

'Weekday toil!' Jonah snorted in an undertone. 'The man's a solicitor for goodness sake! What did he ever know about toil?'

'I don't know,' Bernie whispered back. 'All those long working lunches must be quite burdensome!'

Jonah opened his mouth to reply, but broke off when he saw that the judge was looking down on them disapprovingly. He looked back apologetically and favoured her with one of his winning lop-sided smiles.

'Now let us consider what motive there could have been for anyone to wish to do harm to this exemplary family man,' boomed the prosecutor. 'You have heard that he was well-regarded in his profession and liked and respected by those with whom he worked. However, like all of us, he was not without flaw. He had an eye for a pretty woman; and he had been known to allow more than just his eye to rest upon their persons. It would be only natural for his wife to feel resentment – anger even – at this behaviour. But that is not sufficient, I hear you say, to prompt an attack such as was launched on poor Mr Wellesley. And I would be forced to agree with you, were it not for the fact that we have very clear evidence that Mrs Wellesley did indeed harbour very strong feelings against her husband – and not without cause.

'I ask you to recall the evidence of Mr Lampard, the consultant obstetrician who attended Mrs Wellesley at the birth of her second child. He testified that, in his opinion, the child was born dead as a result of injuries sustained in the womb when premature labour was induced by heavy blows to the abdomen inflicted upon Mrs Wellesley. He suspected domestic abuse and made a report to Social Services, suggesting that the Wellesley's older child might be at risk. Sadly this was not, apparently, followed up. If his surmises were correct, can anyone be surprised if Mrs Wellesley felt anger towards her husband, and desired to be free of him? And, it would seem that she did, indeed, harbour such feelings against him!'

With a dramatic flourish, he snatched up a newspaper from the desk and held it high for all to see.

'Here, we have the words of the defendant's own sister, describing Mrs Wellesley's feelings towards her husband, in an interview that she gave to a reputable local newspaper. You all have copies of the article, which I encourage you to read in its entirety and to keep in mind when the time comes for you to consider your verdict. Meanwhile, I would like to draw your attention to some key phrases, which illuminate the relationship between Mrs Wellesley – the defendant – and her husband.'

A few members of the jury began diligently searching through the papers in front of them, looking for the article. The judge helpfully announced the number of the document and an usher stepped forward to assist the jury to identify it for those who wished to read it. Most, however, opted to keep their eyes fixed on the prosecuting barrister, who seemed ready to read out all the important points – and probably much more than was strictly necessary in their opinions. In this, they were not disappointed.

'I wouldn't blame Vanessa if she had killed him,' he intoned lugubriously. 'He was a vicious bully and made her life hell. He deserved what he got. I tried to get her to leave him, but she was frightened that he'd get custody of Leah. It would have been a complete travesty if he had, seeing as it was all his fault that she lost her baby.'

He held the newspaper high above his head and gestured with it towards Vanessa, who was sitting rigidly in the dock with lips pressed tightly together and eyes staring straight ahead.

'The defendant's own sister openly declares that she had every reason to want her husband dead!' he proclaimed. 'And she goes on. In answer to a question about the Wellesleys' marriage, she says, and I quote, "It was never anything more than a sham. He treated her like a slave and she was too scared to stand up to him. I just know that she hated every minute of it-"'

He broke off suddenly as Vanessa gave a sharp intake of breath behind him. Christabel was on her feet immediately.

'Your Honour, I must object! This article is mere hearsay. Whatever opinions my client's sister may have expressed to a journalist – who, like most journalists, was no doubt encouraging her to exaggerate the situation in order to provide interesting and salacious reading that would attract more customers to buy the newspaper – cannot be submitted as evidence of my client's state of mind or of the state of her marriage.'

The judge looked down gravely on the prosecuting counsel.

'I have to agree with the counsel for the defence,' she said firmly. 'And if this is the only purpose that you have for submitting this as evidence, I will ask the ushers to take back the copies and instruct the jury to ignore what they have read.'

'I bow to your superior judgement,' prosecuting counsel said, 'and I will move swiftly on to my main reason for drawing this document to the attention of the jury.'

'Please do,' the judge urged.

'Members of the jury,' he began, but before he could

get any further, he was interrupted by a whispered, "Please!" from Vanessa, who was standing up with her hand raised, looking towards the judge.

'Mrs Wellesley,' Judge Antonia Freeman said to her in a kindly voice, 'you will have your opportunity to speak later. Meanwhile, please be silent and allow the learned counsel to complete his presentation of the evidence for the prosecution. We are all hopeful that it may be over before it is time for lunch.'

'I'm sorry,' Vanessa said in a whisper, her face going red and then white again, 'I just wanted to say that Christopher wasn't ... I mean, I don't want people to think ...'

She tailed off into incoherence, stood for a moment in silence staring round the room with a bewildered expression, and then collapsed back into her seat.

'I draw your attention to the final paragraph of this article,' the barrister resumed, 'in which the sister of the accused states that she, and her parents, both repeatedly urged her to leave her husband and come to live with them. She may have been angry with her husband – and perhaps with good cause. She may have been fearful of him, and may even have suffered at his hands. She may have had every reason to dislike and despise him. But even if she felt all these emotions, there can be no excuse for the action that she took to rid herself of him – because she could simply have walked away! She could have taken her child and gone to her parents or her sister, as they repeatedly urged her to do. They would have taken her in and protected her.'

He put down the newspaper and clasped his hands behind his back. Then, drawing himself up to his full height and looking directly towards the jury, he continued in dramatic tones.

'If – as you inevitably must – you conclude that there is no one else who could have inflicted the wound that caused Mr Wellesley's death; if – as you surely will – you decide that there can be no one else with sufficient motive to wish him dead; if, I say, you deduce by rational thought and consideration of all the evidence, that the defendant did, indeed, kill her husband … then you have no choice but to find her guilty of murder. The defence may try to suggest that she had no alternative; that her life – or her safety or her sanity – was in danger; that she acted, in effect in self-defence. However, I say to you: if she was in fear for her life that Saturday morning, why did she not simply drive, with her daughter, to the sanctuary of her parents' home? She had the use of a car. Her husband thought that she was going shopping. If she was a prisoner in her own home, she had the means of escape. Why did she not take it?'

He looked towards the jury as if expecting them to reply. Then, after holding them in his gaze for several seconds, he concluded his address.

'I shall tell you why: she did not walk away, because she wanted him to suffer – as he had made her suffer when she lost her baby. You may sympathise with her desire for revenge, but it is your duty, as members of the jury, to set aside such feelings and to try this case in accordance with the law. And the law leaves no room for individuals to take revenge on those who have wronged them. Her proper course of action was to report what he had done to the police and to allow the process of law to ascertain the truth and to mete out just punishment in accordance with the law of the land.'

He paused again and again fixed the jury with his eye, declaiming dramatically, 'I know that I can trust you all to do your duty in upholding the law!'

Then he turned to the judge and announced, 'That is the case for the prosecution.'

He flung himself down into his seat and mopped his brow dramatically with a silk handkerchief, as if exhausted by his own eloquence.

The judge looked across at the clock and then, judging

that there would not be time before lunch for the defence to make any significant headway, announced that the trial was adjourned.

***

The afternoon session opened with the defence putting forward a formal application of *no case to answer* to the judge, who looked towards Vanessa with an expression of sympathy, but declined to accept the application and instructed Christabel to proceed with presenting the case for the defence.

'I trust that the new list of defence witnesses, which you provided to the court yesterday, is now your final offering?' she added drily, giving the defence team a hard stare. She liked trials to proceed predictably in accordance with a pre-agreed plan and had been considerably annoyed by the way in which the defence in this case had pushed to the limit the boundaries of the rules requiring a definitive list of witnesses to be supplied in advance.

'Yes, Your Honour,' Christabel said meekly. 'I'm sorry not to have been able to finalise the list prior to the start of the trial, but some important information has only recently come to light – information that will completely exonerate my client – which requires the testimony of additional witnesses, whom the police failed to interview during the investigation of this heinous crime. I did consider asking for an adjournment to allow more time for the paperwork to be completed, but that might have proved even more disruptive to the smooth-running of the court.'

'Very well,' muttered Judge Freeman. 'I have accepted your new list, now please proceed with putting the defence case – and please attempt to be succinct.'

'Thank you, Your Honour. My client will now enter the witness box to give evidence.'

Looking very nervous, Vanessa got to her feet and was escorted from the dock to the witness box by an usher. She stumbled over the words of the oath, but managed to get them out at last and handed the testament back with evident relief. Smiling encouragingly towards her, Christabel began her examination.

'Mrs Wellesley,' she said gently, 'or would you prefer us to call you Vanessa?'

'Vanessa – yes please,' her client responded, almost inaudibly.

The judge leaned forward and said, in a kindly tone, 'I know this is an ordeal for you, but if you wouldn't mind raising your voice a little when answering. It's important that the whole jury can hear you, and we are none of us getting any younger I'm afraid!'

'Yes, please,' Vanessa repeated a little louder. 'I'd like you to call me Vanessa.'

'Thank you,' Judge Freeman said, leaning back in her chair and indicating with her hand that Christabel should continue.

'Now Vanessa,' Christabel resumed, 'I would like you to tell the court exactly what you did on the morning of Saturday the twelfth of May. Take your time and tell us everything that happened, starting from when you woke up that morning.'

'I – I was woken by Leah – that's our little girl – singing in her cot. I got up and went to her.'

'And can you remember what time that was?' asked Christabel.

'It was half past five. I looked at my watch when I woke, because I didn't know if it was time to get up. It was already light, you see, so it could have been later.'

'I see.' Christabel continued to speak in a low, unthreatening voice. 'And you say that you went to your daughter. She was sleeping in a different room from you, I take it?'

'Oh yes!' Vanessa sounded surprised that this might not be obvious. 'I was with Christopher in our room and Leah was in her room across the landing. We never had her in our room – not even when she was tiny – because it might have kept Christopher awake. He was very sensitive about sounds in the night and the least little thing disturbed him. I got up right away and went to quieten Leah down, so that he could sleep in.'

'That's very considerate of you,' Christabel commented. 'And after you had settled the child, did you stay with her or did you come back to your husband?'

'Oh, I stayed with Leah. I knew she wouldn't go back to sleep so I stayed and played quietly with her, to make sure she didn't wake Christopher up. And then she started to get noisy again, so I dressed her and took her downstairs for breakfast.'

'About what time was this?'

'I – I don't know exactly,' Vanessa replied anxiously. 'We'd finished well before Christopher got up, that's all I can remember.'

'That's OK. Don't worry about it,' Christabel said, reassuringly. 'Do you remember what time it was when your husband got up?'

'I don't remember looking at the time, but he usually gets up between half eight and nine on a Saturday.'

'Thank you. Now go on – tell us what you both did after that.'

'I got Christopher his breakfast, and then, while he was eating it, I went upstairs and had a shower and got dressed ready to go out. Then I came down and put the breakfast things in the dishwasher and got ready to go out. I always do the week's shopping on a Saturday morning.'

'And why is that?' Christabel asked innocently. Then, seeing Vanessa's puzzled expression, she continued, 'I mean – you don't work, so you could do the shopping on a weekday, when the supermarket would be less crowded.'

'Oh, but Christopher wouldn't have liked that! He always gave me the money for the shopping just before I went and I gave him the change when I got back. He couldn't do that if he was at work, could he?' Vanessa spoke as if this were the most natural behaviour in the world for a man with a stay-at-home wife.

Bernie looked towards the jury. The woman, whom she suspected of being an arch-feminist, bore an expression of mixed amazement and outrage; the other women seemed to be indignant, but not surprised; most of the men looked sheepish but one or two nodded complacently. It was clear that sympathy for the victim was beginning to wane.

'And what time did you leave the house?' Christabel asked, 'as far as you can remember.'

'Half nine – something like that.'

'And how did you go?' Vanessa looked puzzled at the question, so Christabel added, 'I mean – by what means? On foot? In a car? Or …?'

'Oh! I see what you mean. We went in the car.'

'We?' intervened the judge. 'Do you mean that your husband went with you?'

'Oh no! Christopher didn't like shopping. He said it was women's work. I meant me and Leah.'

'I see. Thank you. Carry on.' She waved to Christabel to continue.

'And where was your husband when you left the house to go to the shops?'

'He was in the kitchen,' Vanessa replied promptly. 'He poured himself another cup of coffee and took it through to his workshop. He said he was going to finish the shelves that he was making for Leah's room. I tried to get Leah to come and say goodbye to him, but she was playing in the hall and she wouldn't come.'

'And what was this game that your daughter found so fascinating that she was unwilling to leave off for a few minutes to see her father?' Christabel asked.

'She was hiding behind one of my coats,' Vanessa explained. 'It was a long one that I kept for when it was raining hard.'

'Would you describe this coat to the court, please?'

Looks of puzzlement passed across the faces of the jury. The prosecuting lawyer half-rose to his feet, and then thought better of it and subsided back into his seat. The judge leaned forward to address Christabel.

'I am at a loss to understand,' she said, 'what bearing this may have upon the case.'

'I beg Your Honour to be patient for just a few minutes,' Christabel replied with relish, clearly enjoying herself, 'and I will show the court that this coat forms a vital piece of evidence, which clearly demonstrates that my client was not – as the prosecution alleges – the only person to enter the house and speak with the victim that morning.'

'Very well – proceed.'

'The coat?' Christabel prompted Vanessa. 'What was it like?'

'Well, like I said, it was a long waterproof that I used to put on over my other things when it was raining.' Vanessa thought for a few moments. 'It was green and it had a hood. I can't think of anything else to say about it.'

'Thank you,' Christabel responded quietly, and then a little louder, turning towards the jury, 'It was a long, green waterproof coat with a hood. Please make a note of this description, because it will feature again later. Meanwhile, Vanessa, I have just one more question for you about this garment. When do you next remember seeing it?'

'I – I – well, I don't,' Vanessa stammered, taken aback by the question. 'I *never* saw it again.'

'And why was that?' asked Christabel.

'Because it wasn't there anymore. I asked Mum to get it for me – that was after the police shut up the house and I had to go to stay with them – and she couldn't find it.'

'Can you explain this disappearance?'

'No.' Vanessa shook her head. 'I can't understand it at all. I just *know* it was there, hanging up in the hall when we went out!'

'You couldn't have moved it somewhere else after you came home?' Christabel suggested.

'No. I'm sure I didn't. I was too busy getting the

shopping in and putting it away and then … then I found Christopher!'

'So, it is your belief that it must have been removed by someone else, while you were out that morning.'

'Yes.' Vanessa nodded. 'I can't think of any other explanation.'

Christabel turned to address the jury.

'At this point, 'she said to them, 'I would like to remind you of the evidence that the police witnesses gave earlier, stating that the house was designated a crime scene as soon as PC Evans arrived that morning and it remained sealed until after the defendant's mother visited – under police escort – to collect her daughter's belongings. It is inconceivable that any item could have been removed from the scene during that period without the police being aware of it.'

She turned back to face Vanessa. 'Now, please go on. Tell us about the rest of your morning.'

'I went to Tesco on Worcester Road,' Vanessa resumed. 'It always takes a long time to do the shopping, because we always have so much to get and it isn't always easy to find the things we like. I remember talking to the girl on the cheese counter about Christopher's special blue cheese and the boy at the checkout commented on how good Leah was being.'

'Don't worry,' Christabel told her. 'Your movements aren't being disputed, and the jury has the police accounts of their interviews with the shop assistants. Tell the court about what you did after you left the supermarket.'

'I parked under the carport,' Vanessa related. 'I took the bags inside and then I went back for Leah. I gave her a biscuit to keep her quiet while I unpacked. I took the frozen food through to the freezer in the utility room and that was when … that was when I looked into the workshop and … and I saw Christopher!'

'Do you remember what time that was?' Christabel asked gently.

'No – not really. I wasn't thinking about it. I was just – just shocked and frightened at what had happened to Christopher. I went over and knelt down to see closer. I couldn't really believe that it was true.'

'I know this is difficult for you,' Christabel said kindly, 'but can you describe exactly what you saw?'

'Christopher was lying on the floor with this big screwdriver sticking out of him. He was white in the face and not moving and he didn't seem to know I was there. At first I thought he was dead, but I knew he couldn't have been when I pulled out the screwdriver and blood went everywhere. I realised at once that I shouldn't have done it, but by then it was too late!' Vanessa looked towards the jury with a pleading expression as if begging them to believe her.

'And then?' prompted Christabel.

'Leah called out and I turned round and saw her there watching me. Then she ran towards me and fell over and banged her head. She started crying really loudly, so I got up and took her away upstairs. I was afraid she'd annoy Christopher with her noise – he does – did – get so irritated when she started whining. I settled her down in her cot and then I rang for the ambulance.'

'Which, as we have heard, arrived shortly afterwards,' Christabel concluded for her. 'Thank you. You have described what happened very clearly. Now, for the avoidance of any doubt, please will you tell the court all that you know about how your husband, the victim, Christopher Wellesley came upon his injuries?'

'I have no idea!' Vanessa answered, shaking her head and looking completely at a loss. 'He was fine when I left him and then, when I got back, there he was! Someone must have come in and done it to him – unless he could somehow have fallen on to the screwdriver and done it himself by accident.'

'You categorically deny that you yourself stabbed him before leaving the house that morning?'

'Yes.'

'And you also deny having done so, after you returned from your shopping expedition?'

'Yes,' Vanessa confirmed, sounding more sure of herself now. 'I don't know who did it, but it was not me.'

15. ON TRIAL: DAY 5

"Judgement does not come suddenly; the proceedings gradually merge into the judgement."

Franz Kafka,
The Trial

During the journey to Worcester the following day, Peter, Bernie and Jonah discussed the progress of the trial.

'It's all very well Christabel saying that she can get Vanessa off by convincing the Jury that some mystery woman got into the house while she was out and that she *may* have killed Christopher,' Peter complained, 'but even if she's successful, that won't stop people continuing to think that the chances are she did do it really.'

'You're right,' Bernie agreed. '*Reasonable doubt* just isn't good enough. But surely, if she's acquitted the police will have to re-open the investigation?'

'Of course they will!' Jonah said forcefully from behind her, 'but, as I said, that doesn't stop us trying to get there first. Who have we got? Green ruled out Vanessa, Deborah and Louise, but could Paula have been the woman he saw? She has several hours unaccounted for that morning.'

'Yes,' Peter agreed. 'And I checked the train times. She could've got to Evesham and back by public transport within the time available.'

'But, if she was the woman in the green coat, where did she get the red car from?' asked Bernie.

'Alright then,' Jonah conceded, 'What about Lesley

Binns? We've said before that she might have had Leanne's key – assuming that she kept one.'

'There's Kelly Philips too,' Peter added. 'You know – the typist from the temp agency. The agency agreed to give her Christabel's number and, apparently, it's all arranged that she's going to give evidence about Christopher's behaviour at work.'

'Is that a good idea?' asked Jonah. 'After the way the prosecution twisted Linda's evidence into a reason why Vanessa might want her husband dead, I'd have thought the defence might want to back-pedal on that aspect of things.'

'I don't know,' Peter admitted. 'That thought did strike me when she told me, but it's not my business to argue with her expert opinion. I wonder what exactly Kelly is going to say. Christabel did sound ever so smug on the phone, as if it was going to be something quite spectacular.'

'Maybe she's going to confess that she did it herself,' Bernie suggested facetiously. 'Does she fit postman Green's description?'

'I don't know,' Peter shrugged. 'I didn't get to meet her. The agency are very protective of *their girls* as they call them. All they were prepared to do was to pass on Christabel's phone number to Kelly and leave it to her to decide whether or not to get in touch. She did, and Christabel convinced her to give evidence – that's all I know.'

'I suppose, if she was guilty, she wouldn't have agreed to be a witness,' Bernie commented.

'That depends,' Jonah disagreed. 'She might feel that to refuse would make her look guilty, so she better had. Or she might just be so cocksure after having got away with it for this long, that she's enjoying cocking a snook at everyone, by playing along with it.'

'Or she might want to help prevent someone else being convicted of a crime that she committed,' Peter added quietly.

***

The morning session began with cross-examination of Vanessa by the prosecution. The barrister got ponderously to his feet, turned slowly to face the dock and addressed her politely.

'Mrs Wellesley, I would like to take you back to the point in your narrative where you say that you bade your husband goodbye, before leaving the house. I have a simple question for you: did he mention to you that he was expecting any callers while you were out?'

'No,' Vanessa said confidently. Then, when he remained silent as if expecting more, she added, 'he didn't ever invite people to the house. If he had to meet someone, he went to the golf club – or he met clients in his office.'

'So any visitor must have been unexpected?' the lawyer suggested. 'And unwelcome?'

'Yes. I suppose so,' Vanessa answered, looking shaken and glancing towards Christabel, who was already on her feet.

'Your Honour, I must object to this line of questioning. How can my client be expected to know the inner workings of her husband's mind? What possible bearing can it have on the case, for her to speculate on whether or not he would be pleased to see an unspecified person arriving at his home, whether expected or not?'

Judge Freeman gave a small nod in Christabel's direction in acknowledgement of her complaint, and then turned to the prosecutor.

'Do you intend to pursue this point any further? I must warn you that I am inclined to agree with the learned counsel for the defence that you appear to be encouraging the defendant to indulge in fruitless speculation.'

'No, Your Honour, I have no further questions on this

particular point.' He bowed towards the bench and then turned back to address Vanessa again. 'Let us now move on to the moment when you claim that you discovered your husband lying unconscious on the floor. When you gave evidence yesterday, you told the court that you thought he was dead, and you only realised that he was still living after you pulled the screwdriver from his chest and saw that his blood was still flowing. Do you remember saying that?'

'Yes, I suppose so,' Vanessa answered almost inaudibly.

'Mrs Wellesley,' the judge intervened gently, 'I'm afraid I must ask you to speak up, so that the jury can hear your answers.'

'Yes,' Vanessa repeated, a little louder. 'I think that's what I said.'

'And yet, in the statement that you made to the police at the time,' the prosecutor said aggressively, brandishing a sheaf of type-written papers, 'you said, and I quote, "I pulled the screwdriver out because I thought it must be hurting him." Do dead people feel pain? How can you both have believed him to be dead and, at the same time, have thought that removing the weapon from his chest would relieve his suffering? I put it to you that you knew that he was still alive when you returned home. Is that not the truth?'

'I – I – I really don't know what I thought,' Vanessa stammered.

'And yet, you swore on oath that you believed your husband to be dead,' the prosecutor retorted implacably. 'Do you now wish to retract that testimony?'

'I – I –,' began Vanessa, looking round in bewilderment, but Christabel was on her feet, cutting across her client's incoherent stammering to address the judge.

'Once again, Your Honour, I must object to this unnecessary harassment of my client, who has answered all of our questions to the best of her ability. She has admitted that she can remember little of what happened on that unimaginably traumatic day when she found her husband dying on the floor of his own workshop. Those attending the scene have confirmed that she appeared to be in a state of deep shock. Surely it is only natural that she should find it difficult to assess in detail her precise thoughts at such a time?'

The judge looked enquiringly towards the prosecuting counsel.

'With all respect to my learned friend,' he replied to her unspoken question, 'it is of crucial importance whether the defendant truly believed her husband to be dead when she pulled out the weapon from his chest, thus opening the wound and, as confirmed by the medical evidence, hastening his demise.'

The judge nodded and said, somewhat grudgingly, 'very well. You may continue.'

'Mrs Wellesley,' counsel for the prosecution resumed, 'I must ask you again: at the moment that you removed the weapon from the wound, did you believe your husband to be still living or already dead?'

'I – I – I really don't know,' Vanessa stammered. 'I didn't know what to think. I *didn't* think about it – I just – I just pulled it out instinctively – because it looked so awful sticking out of his chest like that.' Her knuckles went white as she gripped the front of the witness box, and her bottom lip began to tremble as if she were fighting back tears. Then, with a great effort, she lifted her head and turned to face the jury. 'You've got to believe me,' she pleaded, 'I didn't mean to kill him! I didn't realise he would bleed like that.'

'Very well, Mrs Wellesley,' the prosecuting counsel said gently, 'we will accept your protestations. Let us suppose – for the time being – that you did pull out the weapon in all innocence, genuinely believing that your husband was dead, or else that so doing would relieve his pain. There still remains to be explained what you did after that. By your own admission, several minutes passed – perhaps as much as a quarter of an hour – between your realisation that your husband was bleeding to death and your summoning an ambulance. Why the lack of urgency?'

'Leah was crying,' Vanessa answered. 'I was just about to get my phone to ring for help when I heard her. And then I turned round and saw her watching. So I wiped my hands on my skirt and picked her up and took her upstairs out of the way.'

'I'm sure we can all understand your concern to remove your daughter from such a horrific scene,' the barrister sympathised, 'but I am still at a loss to understand why it was so long before you made the 999 call. It can have taken no more than a minute to carry the child upstairs. Why did you not make the call immediately?'

'I put her in her cot, but she wouldn't settle,' Vanessa gabbled. 'She doesn't have a nap in the morning any more – only after lunch. She just wouldn't stop crying, and all I could think of was how angry Christopher would be if she kept on. He did hate hearing it so much. In the end, I did just leave her there. I closed the door and hoped the sound wouldn't get down to the workshop. And then I rang for the ambulance right away.'

'Right away,' the prosecutor repeated lugubriously. 'That is, right away after fifteen or twenty minutes – vital minutes during which your husband's life was draining away and his lungs were filling with blood. Thank you Mrs Wellesley. I have no more questions.'

At the judge's invitation, Christabel rose to re-examine Vanessa. She smiled at her reassuringly and spoke calmly and quietly.

'I know that it is painful for you to reflect on these things, but it is important that the jury appreciates how things were with your husband regarding your daughter and her natural tendency to make a noise in the house. Otherwise, they may find it hard to understand your anxiety to quieten her at all costs. So, please, think back and give us an example of his behaviour in the past when she continued to cry for a lengthy period of time.'

'Well,' Vanessa began, her mind racing as she tried to remember the incidents that she had rehearsed with Christabel before the trial started. It seemed such a long time ago now, and so much seemed to have happened in between. 'Well,' she repeated slowly, playing for time. 'There was … there was the time he locked us both in the bathroom while I was changing her and went out and played a round of golf before he let us out.'

'And his rationale for doing that was …?' Christabel prompted.

'He said, he couldn't stick it in the house with that row going on and it was time I learnt how to control her and stop her disturbing him.'

'I see,' Christabel looked round at the jury before continuing, 'and was this an isolated incident?'

'Well, that was the only time he locked us in,' Vanessa admitted, 'but he often shouted at Leah to be quiet, and … and there was the time he threw a hammer at us. He was chiselling out a design on some furniture he was making and Leah called out behind him and made him jump and he messed it up. He'd been working on it for hours, so he was upset that it was spoilt.'

'And was it remembering occasions such as those that made you so anxious to quieten your daughter before calling for help that morning?' Christabel asked.

'Yes.'

'Thank you. That's all now.'

An usher stepped forward and escorted Vanessa back to her seat in the dock.

Christabel turned back to face the judge and announced in a clear ringing tone, 'I now call Mr Russell Cochrane to give evidence.'

Russell entered the court in answer to the summons, looking much calmer than when he had met with Peter in Yasmeen's office. He was dressed in a dark suit with a white shirt and a pale blue tie. His hair was immaculate and his face looked as if it had been freshly scrubbed. He repeated the oath in a calm, clear voice, looking towards the jury as if emphasising to them that what they heard from him would be the truth, the whole truth and nothing but the truth.

'Mr Cochrane,' Christabel began, 'You have asked to be permitted to give evidence in this case. Please tell the court why you did this.'

'Because I know something about what it's like for a woman to be in a relationship with Christopher Wellesley, and I'd like the jury to understand how impossible it would be for them to kill him or to walk away from him,' Russell answered calmly and confidently.

'I see,' Christabel answered in a similarly calm voice. 'And would you please explain to the jury how you come to know this?'

'My partner, Leanne, used to live with him,' Russell replied, still keeping his voice calm and measured, as Christabel had coached him to do. 'Even now, years later, she still blames herself for the relationship breaking down. She thinks it was all her fault that he got tired of her and turned her out. And she thinks it's all a punishment on her that she can't have kids – when it's really because he forced her to have an abortion when she was only a very young girl. She was so much under his thumb that she could never have got up the courage to run away. She was just lucky that he decided he could do better than her. Otherwise, she'd still be living with him.'

'And why would that have been such a bad thing?' Christabel asked mildly.

'Because of the way he treated her!' Russell's voice rose and he visibly fought down a temptation to become agitated and angry. 'He kept her a virtual prisoner in the house and tried to stop her seeing her family, and he knocked her about too – not enough that people would notice, but enough to keep her under.'

'I must protest!' counsel for the prosecution exclaimed, getting to his feet and looking towards the judge. 'What possible relevance can this person's testimony have? The issue before the jury is the guilt or innocence of Mrs Wellesley – not the details of some prior relationship that the victim may have had many years before their marriage!'

Russell opened his mouth to argue, but Christabel was there before him.

'If it please, Your Honour, the purpose of calling Mr Cochrane was in order to establish the type of relationship that the victim had with the women with whom he chose to share his life. However, since my honourable friend has raised an objection, I will ask no further questions of Mr Cochrane.'

'Very well,' Judge Freeman turned to the prosecuting counsel. 'Do you have any questions for this witness?'

'No, Your Honour.'

'In that case, Mr Cochrane, you may stand down.'

In the lull while one of the ushers escorted Russell outside, Peter whispered to Bernie, 'Hat's off to Christabel. She did a good job preparing him for the witness stand. I'd never have thought he could keep calm and not start raging against Christopher's enormities towards his girlfriend.'

The next witness was Kelly Phillips. The three friends watched with interest as she entered the court and made her way to the witness stand, wondering what she would be like.

'She certainly can't be our mystery dark-haired woman,' Jonah observed as she negotiated with the usher that she would prefer to affirm, rather than to swear on the Testament.

She was a natural blonde, with a peaches-and-cream complexion to match the shining gold of her long straight hair, which was parted at the side so that it kept falling over her right eye and she repeatedly pushed it back with her hand. She was dressed in a very short pink dress over scarlet leggings. Despite having two-inch heels on her dark red ankle boots, she still looked very small and young – almost like a child – standing in the witness box.

'Miss Phillips,' Christabel began gently.

'Kelly, please!' the witness interrupted. 'Everyone calls me Kelly.'

'Kelly,' Christabel resumed. 'You work for the *Type and Go* temporary secretarial agency. Is that correct?'

'That's right,' Kelly nodded. 'I've been with them for three years now.'

'And last April you started work at *Wellesley, Bracknell and Wellesley*, solicitors, in Evesham?'

'That's right,' Kelly repeated. 'April the second, it was. I was doing audio-typing and helping out with general office duties.'

'And how long were you working there?'

'Just on six weeks. I finished on Friday the eleventh of May.'

'I see. And was this the date that was planned for you to finish there?'

'Oh no! It was supposed to be a six month contract to take them over the summer holiday period.' Kelly smiled back mischievously, clearly pleased to be the centre of attention.

'So what happened to change that?' asked Christabel, as if she were unaware what answer to expect.

'I asked to go somewhere else,' Kelly replied promptly. 'I didn't like the way Mr Wellesley kept coming on to me. Linda – I mean Mrs Hayes – warned me to be careful, and I know how to stick up for myself and avoid being bothered by men without offending them, if you see what mean. But when he asked me to go round to his house on a Saturday, to work on some urgent business he said he had … Well! I'm not stupid – I knew what sort of business he had in mind, the dirty old git – specially when he started talking about how his wife wouldn't be there, 'cos she always went out on Saturday mornings. So I said, "no way!'"'

She paused and looked towards Christabel with a knowing grin on her face.

'And then,' she continued, 'over the weekend, I thought about it, and I decided I didn't want to go back there, not if he was going to carry on like that. So I went to Miss Appledore – she's my boss at the agency – and told her about it, and she rang Linda and told her I wasn't available anymore and she'd send them a replacement. She did too!'

Kelly giggled and looked round the court triumphantly.

'She sent Gary Capstick! I'd like to have seen the look on Mr Wellesley's face when he turned up instead of me! Talk about gobsmacked! I bet he'd never seen anything like it!'

'Thank you,' Christabel said when Kelly finally fell silent. 'Just to be quite clear, Christopher Wellesley asked you to go to his house that Saturday morning – the twelfth of May?'

'That's right! He asked, but he didn't get.'

'And did anyone else in the office hear him say this – or find out about it?'

'I told Lin – Mrs Hayes – about it,' Kelly answered promptly. 'And she said I was quite right to tell him "no", and that she'd quite understand if I didn't want to work with him anymore.'

'Did she give you the impression that this sort of thing had happened before?' Christabel asked, sounding casual but with a slightly anxious look on her face that indicated that she was not sure what answer to expect.

'Oh yes!' Kelly grinned. 'I reckon he tried it on with all the staff – 'cept Gary, of course! That must've really cramped his style! Only, I suppose he was already dead, wasn't he,' she added, suddenly becoming more sombre as she remembered that this was a murder trial.

'Thank you,' Christabel repeated, then to the judge, 'No more questions, Your Honour.'

The prosecution declined to cross-examine this witness and Kelly, looking a little disappointed that her appearance was over so soon, was led out by an usher. The judge looked up at the clock and declared that the court was adjourned until Monday morning.

***

'I should think Christabel will be well pleased with herself after that performance,' Jonah observed as they drove home from the court. 'The jury seemed to be lapping up all that stuff about Christopher being a predatory male and expecting women to be kept under his thumb.'

'I thought the most important bit was when Kelly talked about him inviting her round on Saturday morning,' Bernie said. 'It rather undermined the prosecution argument that he couldn't have been expecting anyone.'

'Except that she said she told him where to get off,' Jonah pointed out. 'So, unless he had a reserve lined up in case she said *no*, her testimony actually supports that idea.'

'I meant it knocks on the head the suggestion that he never invited people to the house,' Bernie argued. She thought for a few seconds, and then added, 'or could she have gone after all, but not admitted it?'

'She certainly can't have been the woman that the postman saw,' Peter objected. 'And surely there can't have been *two* visitors that morning.'

'Three, including Louise,' Jonah pointed out. 'You're starting to make it sound as busy as Clapham Junction!'

'Besides,' Peter added, 'Kelly didn't need to give evidence. She came forward of her own volition, remember? Why would she do that and then lie on oath?'

'To throw us off her scent by making us think that?' suggested Bernie. 'Or simply because she just couldn't resist the opportunity to be the centre of attention – she was obviously loving every minute of it. But I think Jonah's right – the murderer has to be the dark-haired woman that Alan Green spoke to, and Kelly just doesn't fit the bill.'

'She's even too short to be the woman in the green coat,' Jonah agreed, 'assuming that it was Vanessa's coat, stolen from her hall. Hazel Lowndes would have noticed if it was dragging on the ground.'

'So the big question is: who was that dark-haired woman?' Peter summarised. 'And Kelly's testimony made me wonder if it could have been Christopher's mistress – or whatever you call it these days. It's now clear that, however keen he is on some aspects of catholic teaching on marriage, he doesn't take seriously his vow to *forsake all others*. What if he had a girlfriend who came round regularly on Saturday mornings?'

'Except, if he was expecting her that Saturday, why would he ask Kelly as well?' Bernie argued.

'Maybe he wasn't expecting her, but she came anyway,' Peter answered. 'Or maybe he was planning to put her off if Kelly agreed to come. And then she didn't, so he didn't need to.'

'You mean, he was hoping to have Kelly, but if not, he was willing to put up with the regular girlfriend instead?' Bernie queried.

'That's right. I was thinking that Kelly's young and pretty and she's not going to be available for long, so-'

'And Green said the woman he spoke to was older,' Jonah cut in. 'What if she was an old girlfriend that he'd been seeing since before he met Vanessa?'

'The person he left Leanne for, for example?' Bernie asked.

'Maybe,' Jonah agreed. 'The point is, if she was in the habit of coming over to see Christopher while Vanessa was out, he could well have given her a key to let herself in. She'd be able to tell if the coast was clear, by looking for the car in the carport.'

'That's all very well, but it doesn't get us any closer to finding out who she was,' Peter said gloomily. 'And if it is a regular arrangement that's been going on for years, what made her kill him on this occasion?'

'Finally got fed up with playing second fiddle to Vanessa?' Jonah suggested without conviction. 'Or maybe just one of those pointless arguments that people have over nothing much and his getting seriously injured was an accident.'

'Is there anything we can do to find out who the dark-haired woman was?' Bernie asked wearily. 'We seem to have got to a brick wall.'

16. PAUSE FOR REFLECTION

For now we see in a mirror, dimly, but then we will see face to face.
Now I know only in part; then I will know fully, even as I have been
fully known.
1 Corinthians 13:12, NRSV Anglicised Edition

'Aren't you going to ask me if I killed my brother?' Paula enquired, leaning against the rail at the stern of the *Maid of Saxony* and watching Martin as he stood with the tiller in his hand guiding the boat along the tranquil waters of the Oxford Canal.

'Why would I want to do that?' Martin responded, smiling back at her.

'Isn't that what this is all about? Inviting me out here – plying me with *kaffee und kuchen* – all devised to put me off my guard, so that I'll open up and admit that I did it?'

'If that's what you think, why did you come?'

'Dunno – curiosity maybe.'

'What about?'

'You. Why you're still living with your mother-'

'I explained about that.'

'Who those friends of your are-'

'I explained that too.'

'Hardly! But never mind. What I'd really like to know is why you're all so dead set on proving Chris's wife didn't kill him. It seems like the obvious explanation to me – and the police must have thought so too, or she wouldn't have been charged.'

'I don't know much about it,' Martin shrugged. 'Bernie

asked me to introduce you to her and I went along with it, that's all.'

'But what does it matter to any of you?' Paula persisted.

'Well, don't you think it matters if someone's locked up when they haven't done anything wrong?'

'But why would you think this Vanessa woman isn't guilty? According to the newspaper reports, she was found with blood on her hands and the murder weapon beside her. Doesn't that rather suggest she did it?'

'Peter's convinced she didn't,' Martin answered quietly, 'and I trust his judgement. And, even if she *did* do it after all, it can't do any harm for them to look for alternative explanations – just in case.'

'It might,' Paula argued, 'if it gets all sorts of people involved who don't need to be, or dredges up things from the past that would be better forgotten.'

'Such as?'

'That girl – Leanne – that I told them about. I wish I hadn't now. Why should she have to put up with having them descending on her with questions about a part of her life that she's probably trying to forget?'

'Bernie told me they've given up on that line of enquiry. Apparently she was safely locked away in a secure mental unit when your brother was killed.'

'Poor kid! Was it what Chris did to her that …?'

'I didn't ask. It's none of my business. All I know is that Bernie said she had a perfect alibi, so they had to rule her out.'

'So much for not wanting innocent people locked up!' Paula muttered. 'We do it all the time, don't we? In mental hospitals and care homes and boarding schools and …'

'Was that how you felt, when your parents sent you to boarding school?' Martin asked. 'Did it feel like being put in prison? Did you think they were punishing you?'

Paula did not answer. For several minutes they stood there without speaking, listening to the water slapping against the sides of the boat and the diesel engine throbbing as they glided on up the canal. Martin gazed steadfastly ahead, as if he were watching out for some landmark to come into sight. Paula stared down at her feet and fiddled with the keys in her pocket. Eventually she looked up at Martin again and drew in a deep breath.

'Later on – when I was a teenager – it was a relief every term, going back to school and getting away from my father and Chris, and from seeing my Mum being so servile and cringing. But at first, when I was only seven and I hadn't realised how much they resented me and wanted me out of the way – yes, it did feel as if they were punishing me. And the school did seem like a prison.'

'Was your father really as bad as you made out to Bernie?' Martin asked, struggling to understand how any parent could behave in the way that Paula had described.

'Every bit,' she confirmed bitterly, 'and more! He made it abundantly clear that, once he'd got the son he wanted, I was surplus to requirements – an encumbrance – an expensive embarrassment!'

Martin could not think of anything to say. This was something beyond his comprehension. The boat chugged on.

'When I was little, I used to try to please him,' Paula resumed at last. 'I brought him his slippers when he came in from work, and I made little presents for him, and … but somehow I never managed to get it right. Whatever I did only annoyed him. I thought I must be really stupid to make so many mistakes! Then … it was Chris's fourth birthday, so I must have been ten. Our father had taken time off work to be at his party. They'd organised a big party for him with lots of kids from the neighbourhood. I don't know how they found them all.'

She paused, as if wondering whether to go on. Martin continued to hold fast to the tiller while staring ahead, as if all his concentration was needed for steering the boat.

'Anyway,' Paula continued, 'Mum was getting Chris dressed up in the new clothes they'd bought him, and I asked what I was going to wear – some of the girls at school had shown me pictures of their birthday parties with all the girls dressed up in party frocks and I was hoping they might have got one for me. Chris piped up right away, telling me that he wasn't having any girls at his party. And Mum backed him up and told me that she needed me in the kitchen with her to help with the food. And that was when I realised that there was *nothing* I could do to make them want me.'

They glided on in silence for several minutes. Then Paula tentatively took the initiative.

'What about you?' she asked casually. 'Do you ever go back home – to Germany, I mean?'

'No.' Martin paused, as if wondering whether or not to expand on this. 'My mother wouldn't like it. We cut off all ties with our old life when my father was arrested.'

'Why was that?' Paula sounded puzzled. 'I can understand that you'd be bound to lose touch, but I'd have thought, after the wall came down, you'd both want to-'

'But she couldn't trust any of them,' Martin cut in. 'She was convinced that someone must have betrayed us to the Stasi – but there was no way of us ever knowing who it was, so …'

'I'm not sure I understand,' Paula said, furrowing her brow. 'I thought you said he was caught trying to escape to the West.'

'No, he never got that far.' Martin paused for so long that Paula began to think that he did not intend to say any more.

'My mother was a concert pianist,' he resumed at last. 'That was how the two of us managed to get out. She was given permission to go on a tour of Western Europe with an orchestra she used to play with. It was supposed to be a demonstration of Socialist superiority in the Arts. She managed to smuggle me out with her, but there was no way my father would ever get an exit visa. He was a physicist and may well have known state secrets or at least have been a loss to the country's scientific establishment.'

He sighed, continuing to stare ahead as if transfixed by something far beyond the prow of the boat.

'Mutti agreed to take her chance, on the understanding that he would follow us somehow, but I don't think they ever had a clear plan how he was going to do that. When we heard that he'd been arrested by the Stasi, she was convinced that someone must have tipped them off that she was planning to defect. She thought that they arrested him in the hope that she would change her mind in order to save him.'

'But she didn't?'

'No. That same day, she claimed political asylum for both of us. The fact that my father was in the custody of the Stasi counted in our favour and we were granted leave to remain in the UK. I think that my father engineered his arrest deliberately, partly in order to push my mother into taking the plunge and partly to convince the authorities that we were genuinely at risk if we went back.'

'It must have been very hard for you both, leaving everything you'd ever known behind and starting again in a foreign country,' Paula commented.

'Not so very hard. People were very kind. I was young and I soon picked up the language. My mother had her music. No, the only hard part was that my father was not there. My mother missed him very much. She still does, even now.' He flashed a brief smile towards Paula. 'So you see: we men are not all monsters!'

'I never said that you were,' Paula protested, returning his smile.

'But you have never found one that you could trust enough to share your life,' Martin pointed out.

'Thus speaks a bachelor, who still lives with his mother,' Paula retorted in gentle mockery.

'Yes,' Martin laughed. 'I suppose you have a point there. But it's not that I don't trust women; it's just that none of them has ever proposed to me – and of course, I couldn't risk offending their feminine right to autonomy by presuming to pop the question myself, could I?'

'Are you laughing at me?'

'No – just pointing out the difficulties faced by a man who prefers women who have a mind of their own.' Martin looked round at last and smiled at Paula. 'Your father sounds awful and I'm sure you and your mother both had a dreadful time; but don't you think it might not have been that brilliant for your brother either? Think of the weight of expectations heaped on him.'

'There were no expectations as far as his morals were concerned,' Paula snorted. 'Shacking up with a sixteen-year-old! And he had everything given him on a plate – a house, a partnership-'

'What if he didn't want to be a solicitor?' Martin asked gently. 'But I was thinking more of earlier, when you were children. It's all very well knowing you're the apple of someone's eye, but there's always the worry that you might let them down.'

'Is that how you felt – when you were a kid?'

'No, not exactly.' Martin paused briefly and then took a deep breath and continued. 'Don't get me wrong – I always knew with *absolute certainty* that there was nothing – nothing in the world – that would ever make my mother stop loving me. But … there was always that nagging feeling at the back of my mind that I owed it to her – and to my father – to make the most of what they'd done for me. They'd sacrificed everything to give me a better life and it was … I always felt I had to make sure I didn't screw up and turn it all into a waste. Does that make any sense?'

'Yes,' Paula assured him. 'It makes perfect sense.'

'And getting back to your brother,' Martin persisted. 'Of course, I don't really know anything about it at all, but I did just wonder if he might have felt the pressure without the assurance that … well, he may have thought that if *he* screwed up his dad would reject him.'

'The way he did to me?' Paula suggested.

'Well,' Martin shrugged, 'that did set a precedent, didn't it? Your brother may have been made of sterner stuff, but I know I'd have been worrying that I might fall from grace too.'

'I never thought of it that way,' Paula mused. 'Chris always seemed so arrogant and sure of himself. Do you honestly think it could've all been just a front?'

'How would I know?' Martin shrugged again. 'I never met the man. For all I know, he *was* arrogant and sure of himself – not to mention a woman-hater and a bully. I was just … I just thought, if your father was the way you describe, how could he have turned out any other way?'

He turned his gaze back to the distant scenery, slightly increasing the speed of the boat so that the water lapped more loudly against the sides. They continued in silence for perhaps five minutes, before Paula spoke again.

'It said on the radio that the trial might end on Monday. Would you be free to come with me to watch what happens?'

***

Peter, Bernie and Jonah, meanwhile, were sitting in their car outside twenty-six Wilbraham Avenue, debating what to do next. The two days of the weekend seemed too valuable a breathing space to be wasted, but it was unclear what steps they could take to identify the real killer before the defence case was completed and the jury retired to consider its verdict.

'What makes you so sure the woman Green saw was Lesley Binns?' Peter asked wearily. 'As far as I can see, it could have been anyone.'

'Except Vanessa, Deborah or Louise,' Bernie pointed out, 'thankfully.'

'First off – she may well have access to a key,' Jonah replied. 'Leanne surely must have had one, and the chances are she didn't give it back when she left, or was chucked out or whatever happened.'

'That's only speculation,' Peter argued, 'but go on.'

'Secondly,' Jonah continued, smiling at Peter's exasperation. 'He said it was an older woman-'

'Only older than Vanessa,' Bernie interrupted. 'There's nothing to stop it having been Paula. And anyway, there could be any number of his girlfriends and ex-girlfriends who might have gone calling if Kelly Phillips' testimony is anything to go by – and they could well have been given keys.'

'Maybe,' Jonah conceded, 'but there's nothing we can do about any of them, whereas, we *can* have another go at checking out Lesley Binns.'

'But we've already established that her account of that morning is consistent with her being the woman in the green coat,' Peter argued. 'What's the point of going through it all again?'

'In case we uncover something that we didn't spot before,' Jonah insisted. 'Or in case she gets jumpy and gives something away.'

'OK.' Bernie looked at her watch. 'It's ten twenty-one. Alan Green would be just knocking on the door of number twenty-three. Imagine we're the woman in the green coat. We've just stabbed Christopher with the screwdriver and grabbed the coat from the hall to cover up the bloodstains on our clothes. We come out of the house, get into the car and off we go!'

She released the handbrake, let in the clutch and moved off. Soon they were on Greenhill Road, heading into the centre of Evesham. They passed a sign to the railway station. The traffic increased as they continued south along the High Street.

'Ten twenty-seven,' Peter said as they waited for the traffic lights to change at a busy junction. 'And there's a camera up there that could confirm when she passed – if only they keep the tapes for long enough.'

'Not much chance of that, surely?' Bernie commented.

'What about data protection and stuff?'

They moved off again – but not for long. Soon they were in a queue of cars waiting to cross the river.

'Ten twenty-nine,' Peter announced as they came off the bridge and turned right into Pershore Road. 'Not much further now.'

Two minutes later, they were cruising past the pharmacy where Lesley Binns had collected her husband's prescription.

Bernie pulled in a few yards further on and turned to Peter. 'How're we doing?'

Ten thirty-two,' he replied. 'That's twenty-one minutes before the time-stamp on the prescription. If she *was* the woman in the green coat, something seems to have held her up on the way here.'

'There could have been a queue in the chemist's,' Bernie suggested. 'Or she may not have set off for a few minutes after she got in the car.'

'Or the traffic may have been worse,' Jonah agreed. 'The main thing is that neither the pharmacy time stamp nor Russell's telephone call establish an alibi for her. So, I vote we call on her again and see what she has to say for herself.'

'I don't know,' Peter sounded dubious. 'It feels a bit like harassment to me.'

'Or giving her an opportunity to establish her innocence,' Jonah insisted. 'If she can produce the till receipt from the supermarket, that may prove that she couldn't have got to Wilbraham Avenue in time to be the woman that Green saw going into number twenty-six.'

'Or it might prove that she left the supermarket in plenty of time to get there,' Bernie added brightly, 'and, if she did, then she would need to explain how it took her so long to get to the chemist.'

'In which case, she will almost certainly have lost the receipt,' Peter commented drily. 'If she's guilty, she's not going to hand over anything that confirms that she was in that part of Evesham at the critical time. That's quite apart from it being highly unlikely that she's still got a receipt from five months ago!'

'I still think we ought to interview her again,' Jonah insisted stubbornly. 'If she's guilty, she may let something slip, and if she's not, she may be able to suggest who else it might be.'

'Oh very well!' Peter conceded. 'I can see you won't give us any peace if we don't, but I don't want you asking her about that till receipt. If she *is* guilty and she realises it could incriminate her, she'll say she's lost it, and by the time the police come with a warrant, it *will* be lost and gone forever.'

Bernie drove the car the short distance to the Binns family home, parking a few doors further down the road. They got out and Peter took out the portable ramp. They walked back to the house. Then they stopped. There was a small red car parked in the centre of the drive. Jonah attempted to manoeuvre his wheelchair past it on the left, but there was not enough space between the car and the thick hedge that divided the front garden from the pavement. He tried the other side, but this was worse, because although the larch-lap fence between the drive and the garden next door was just far enough away from the car for the wheelchair to pass, it was supported by unyielding concrete posts, which restricted the width at intervals, preventing Jonah from getting through. He went back to try the left-hand side again, but it was no good. Unless the vehicle was moved a few inches to one side, he would not be able to approach the front door.

'I'd better wait in the car,' he said after a few moments' thought. 'Let me know how you get on.'

Lesley Binns invited in Bernie and Peter readily enough when they rang the bell a few minutes later, having escorted Jonah back to the car and settled him into the back. She chatted brightly as she led them into a small sitting room at the front of the house.

'Go on in and make yourselves comfortable. I'll be with you in a moment. I just need to get some scones out of the oven.'

While they waited for her return, Bernie looked round the room. On the mantelpiece, above a modern wood-burning stove, there was a line of photographs. Centre stage was a large portrait of a teenage girl smiling merrily towards the camera. That must be Leanne before she met Christopher Wellesley. On either side of it were snaps of happy family scenes: a picnic by the river, riding a donkey on the beach, a children's birthday party. Leanne had clearly been the centre-point of this household while she was growing up.

Russell had told Lesley about his performance in the witness box and about Christabel's assurances to him that his evidence would contribute to exonerating Vanessa, or at very least ensuring that she got a light sentence.

'Mind you, he was disappointed that the judge stopped him before he could say everything he wanted to,' she finished, sitting down on an easy chair and looking across at Peter and Bernie, seated together on a matching sofa. 'He thinks – we all think – Christopher Wellesley ought to be exposed for the brute that he was.'

'And yet you said you weren't prepared to be a witness yourself,' Bernie pointed out. 'Why was that?'

'Like I said before, I didn't want Leanne to know about it. I was afraid it would set her off again.'

'We now think that whoever it was who killed Christopher let themselves into the house with a key,' Peter said gently. 'That's really why we came back to talk to you again. We thought that Leanne might have had a key – from when she lived with Christopher – and that–'

'She didn't kill him,' Lesley interrupted sharply. 'I told you – she was still in hospital that weekend. And I don't know anything about any key, either,' she added defensively.

'No, we know it can't have been Leanne,' Peter assured

her kindly. We just wondered if she had had a key, and if she did, whether you knew where it was. We wondered if it could somehow have fallen into the wrong hands – if she threw it away because she didn't need it anymore, for instance.'

'No,' Lesley said firmly. Her initial affability had evaporated now and her expression was distinctly hostile. 'I'm sure Leanne never had any key. He didn't like her having any freedom. He wouldn't want her to be able to let herself in, because then he wouldn't know where she was, would he? He'd have wanted her to have to ring the bell to be let in, so that he could tell when she'd been out and how long. Now, if that's all your questions, I've got a lot of ironing to get done before John comes home.'

'Your husband's out then?' Peter asked innocently, getting to his feet. 'I don't know why, but I'd assumed that was his car on the drive.'

'No. He has a van. It's more convenient for his fishing tackle. That's where he is at the moment,' Lesley added, opening the door and holding it, waiting for them to go through it into the hall.

'I see. Well, thank you for your time,' Peter held out his hand and Lesley shook it grudgingly. 'We won't keep you any longer.'

Lesley hurried to open the front door for them. As she passed, Bernie spoke earnestly to her in a low voice.

'Mrs Binns, I know it's hard for you to think about these things, but it will be a terrible thing for her daughter if Vanessa is sent to prison. If you think of anything that could help us to find out who really killed Christopher, you will tell us, won't you?'

17. ADMISSION OF GUILT

For I know my transgressions, and my sin is ever before me.
Psalm 51:3, NRSV Anglicised Edition

On Monday morning, Bernie looked around the court as she waited for the trial to resume. On the row in front of her, the prosecuting counsel was having a whispered conversation with his junior colleague. Christabel and Justin were sifting through a pile of papers on the desk where they were sitting. Yasmeen leaned across to speak to Christabel in an undertone.

There was a low murmur of voices as the public gallery began to fill up. Bernie turned in her chair and scanned the rows of seats. Patrick and Deborah O'Shea were at the front. They appeared to be holding hands. Next to them, she recognised Father Gerard, his brightly-coloured blazer contrasting starkly with Patrick's navy blue suit and Deborah's dark purple coat. A man that she did not recognise stood up to allow Louise and her partner, Thomas Hazle, to pass along the row in order to sit next to them. He took his seat again, enabling Bernie to see the faces of the people on the tier behind. She stared in surprise as she recognised Paula Wellesley and …!

'Look up there,' she said quietly, nudging Peter and nodding towards the public gallery. 'On the second row, behind Louise and her bloke.'

'Martin!' Peter breathed, sharing Bernie's surprise. 'And Paula, who doesn't care what happened to her brother so long as she isn't expected to feel sorry for him. What d'you think they're doing here?'

'Dunno,' Bernie shrugged. 'But that's not the only surprise. Look who's just come in!'

Peter watched as a lone woman crept in and sat down at the back of the public gallery. Her black coat and a black felt hat made her look as if she were dressed for a funeral. They also made her appear older than she was in reality, but Peter had no difficulty recognising her.

'Lesley Binns!'

'Are you serious?' Jonah asked sharply, catching the name and turning his wheelchair to see for himself. She glanced towards him and he turned back hastily to avoid catching her eye. 'Well, well, well. I wonder what's brought her here!'

'Be upstanding!' The usher's stentorian command brought silence to the court as everyone present, with the exception of Jonah, scrambled to their feet. The judge entered and took her place at the bench. At a glance from her, the company subsided back into their seats. The judge announced that the court was now in session and invited Christabel to continue presenting her evidence.

Christabel called her first witness, who, as expected, was Alan Green. He was wearing his Royal Mail uniform. Bernie wondered idly whether this was because he would be returning to his round after giving evidence or if he thought that it was pertinent to the role that he had played in the events of that fateful Saturday.

He confirmed his name, address and occupation in a clear business-like voice, and looked towards Christabel for further questions.

'On the twelfth of May this year, you were assigned a different round from normal, is that correct?'

'Well, strictly-speaking, I was assigned the round the day before – the eleventh. Simon – that's Simon Hutchins, one of my co-workers – phoned in sick and we had to re-vamp things a bit. He was still off on the Saturday, so we did the same that day too.'

'I see,' Christabel cut in quickly, before he could expand on the details of the re-allocation of work. 'And on Saturday the twelfth, you delivered to Wilbraham Avenue, which is not part of your usual round – is that correct?'

'That's right,' Green confirmed.

'Do you remember delivering to number twenty-six, Wilbraham Avenue?'

'Yes. I remember it quite distinctly. I didn't realise it was that day, mind you, until that gentleman over there came asking me about it.' He waved his arm in Peter's direction. 'But it was that house for definite, because I remember having to come halfway up the drive before I could see the number on the house, because of this big bush in the front garden. And then, when he started asking about what time it was I delivered a parcel to number twenty-seven, I remembered it was the same day, and then, when we looked it up, it was Saturday the twelfth. There's records, see – times and dates, so people can track their letters and parcels. That's technology for you,' he added in a satisfied tone.

'What time was it that you delivered to number twenty-six?' asked Christabel, as soon as she could intercept his flow of words.

'We worked it out, it must have been about ten on the dot. You see, I had tracked items for number ten and number twenty-seven. So I know I was at number ten at nine thirty-eight and I got to number twenty-seven by ten twenty-three, which means that I must've called at number twenty-six somewhere in between.'

'Tell the jury about what happened while you were at number twenty-six,' Christabel instructed.

'Like I said, I came up the drive a bit to check the number, and I saw this woman standing there with her hand up to the door, just putting the key in the lock. I called out to her that I'd got her post, and she turned and took the letters and said thanks and then she carried on unlocking the door and went in and closed it behind her.'

'You're sure she let herself in with a key?' Christabel pressed him.

'Yes: certain. She was just putting it in the lock when I called to her and she left it there while she took the letters and then she turned it to open the door. I didn't think anything of it, because, with me not usually delivering there, I didn't know it wasn't the lady of the house.'

'Did you see this woman clearly?' Christabel asked.

'As plain as I can see you now,' Green replied confidently.

'Would you recognise her if you saw her again?'

'I reckon so. I'm good with faces, because I get to see a lot of them in my line of work.'

'Good. Now, Mr Green,' Christabel's tone became more sombre and she looked at him gravely, 'I want you to look round this room and tell me if you can see that woman now. Take your time and consider your answer carefully.'

Green obediently turned round slowly in the witness box, fixing his eyes in turn on the judge, the clerk and stenographer, the legal teams and the members of the jury. Then he turned his attention to the defendant and the police officers sitting on either side of her. Finally, he raised his eyes to the public gallery, scanning along each row in turn, before turning back to address Christabel.

'Yes,' he said firmly. 'She's here. I'm certain of it.'

There was an audible gasp from both the public gallery and the jury box. The judge frowned and ordered silence. Christabel, visibly shaken by this unexpected development, addressed the witness sternly.

'Are you quite sure? Remember that a person's liberty may depend upon your answer.'

'Yes,' Green repeated doggedly. 'I'm absolutely sure.'

'In that case,' Christabel replied, displaying the first sign of nervousness that Bernie had seen in her since they first met, 'please point her out to the jury.'

Green turned towards the dock and for a moment it

seemed that he might be about to denounce Vanessa. Then he raised his eyes to stare into the public galley above and put up his arm to point towards a figure sitting at the back.

'She's up there in the back corner, dressed all in black. Can you see her? She's the one with the little black hat.'

For a few minutes, the court was in uproar. Judge, jury and lawyers all turned to look up at the public gallery, where people were on their feet pointing and staring at the woman in black, who shrank back against the wall and held up her hand to cover her face. Ushers called for silence and for people to return to their seats.

As the hubbub gradually subsided, the judge ordered one of the ushers to bring the woman down to speak to her privately and announced that the trial was adjourned for thirty minutes to allow her time to consider what to do.

'Whew! Bernie whistled when the judge finished speaking. 'Christabel got a bit more than she was bargaining for there, I reckon.'

'Yes,' agreed Jonah with a grin. 'She brought Green in to prove someone other than Vanessa had been in the house that morning; she never thought he'd be able to tell us who it was!'

'I have to admit,' Bernie went on, 'I did have a nasty moment when he looked up there and said he could see her. For a split second, I thought he was going to say it was Paula.'

'I was afraid he was going to pick Deborah,' Peter chipped in. 'I had this feeling he was checking her over carefully before moving on.'

'I wonder what it was that made Lesley decide to come today,' Jonah mused.

***

'I never meant to kill him,' Lesley Binns insisted, looking round with pleading eyes at the two police officers sitting opposite her across a table in the interview room. 'I was frightened, and I just grabbed the screwdriver to try to fend him off. I can't really work out how he ended up on top of it. Everything just happened so quickly.'

The trial had now been adjourned until the following day, while DI Scott Wilding and DC Amanda Burgess interviewed this new, and unexpected, suspect. Jonah was also present; DI Wilding having soon discovered that saying "no" to a police hero was a mug's game, even when that hero was responsible for showing up serious flaws in the most important investigation of your career so far.

'We'll come to that later,' Wilding said firmly. 'First, I'd like to get a few things clear – starting with how you came to have a key to the Wellesleys' house.'

'I was going through Leanne's things,' Lesley explained. 'She'd been admitted to hospital the day before and Russell – that's her boyfriend – asked me to sort out some clothes for her. He thought I'd have a better idea what she'd like than he did. I found this envelope in the bottom of her underwear drawer. I suppose she'd put it there because it was one place that Russell would never look. It had some photographs of Christopher Wellesley and some old love letters he'd sent her – and this key! I couldn't believe she'd still kept them, after all she'd gone through with him.'

She paused and took a sip of water from a plastic cup on the table in front of her.

'Go on,' Jonah urged gently.

'I didn't know what to do. I hated the idea that she was still thinking about him, but I was frightened that, if I took them away, she might get upset when she came home and couldn't find them. And then I decided that I didn't care! I thought: it's thinking about him that's got her into this state. I thought that, if I took them away and destroyed them, then she wouldn't be able to keep looking at them and reminding herself about him. So I put the envelope in my pocket and took it home with me.'

'What did you do with it?' asked DC Burgess. 'Do you still have the envelope?'

'No. I burned it along with the photos and the letters. I wanted to make sure Leanne could never see them again.'

'And the key?' enquired DI Wilding.

'I was fairly sure it must be for the house where she'd lived with Christopher – the family home that he made clear was so much more than she had any right to expect!' Lesley's tone was bitter. 'I put it in my purse, thinking I'd better get rid of it somehow. I didn't like to just throw it away in the bin, in case it got into the wrong hands; so I just put it in there while I thought what to do with it.'

'When exactly was this?' DC Burgess asked. 'I mean, how long before Christopher Wellesley was killed?'

'It was the Friday. Leanne was sectioned on the Wednesday evening, and I went round to sort out her clothes on the Friday morning.'

'That's Friday the eleventh of May?' Burgess queried.

'That's right,' Lesley nodded. 'It was still in my purse on the Saturday morning when I went shopping. I went to the big Tesco on Worcester Road. I was just coming out, back on to Greenhill Road, when it struck me that I was only a couple of minutes away from Christopher's house. I thought I might as well just go and check if that was what the key was for, seeing as I was almost there anyway.'

'What were you going to say to Christopher if you met him?' Jonah asked with interest.

'I don't know.' Lesley appeared nonplussed. 'I never really thought about it. I think I was expecting to just try the key in the door and then … I suppose, if it fitted, I could've dropped it through the letterbox, and nobody would have been any the wiser.'

'You mean, you intended to return the key anonymously?' Wilding jumped in quickly to forestall any further questions from Jonah.

'Yes – I think that's what I meant to do.'

'So, when did you change your plans?' demanded Burgess. 'And why?'

'It was that postman,' Lesley explained, sounding rather

flustered. 'I – I'd just put the key in the door, and found that it fitted, when up he came holding out a sheaf of letters. I didn't want to go into all sorts of explanations with him, so I just took the letters and said *thank you* and … He went back down the drive, but I thought he'd see me if I followed straight after him, and he'd think it was odd. So …,' she tailed off into silence and took another sip of water.

'Go on,' Jonah prompted her. 'What did you do next?'

'Well, it was like he said,' she replied. 'I unlocked the door and went in. I couldn't see anywhere in the hall to put the letters, so I went on down to where there was a door open on the right. It was the kitchen, so I thought I could leave them on the worktop in there.'

'And you were still not planning to speak to Christopher Wellesley?' Wilding cut in sharply. 'Or had you changed your mind about that by then?'

'I don't know. I don't think so. I think it was only when I heard him whistling to himself that I … It seemed so unfair that there he was, without a care in the world, and there was my Leanne, locked away in a mental hospital with her arms all bound up where she'd been punishing herself because … because she thought it was all her fault!'

Lesley's face crumpled and she broke down in tears. Burgess reached into her pocket and pulled out a small packet of tissues, which she pushed across the table towards her.

'Take your time,' Wilding said kindly, flashing a brief glance at Lesley's solicitor, who had so far played no part in the proceedings.

***

Meanwhile, Peter and Bernie were wandering around the museum, killing time while they waited for Jonah to call them to say that he was ready to be collected. Martin and Paula were with them, also at a loose end following the morning's dramatic events. They had returned to the court after lunch, expecting that the trial would resume, only to be told that it was now over for the day. Then, going back outside, they had bumped into Peter and Bernie who were on their way back from dropping Jonah at the police station, and all four had decided to retire to the museum to compare notes.

'Who is she?' Paula asked, as they studied a large stuffed sturgeon, which, according to the information board next to it, had been caught in the River Severn in 1835. 'The woman in black, I mean. The one the postman pointed out. And, if she killed Chris, why was she up there watching the trial?'

'She's Lesley Binns – Leanne's mother,' Bernie told her. 'We went to see her on Saturday. I suppose that's probably what prompted her to come to the trial.'

'A guilty conscience, you mean?' Paula continued to sound puzzled. 'Because she'd allowed Vanessa to take the blame?'

'We don't know for certain that she did kill Christopher,' Peter pointed out. 'Only that she went to see him that morning.'

'But if she didn't kill him, why didn't she come forward earlier?' Bernie argued. 'Especially after we told her that Vanessa might be innocent. She was an important witness, whether Christopher was already dead when she got there or if she left him fit and well and he was killed later. And what about the coat? How do you explain her taking that away, if it was just a social call?'

'But why would she want to kill him?' Paula persisted. 'And where did she get a key to his house?'

'I think we told you that Leanne had mental health issues,' Bernie answered. 'Her mother blamed them on your brother's treatment of her when they were together.'

'But that was years ago!' Paula protested. 'Surely she must have got over it by now.'

'Do you mean Leanne or her mother?' Peter asked. 'Either way, it's not as simple as that. According to Mrs

Binns, Christopher forced her to have an abortion when she was only eighteen, and there was some damage done in the process that caused her to have a sequence of miscarriages quite recently. And that's a contributory factor to her depression and self-harming.'

'Oh.' Paula fell silent, feeling suddenly ashamed of having dismissed Leanne in her own mind as simply weak and silly.

***

Lesley blew her nose and wiped her eyes. Then she looked round at all three of her inquisitors with a rather hopeless expression on her face.

'I put the letters down on the worktop, like I meant to,' she resumed eventually. 'And I followed the sound of the whistling – through the room with the washing machine and things, and out to that workroom place at the back. And there he was! He was planing down a piece of wood, and whistling and smiling to himself all the while as if he was pleased with himself about something. He looked up when he heard me come in, and I could see he didn't know who I was.'

She paused to dab her eyes with a tissue and take another draught from the plastic cup.

'I said to him he might be interested to know that Leanne was in hospital, and he – he – he just looked at me as if I was mad; and then he said, "who's this Leanne?" just like that! He didn't even remember her name, she meant that much to him!'

For several minutes, she was consumed by uncontrollable sobbing. Seeing the solicitor sitting impassively, Burgess got up, walked round the table and put her arm round Lesley's shoulder.

'It's alright,' she assured her. 'There's no hurry. Just take your time.'

***

'What about you?' Bernie asked as they entered a room full of colourful military uniforms and ancient swords and pistols. 'Why did you decide to come to watch the trial?'

'I don't know really,' Paula answered. 'Curiosity, I suppose – and I am Chris's only living relative, so … Well, I suppose I thought I ought to take a bit of interest. What'll happen now? Is the trial over, or …?'

'That rather depends on what Lesley Binns tells the police,' Peter told her, 'and whether they believe her. My guess is that either the judge will stop the trial, while they carry out a further investigation or else the crown will withdraw the charge against Vanessa and that'll be the end of it as far as she's concerned.'

'So much for this entertaining day out that you promised me!' Martin joked in an attempt to lighten the mood. 'The show folded almost as soon as it had started.'

'It could hardly have been more dramatic though, could it?' Paula retorted with a laugh.

***

Lesley's weeping subsided and she blew her nose again. She looked earnestly across the table at the three detectives.

'I honestly don't remember much about what happened after that,' she told them, clasping her hands together very tightly where they lay on the table in front of her. 'I know I started shouting at him, telling him what he'd done to Leanne and where she was now and telling him he ought to be ashamed of himself. At first, he just laughed, and then he got angry and ordered me out of the house. I told him I wasn't going until he apologised; so then he came at me and grabbed my arms to get me out by force. I fought back and he pulled my arm up behind my back until I thought it was going to break.'

She paused and took another sip of water.

'I know you probably won't believe me, but I really did think he was going to kill me. I grabbed the screwdriver to try to fend him off. I really didn't know what I was doing by that time. And then the next thing I knew, he'd fallen on top of it and then he dropped down on to the floor and I saw it sticking out of him and blood oozing round it. He looked like he was dead. I thought it must've gone into his heart. And then I realised how bad it would look if anyone came in and found me there, so I went back through the kitchen and out of the front door and home again as fast as I could.'

'Did you pick anything up on the way out?' Jonah asked quietly.

'How did you know about that?' Lesley looked at him wonderingly. 'Yes, there was blood on my hand and I wiped it off on my skirt without thinking. Then I looked down and I thought someone might notice it – and I had to call at the chemist on the way back for John's prescription. I couldn't think what to do – and then I saw this long green coat hanging up near the door. I put it on over my skirt, and then I thought that, if I put the hood up, nobody would recognise me if they saw me coming out of the house.'

'It worked,' Jonah told her. 'One of the neighbours did see you, but all she could describe was the coat – and your car.'

'What did you do with the key in the end?' Burgess asked suddenly. 'You said you were going to drop it through the door. Did you leave it somewhere in the house?'

'No, I put it back in my purse after I'd got the door open and then I forgot about it until I was on the way back in the car. I stopped off at the car park, just before the bridge, and I threw it in the river.'

'And the coat?' Burgess enquired.

'I put it in the wood burner with the rest of the clothes I was wearing. I'd seen all those TV shows about murderers being identified by minute drops of blood on their clothes. Most of them looked clean to me, but I didn't want to take any chances.'

'Why didn't you summon medical help?' Wilding asked coldly. 'Why did you just leave him to die?'

'I thought he already *was* dead,' Lesley answered. 'Please! You've got to believe me – I never meant to hurt him and I didn't realise he was still alive afterwards. I was in shock. I didn't know what I was doing!'

'Apart from remembering to cover up to stop anyone seeing the blood or recognising your face,' Wilding commented implacably.

'I – I – I don't know how I thought of that. I was just … just …'

Lesley's voice faded away into more sobbing.

'I think we'll stop there,' Wilding said, 'unless there is anything else that you wish to add?'

Lesley shook her head vigorously.

'Very well.' Wilding announced that the interview was over. Then he stated the time and stopped the recorder, before turning back to address Lesley again. 'As I explained at the beginning, this interview has been recorded. There are two copies of the CD in this machine. I will now take one and seal it, and then it will be signed by everyone here, so that it can be produced at your trial, free from any danger of tampering. Do you understand?'

18. LIFE SENTENCE

Murder has always been regarded as the most serious criminal offence and the sentence prescribed is different from other sentences. By law, the sentence for murder is imprisonment (detention) for life and an offender will remain subject to the sentence for the rest of his/her life.

Sentencing Guidelines Council
Reduction in Sentence for a Guilty Plea
Definitive Guidance, 2007

'Mrs Lesley Binns was today sentenced to life imprisonment, at Worcester Crown Court, for the murder of her daughter's ex-lover,' the newsreader said, across a view of the pillared magnificence of the front entrance to the court building, 'with a minimum term of seven years. In sentencing, the judge cited, as mitigating factors, the lack of premeditation, provocation by the victim, and the possibility that Mrs Binns was to some extent acting in self-defence.'

'Do you think the judge believed what she said about it being more or less an accident?' Bernie asked. 'The jury went for murder rather than accepting her plea of guilty to manslaughter, which rather suggests that *they* didn't.'

'Who knows?' Peter shrugged. 'My guess is that the jury were influenced by the way she did nothing to prevent Vanessa being convicted – especially in view of the fact that *she* was just as much a victim of Christopher's controlling behaviour as Leanne had been.'

'The absence of fingerprints on the handle of the screwdriver must have counted against her too,' Jonah

231

observed. 'The prosecution played that for all it was worth – and it *is* odd that she should have thought of wiping it clean when she was supposed to have been all in a daze and a dither!'

'After the hearing, the victim's wife, Mrs Vanessa Wellesley, who had herself previously been accused of killing her husband, released this statement, which was read to the press by her solicitor,' the television reporter continued.

They watched as Vanessa and her parents emerged from the court and stood together on the steps. Yasmeen stepped forward holding a piece of stiff paper in front of her. Microphones on long poles appeared from amongst the waiting crowd of media representatives.

'It is now nearly one year since I returned home to find my husband dying from injuries that he had received while I was out on a routine shopping trip,' she read out. 'My most conspicuous emotion at this time is relief that it is all now over. My husband had many faults and I will not deny that he was capable of making life with him unbearable at times.'

She paused and looked around at the eager journalists.

'She's about to say "but", isn't she,' Bernie murmured. 'Don't say she still thinks it was her fault that-'

'Sshh!' Peter hissed. 'Let's hear her out first.'

'However,' Yasmeen continued, prompting a smug smile from Bernie, 'he could also be loving, generous and loyal. He did not deserve to be killed in the manner in which he was. I believe that justice has now been done.'

'Loving, generous and loyal!' Bernie repeated scornfully. 'In between knocking her about, making her account for every penny she spent and having it off with any woman who'd have him!'

'I am grateful,' Yasmeen continued to read, 'to everyone who has supported me over the past year: my parents and sister, who never doubted my innocence-'

'Hmmph!' Bernie snorted sceptically.

'... my legal team, the police, Father Gerard and his friends who eventually uncovered the truth, and Judge Freeman who presided so fairly over my trial.'

'It's starting to sound like an Oscar acceptance speech,' Jonah muttered.

'I would like to extend my sympathy to Mrs Binns' daughter, Leanne, who suffered unimaginable wrongs at my husband's hands,' Yasmeen went on. 'Like her, I have experienced the pain of losing a child. These past months, since her mother was charged with murder must have been tremendously stressful for her. I hope that she, like me, will now be able to move on and put the past behind her. Finally, I would appeal to you all to allow me and my daughter the privacy that we need to re-build our lives.'

Yasmeen lowered the paper and looked round at the audience again. 'Thank you all for listening to my client's statement.'

'Now that's more like what I would call loving and generous,' Bernie declared. 'How can she talk about *unimaginable wrongs* at the same time as describing him as-'

'Hang on, she hasn't finished yet,' Peter interrupted.

'And now,' Yasmeen continued in a louder voice, 'I have been asked to read the following statement from Mrs Wellesley's parents and sister.'

She swapped over two papers in her hand and then proceeded to read aloud again.

'We are pleased that justice has, at last, prevailed. Christopher Wellesley was a callous, manipulative and often violent man. Although the taking of a human life can never be justified; in our opinion, the world is a better place now that he is no longer in it. We completely understand why Mrs Binns felt towards him as she did. However, we are struggling to forgive her for allowing Vanessa to be put through the trauma of being charged and tried for a crime that *she* committed. For that reason, we are glad that she will be spending at least seven years in jail. We extend to her daughter Leanne every possible good wish, and hope that she will succeed in making a happy future life for herself and her partner. We too are grateful to Father Gerard and his friends, who were instrumental in exonerating Vanessa and bringing the true perpetrator to light.'

Yasmeen looked up from her reading and folded the papers in half.

'That's all. Thank you again.'

The press surged forwards, calling out questions and clamouring for interviews with Vanessa and her family. Two uniformed police officers escorted them away through the crowd to a waiting car. The camera followed it as it drove away and then panned back round to the steps of the court building.

'That was a very unfortunate statement,' Peter groaned. 'Why couldn't they have left well alone?'

'I bet it was Louise's idea,' Bernie agreed. 'She hated Christopher with a passion and thought Vanessa was too easy on him.'

'I can't think why Yasmeen didn't advise them against it, though.' Jonah agreed with Peter's assessment. 'It makes them seem vindictive.'

'I was thinking more of how Vanessa will react,' Peter said with a sigh. 'It's as if they haven't realised that she really did love the bastard.'

'Hang on! There's more!' Bernie called out, pointing towards the television screen. 'That's Paula coming out now.'

They watched as two figures emerged from the building and started down the steps. They were both dressed casually in jeans and sweatshirts and were of similar height and build, but one had dark brown hair and eyes while the other was blond-haired and had pale blue eyes behind metal-framed glasses.

They attempted to skirt round the cluster of journalists, but they were intercepted by a young man with a microphone in his hand, who stepped in front of them barring their way.

'Miss Wellesley,' he said breathlessly, 'please will you tell us what you think of the sentence? Do you think your brother has had justice?'

'Professor Wellesley has nothing to say to you,' Martin answered firmly, pushing the microphone to one side. 'Now, if you will excuse us, we have to get back to Oxford.'

He took Paula's hand and, sidestepping the journalist, led her swiftly down the path towards the road. The camera followed them for a moment or two and then the picture snapped back to the news studio.

'Well, well, well!' Jonah chuckled. 'What d'you think of that?'

'Martin's a dark horse,' Peter agreed. 'I have to admit, I didn't see that one coming!'

'I hope he realises what he's letting himself in for,' Bernie grinned. 'These strong-minded academic women can be difficult to live with – or so I've heard!'

THANK YOU

Thank you for taking the time to read Admission of Innocence. If you enjoyed it, please consider telling your friends or posting a short review. Word of mouth is an author's best friend and much appreciated. Thank you,

Judy

ACKNOWLEDGEMENTS

Many Facebook friends contributed ideas to this book. Special thanks go to Heather Rotherham, who came up with the title "Admission of Innocence". Maryalice Hogg-O'Rourke and Marion West were also great sources of encouragement and provided ideas for the cover design.

I would like to thank Gillian Gilbert for reading the manuscript, giving helpful comments and pointing out typographical errors.

I am indebted to the authors of a wide range of internet resources, which have been invaluable for researching the background to this book. These include (among others):

- The ministry of Justice (www.justice.gov.uk)

- The Crown Prosecution Service (www.cps.gov.uk)

- Wikipedia (https://en.wikipedia.org/)

- Google Maps (www.google.co.uk/maps)

Scripture quotations are from New Revised Standard Version Bible: Anglicized Edition, copyright © 1989, 1995 National Council of the Churches of Christ in the United States of America. Used by permission. All rights reserved worldwide.

DISCLAIMER

This book is a work of fiction. Any references to real people, events, establishments, organisations or locales are intended only to provide a sense of authenticity and are used fictitiously. All of the characters and events are entirely invented by the author. Any resemblances to persons living or dead are purely coincidental.

Most of the locations and institutions that feature in this book are real. Their inhabitants and employees, however, are purely fictional. In particular:

- Lichfield College, while intended to be typical of many Oxford colleges, is not based on any specific one of them;

- There is no St Monica's Church in Evesham, and Father Gerard and his parishioners are not based on any church there or anywhere else;

- None of the police officers featured here are representative of any members of the police service in West Mercia, Thames Valley or anywhere else.

MORE ABOUT BERNIE AND HER FRIENDS

There are now eleven **Bernie Fazakerley Mysteries**. The other ten (in chronological order of the action) are:

1. **Two Little Dickie Birds**: a murder mystery for DI Peter Johns and his Sergeant, Paul Godwin.

2. **Murder of a Martian**: Peter and Jonah solve a double murder and Peter meets Martin Reiss for the first time.

3. **Grave Offence**: Peter investigates an assault and a suspicious death, while Jonah is in rehab in the spinal injuries centre.

4. **Awayday**: a traditional detective story set among the dons of Lichfield College.

5. **Death on the Algarve:** a mystery for Bernie and her friends to tackle while on holiday in Portugal.

6. **Mystery over the Mersey**: a murder mystery set in Liverpool.

7. **Sorrowful Mystery**: Jonah investigates a child abduction and Peter embarks on a new journey of faith.

8. **In my Liverpool Home**: Bernie and her friends return to Liverpool to investigate a suspicious death in Aunty Dot's Care Home.

9. **Organ Failure**: a body is discovered under the organ in St Cyprian's Church and Jonah is called in to investigate.

10. **Rainbow Warrior**: One of their friends is injured in a hit-and-run incident and Jonah is convinced that this is attempted murder.

Bernie also appears in two other novels:

- **Changing Scenes of Life**: Jonah Porter's life story, told through the medium of his favourite hymns.
- **Despise not your Mother**: the story of Bernie's quest to learn about her dead husband's past.

There is also a book of short stories, in which Peter narrates his side of the story:
- **My Life of Crime**: the collected memoirs of DI Peter Johns. This includes some episodes that appear in other books, but told from a new perspective, as well as some completely new stories.

You can find them all on Judy Ford's Amazon Author page: www.amazon.co.uk/-/e/B019315B1M
Read more about Bernie Fazakerley and her friends and family at https://sites.google.com/site/llanwrdafamily/

Visit the Bernie Fazakerley Publications Facebook page here: www.facebook.com/Bernie.Fazakerley.Publications.
Follow Bernie on Twitter: https://twitter.com/BernieFaz.

LIST OF POLICE PERSONNEL

The following police officers recur in many of the Bernie Fazakerley Mysteries. This alphabetical list is provided to give some background to them and for reference.

- **Rupert Andrews:** (Thames Valley) Detective Sergeant 2000, Detective Inspector 2012.

- **Malcolm Appleton:** (Thames Valley) Police Constable 2007, Sergeant 2018.

- **Alison Brown:** (Thames Valley) Detective Inspector 1989, DCI 2004, Chief Superintendent 2015.

- **Amanda Burgess:** (West Mercia) Detective Constable 2016.

- **Tracy Burton:** (Thames Valley) Police Constable 1999, Sergeant 2005.

- **Anna Davenport:** (Thames Valley) Detective Sergeant 2007, Detective Inspector 2015. Married in 2001 to Philip Davenport. Separated in 2017. 3 children: Jessica (2001), Marcus (2002), Donna (2017). Archaeology and Anthropology graduate from Cambridge.

- **Karen Evans:** (West Mercia) Police Constable 2010, Detective Constable 2011 Detective Sergeant 2013. Married Paul Godwin in 2018.

- **Sarah Farrow:** (Merseyside) Police Constable 2003

- **Bryony Foster:** (Merseyside) Detective Constable 2016

- **Jordan Fox:** (Thames Valley) Police Constable 2001, Sergeant 2006, Inspector 2018

- **John Gamble:** (Thames Valley) Police Constable 2017

- **Paul Godwin:** (Thames Valley / West Mercia) Detective Constable 1993, Detective Sergeant 2002, Detective Inspector 2008, Detective Chief Inspector 2017. Moved from Thames Valley to West Mercia Police 2008. Married Karen Evans in 2018.

- **Pamela Gregson:** (Thames Valley) Custody Sergeant.

- **Gavin Hughes:** (Thames Valley) Police Constable 1988. Specialises in community policing and building bridges with rough-sleepers.

- **Peter Johns:** (Thames Valley) Police Constable 1969, Detective Constable 1973, Detective Sergeant 1978, Detective Inspector 1993, retired 2011. Married to Angie in 1978 and to Bernie in 2006. Father of Hannah (1980) and Eddie (1982). Stepfather to Lucy (2000).

- **Lee Jones:** Merseyside) Police Constable 2015

- **Arshad Khan:** (Thames Valley) Detective Sergeant 2002, Detective Inspector 2006, Detective Chief Inspector 2014. Specialises in cases involving ethnic minority victims. Married to Anita.

- **Aaron King:** (Thames Valley) Police Constable 2001, Sergeant 2009.

- **Sandra Latham:** (Merseyside) Detective Chief Inspector 2014.

- **Christopher Lucas:** (Greater Manchester / Merseyside) Detective Inspector 2009.

- **Andrew Lepage:** (Thames Valley) Detective Constable 2007, Detective Sergeant 2015. Graduate in criminology (1st class) from Leicester University in 2005. Lives with his mother in Headington Quarry.

- **Janet Morecambe:** (Merseyside) Police Constable 2010

- **John O'Connor:** (Merseyside) Police Constable 2016

- **Monica Philipson:** (Thames Valley) Detective Constable 2002, Detective Sergeant 2008. An ambitious police officer, who studied at Keble College, Oxford.

- **Richard Paige:** (Thames Valley) Detective Constable 1960, Detective Sergeant 1967, Detective Inspector 1973, Detective Chief Inspector 1981, Detective Superintendent 1995, died 1999. Married to Bernie in 1997. Father of Lucy (2000).

- **Joshua Pitchfork:** (Thames Valley) Detective Constable 2015

- **Jonah Porter:** (Thames Valley) Police Constable 1977, Detective Constable 1979, Detective Sergeant 1983, Detective Inspector 1987, Detective Chief Inspector 1996. Married to Margaret in 1982. Widowed in 2014.

- **Louise Otterbourne:** (Thames Valley) Police Constable 2017

- **Thomas Pullinger:** (Merseyside) Police Sergeant 2012

- **PD Q:** (Thames Valley) Police Dog 2014. General Purpose dog. German Shepherd Dog.

- **Oliver Ransom:** (Merseyside) Detective Constable 2015

- **Alice Ray:** (Thames Valley) Police Constable 2015, Detective Constable 2016

- **Charlotte Simpson:** (Merseyside) Detective Sergeant 2015

- **Melanie Stanton:** (Thames Valley) Police Constable 2009 and Dog Handler 2014

- **Ben Timpson:** (Thames Valley) Police constable 2018

- **PD Wesley:** (Thames Valley) Police Dog 2015. Drug and firearms search dog. Spaniel.

- **Melanie Wharton:** (Merseyside) Police Sergeant 2010.

- **Scott Wilding:** (West Mercia) Joined the police from the army in 2008. DI 2016.

ABOUT THE AUTHOR

Like her main character, Bernie Fazakerley, Judy Ford is an Oxford graduate and a mathematician. Unlike Bernie, Judy grew up in a middle-class family in the South London stockbroker belt. After moving to the North West and working in Liverpool, Judy fell in love with the Scouse people and created Bernie to reflect their unique qualities. She has worked in academia and in the NHS.

As a Methodist Local Preacher, Judy often tells her congregation, "I see my role as asking the questions and leaving you to think out your own answers." She carries this philosophy forward into her writing and she hopes that readers will find themselves challenged to think as well as being entertained.